Under

Witch Curse

MARIA E. SCHNEIDER

Bear Mountain Books

A Bear Mountain Books Production
www.BearMountainBooks.com

Under Witch Curse
Maria E. Schneider
Copyright 2013 © Maria E. Schneider

Printing History:
POD printing June 2013
E-format March 2013

ISBN-13: 978-0615831497 (Bear Mountain Books)
ISBN-10: 0615831494

Acknowledgments

Publishing novels has been an interesting road, and I wouldn't be here without the early support of people like Kevin, Wendie and the dog. Not the snake, but the dog. Dee, Heather, Margaret, Irene, Bo, Janet, Ann, Pat, Tibet, Marlene, Kathe, Sherry (both of you) and the rest of the gang at the Amazon cozy forum—you've been bright spots from the very start. Fans like LuvMyKindle, Northern Lights, Burgundy, Marisa and Elisabeth discovered my work and stayed with me for the ride. Thank you for taking the time to get to know me and my work.

A special thanks to April who started as a friend and for some reason, she's decided not to toss me overboard. I owe her and some other special beta readers for trying to set me straight: Dee, Kathy, Karen Cantwell, Jeff Hepple, and Michelle Scott – thanks. LeAnn, you were spot on with the cover. John Levitt, I can't believe you were generous enough to take me under your wing. I'm never going to fly like I should, but your timely advice and generosity made a difference in my world.

Big gratitude to my husband because he picks up the slack when the rope is in tangles all over the floor. And no, I don't know how that knot got there. Ask Junior.

Acknowledgments

Publishing novels has been an interesting road, and I wouldn't be here without the early support of people like Kevin, Wendie and the dog. Not the snake, but the dog. Dee, Heather, Margaret, Irene, Bo, Janet, Ann, Pat, Tibet, Marlene, Kathe, Sherry (both of you) and the rest of the gang at the Amazon cozy forum—you've been bright spots from the very start. Fans like LuvMyKindle, Northern Lights, Burgundy, Marisa and Elisabeth discovered my work and stayed with me for the ride. Thank you for taking the time to get to know me and my work.

A special thanks to April who started as a friend and for some reason, she's decided not to toss me overboard. I owe her and some other special beta readers for trying to set me straight: Dee, Kathy, Karen Cantwell, Jeff Hepple, and Michelle Scott – thanks. LeAnn, you were spot on with the cover. John Levitt, I can't believe you were generous enough to take me under your wing. I'm never going to fly like I should, but your timely advice and generosity made a difference in my world.

Big gratitude to my husband because he picks up the slack when the rope is in tangles all over the floor. And no, I don't know how that knot got there. Ask Junior.

Chapter 1

Before I could blink, his claws pressed against my throat, pinning me to the wall. I wouldn't have been able to breathe easily with a vamp this close to me anyway, but this guy was making sure no oxygen reached my lungs at all.

He growled an order or suggestion, but I was too panicked to understand. From the way his free hand was trailing down my arm, I think he was trying to be sexy. He had the dark good looks for it, but he was a vampire. There was nothing sexy about dead.

The turquoise at my wrist flashed heat, as if I needed the warning. It wasn't as hot as the ring White Feather had given me. Gold channeled even better than silver, sending enough heat and earth power through it that the diamond flared. The bright flash distracted the vampire momentarily, but I hadn't owned the ring long enough to know how to use it to my advantage.

The vamp's eyes returned to bore into me. It was obvious he was attempting to glamour me.

Stupider than he looked. No glamour on earth stood a chance of breaching my fear of the freak, even had I been dumb enough to gaze directly into his eyes. Most witches have some natural protection against vamps because we are tuned to magic. I'd been exposed to vamp glamour before, and all it had done was make me ground to Mother Earth as if my life depended on her, which it did.

The vamp's fingers relented just enough for me to suck in a breath of air. He was damned, and if I didn't do something fast, so was I.

"You think you're powerful now, Adriel the witch?"

Power? I needed a miracle. "God Bless You." I meant to say "God save me," but stress and force of habit had me uttering the more common phrase.

His body was halfway across the room before I managed to suck in another breath. He hit the wall hard enough to crack the foot-thick adobe. Wind, maybe from outside—no, he hadn't breached the wall.

I flicked a glance at the sparkling diamond on my left hand. *The ring?* Wind from White Feather? The stone and setting still radiated warning heat, but that was Mother Earth, not wind. Where the turquoise and silver were clearly a reflection of my ties to earth, the gold and diamond band felt as though a draft circled it, drawing away the warning heat.

I was an earth witch and had no say over wind; that was White Feather's court. Luckily, my blessing pinned the vamp more effectively than either of the elemental powers.

The vamp roared a curse that was swallowed by the spirit force that kept him in check. His fangs glistened like those of a snake, taking up more than half his face.

"God Bless You," I said again, louder. It wasn't possible to put any more conviction into it than the first time. When you're about to be devoured by a blood-sucking entity, prayers don't get any holier or more desperate.

Something in the prayer made the air shimmer. Not only had I never seen such teeth, apparently I had never seen a vamp without some glamour. The beast splayed against the wall went from humanoid to an ugly, hunchbacked, clawed creature. The plaster behind him crumbled as the vamp tried to muscle free.

"God help me," I whispered. I grabbed the silver crucifix from over the fireplace. It would burn him rather than destroy him, but in this case, every little advantage counted. My hands shook so badly I could barely hold the silver cross.

We might have stayed at stalemate until daylight took its toll on him had there not been a knock on the door. The polite tap was about as anti-climatic as snow in the middle of summer.

"Who is it?" My voice croaked.

"Patrick."

"Since when do you vamps need an invite?" I was staring at living proof that a vamp had crossed my threshold without my permission. Why didn't Patrick just pop right in like the other vamp? At least I knew Patrick marginally; I had helped him once, and he had patched me up in his secret hospital room not too long ago. That didn't mean I trusted him.

"The vampire used your blood to get in. Otherwise your power would have held and he would have required a specific invitation."

My fingers cramped around the crucifix. "And how, pray tell," I included the reference to prayer in hopes it would hold the vamp against the wall, "did he get my blood?"

"You recall, perhaps, that I am indebted to you because you disposed of Sheila the witch? She had your blood. And the blood of one of my vampires."

"Sheila's dead. And anything she had is long gone."

Patrick remained patient, but it was probably easier when standing on the other side of a door and not in the direct path of a rabid vamp. "You may also recall she experimented on a coyote shifter, among other creatures."

"Zandy!" It came out a curse. The vamp against the wall surged forward as soon as the word was out of my mouth.

My heart hit my toes and heat flared through the jewelry again. "Bless you," I shouted as though the vamp had sneezed. In this case I wished him all kinds of blessings, especially one from God above to cure his lack of death.

"Yes, Zandy," Patrick said dryly, as the vamp flew backward and smashed into the wall again. Patrick ignored the noise and shaking. "Sheila harvested blood, including yours. She concocted a spell and injected Zandy. Recently the coyote hired himself out as a food source to the vampire in your living room."

"This guy sucked Zandy dry?" I couldn't blame him much for that.

Zandy was an arrogant coyote shifter with no sense. He played any side of the fence that had money, and if he'd ever seen a moral, he'd tried to extort it too.

"Sadly, no, but the vamp fed from him. Some basic blood aura of yours must have remained in Zandy's blood. That allowed the vampire to breach your threshold. Whatever spell Sheila injected into Zandy also rendered the vampire insane. We're immune to most diseases, but not, unfortunately, insanity."

"Wasn't it obvious to berserker here that Zandy was insane?" The coyote shifter had allowed a vampire to feed on him. That was proof right there, regardless of Sheila's lingering spell.

"You must understand it is rare for a shifter to offer blood to one of my kind. Shifter blood has unique regenerative properties. It is incredibly strong, and it is...something of a treat."

"Whatever." I could almost hear Patrick drooling, but I wasn't interested in learning the finer points of vampire cuisine. Extraordinary cook I was not, and it would be a cold day in...there was no point in bringing hell into this. Hell was already in my living room.

"Have you killed Zandy, finally?" I edged a few more steps back.

"I've been rather preoccupied chasing down the complication we're currently discussing." His voice was calm, but there was an undercurrent of anger. It was nothing compared to my own. My home had been violated, spells broken and...I squeaked in protest.

The vamp was changing again, and not for the better. I could hold my faith until I died of starvation, and in fact, as I gained confidence and oxygen, the hold was stronger. But either the shimmer was making it easier for me to see what he truly was or the vamp was losing more of his humanity. When I had first opened the door, not expecting a vamp, there hadn't been time to register more than a handsome human face, dark black eyes, and power.

Now, the creature before me was fangs. His eyes were pushed inside a brow that would have done a Neanderthal proud. Legs that originally had him towering a foot and a half over my own five-six frame were now those of a very large dog ready to pounce. His hunched back had shredded his shirt, revealing transparent skin that stretched over long pointed spines, some of which jabbed repeatedly into the plaster wall as he twisted to free himself.

I backed up another step and muttered the first lines of a Hail Mary. This thing was tearing out my front wall. If my hold faltered...the breeze from my gold ring picked up speed, swirling enough that my black hair lifted. "White Feather?"

Adriel. It was a whisper on the wind.

I almost spun around to find the voice, but instinct and training kept me facing my enemy.

Still, the distraction interrupted my prayer. The vamp pulled away from the wall, fighting hard.

I had faith. It pushed him back, but retreating even as far as my lab to grab a stake was going to be a trick. I slid one foot backwards. He held.

Another. How far could faith hold? Did I have to be in line of sight?

The vamp thrashed violently, gouging a hole in the plaster and leaving a worrisome dent in the adobe.

The gold ring flared warm again, and the scent of White Feather's magic drifted across the room.

"Houston, we've got a problem," I said to no one in particular. White Feather must know I was in trouble. If he wasn't on his way, I didn't know magic.

The vamp's elbow punched against the adobe, knocking another large chunk loose. His claws tore at the bricks even though he still faced me. If he couldn't reach me, he would claw his way out.

Then what? Would Patrick get him? What if Patrick failed?

This spawn from hell could come inside my home. Anytime, apparently.

"Patrick, I think you better get in here and take out the trash."

Patrick didn't need a second invite. The top door hinge snapped with the force of his entry. He may have spared me a glance, but his focus was tight and saved for the vamp. He was within a foot of the guy against the wall when he finally said, "Witch, I don't know what spell you used, but you must cancel it."

His voice was strangled, stunned almost. He did look at me then, and even though I did not meet his eyes, I sensed a new respect. He murmured, "I don't think I've seen this spell before."

"It slipped out." What were the chances anyone had tried to bestow God's blessing on a vampire? Condemn them to hell, yeah, I could see it. That may or may not work, but apparently variations on a plea or blessing were very effective.

The vamp beast snaked out a lethal claw to hook Patrick, but was held back by the spirit in my blessing. Enraged at the failure, it turned its anger back to escaping. It landed a punch that hurt my ears and broke through the adobe to the outside.

"You had best hurry," Patrick advised. His cultured voice was not as calm as usual. Instead of a neatly tied ponytail, strands of black hair floated around his face in a messy tangle. There was a smear on his jeans. His spinal column was as straight as any human, but I knew better. There was a beast within. A very ugly beast, and I had just invited it inside my home.

"Uh, yeah." Whenever presented with a spell that needed undoing, I usually went for the opposite. In this case, the opposite presented a fairly large problem because I wasn't about to beckon anything that was the opposite of the spirit I'd called. "Can you wedge yourself in underneath it?" I asked.

Patrick held out a hand towards the force. His face was nearly white at the best of times. It turned death gray as his hand met resistance. Muscles clenched, but the force did not bend.

I felt nothing, but apparently he did. "No."

"Okay." The problem was worse than I thought. I didn't know how to cancel the spell.

Patrick spared me another glance. "Well?"

"This, uh," I licked my lips. "This is tricky."

"As in you can't do it without harming me? Perhaps you don't need me to remove the trash after all." His unblinking stare regarded me as though he had never seen me before.

I ignored him for the higher priority. I could hold the beast for quite a while, but it was ten-thirty at night. Daybreak was a long way off. The vamp wouldn't die from standing there; he was already dead. The creature snarled and slammed the wall again. Nope, no time for tea to while away the hours waiting for the sun to fry him.

If he beat his way outside my home, he would eventually come back. "He has to be destroyed, Patrick." The throbbing bruise at my throat was more than enough proof for me. I wasn't setting a rabid, insane vamp free. I wasn't even certain it was possible because if I reversed the blessing, that would be condemnation, and he was already condemned. He had overcome the laws of Spirit and Nature. The only answer was annihilation.

"I know that," Patrick said impatiently. He stepped back. "Can you destroy him?"

"I'd rather not."

"You must cancel the spell then."

"Are you faster than him? Are you very, very sure?"

An hour earlier, Patrick probably would have taken the bet with a laugh. Unlike me, he wasn't shocked at the vampire form. But until a few minutes ago, he hadn't known the spell I used existed. Neither had I.

"I'll take care of it," he promised.

If Patrick failed, I'd have two vamps to deal with. But it was impossible to hold a spell forever, even this one. If Patrick didn't come out on top, I'd have to call the spell again, faster. "I'm going to get a stake. If he moves, assume he's freed." I backed towards my lab. "Strike that. Don't allow him to move, Patrick. Don't let him get that far."

He gave me a single, perfunctory nod.

I scurried backwards. There was ash in the lab. It might not be honed to a fine point, but if faith continued to hold with me outside the room, I'd make sure the rogue vamp never showed up uninvited again.

Chapter 2

My lab was meant to withstand spells. Both the inside and outside walls were constructed with spelled chicken wire tucked inside the adobe. The double wall between the lab and house was capable of containing small explosions, thus keeping me from destroying the entire house if a spell went badly wrong.

The moment I stepped inside the haven, there was a loud roar followed by dead silence.

I stopped breathing and listened. One heartbeat...two. My silver went quiet. The ring...I held my hand in front of my face. No breeze. But the gold was warmer than expected. White Feather had designed the gift with my ability to channel power from Mother Earth in mind. The diamond sparked brightly as though the light energy wasn't entirely gone either, but it could have been a reflection from the fluorescent bulbs in the lab.

The diamond was a new source of power, one I hadn't dared tap yet. The very idea terrified me. For one, the ring was a precious gift, containing a stone formed millions of years ago. As if that weren't enough, it also held the love from White Feather's grandparents and even more importantly, love from him. "White Feather?" I kicked the door to the hallway closed. If that thing freed itself, it could follow me in here, door or no door, but I felt safer anyway. I said a prayer and scooted back.

The ring didn't answer, but the tiniest bit of energy tingled across my hand. I was too practiced at witching to attribute it to coincidence. I was also too experienced to waste any further time trying to figure it out.

My lab was storage to raw magical elements that included spools of silver, stones, herbs, and wood, both new and ancient. Most of the tree material was for witching forks, but I never threw anything out, because with magic, you never knew what you might need.

The oak plank was too flat to be of use. "Maple...pine," I tossed them aside. "Is this ash?" It was darker than the maple and more gnarled. I hadn't labeled most of the collection, foolishly assuming that if wood was required for a spell, I'd have time to research and identify. "With a prayer, it'll have to work. If it doesn't, I'll stick it up his ass and light it on fire."

At the lab door, my heartbeat ratcheted up a notch. I clutched the doorknob and prepared to charge out with my best rebel...prayer on my lips. As I twisted the knob, there was a whisper from the ring; an echo of metal against metal when it touched the brass knob that was coated with both copper and silver.

"White Feather?" This was surreal, even for me.

I waited for an answer, but didn't get one.

Nothing had followed me into the lab, but when I yanked open the door, my heart expected vamps to be lined up along the short hallway. With the stake held high, trying not to think about the fact that it wasn't all that pointy, I edged forward.

My own raspy prayer was the only sound in the hallway. Why hadn't I grabbed my silver dagger? My extra crucifix?

Holy water! I back pedaled. My dagger was on the table in its protective leather sheath. Holy water was in one of two places; the small jar on the shelf filed in alphabetical order or a large gallon jug by the outside door.

I snatched up the gallon jug and braved the hallway leading to the living room.

This time, a real voice broke the silence. "Adriel?" The panicked growl in White Feather's call was more obvious in real life than the whisper from the ring.

I charged forward. "White Feather! Vamps!" He had no way of knowing there were vamps afoot. I turned the corner, spear up, ready to defend him.

When White Feather used wind to search ahead for danger, it had a subtle caress. I was expecting it, but unfortunately for both of us, he was moving with his wind, not trailing along behind it.

"Mmmooof." The breeze impacted me a fraction of a second before he did. Neither force was subtle or caressing. The wind jerked the spear out of my right hand. Holy water exploded from the jug with geyser force as it smashed between us. I careened off the wall before White Feather's crashing weight bore me to the carpet.

We were blessed all over. The spear bounced off my head and thumped harmlessly onto the floor.

"Adriel." The voice was in my ear. It was possible the ring tingled, but my arms and hands were throbbing from the fall, deadening everything else.

"Vamps. Living room?" I gasped out.

"Hole in the wall," White Feather growled back. He lifted himself off me, his strong arms pulling me up with him. "Adriel—" He held my shoulders and inspected me from top to bottom. "He came in the wall? As a bat? I thought that was a myth, but that hole isn't big enough for a vamp!"

I peered over his shoulder, scooting him sideways in order to see.

An opening over a foot long yawned like a jagged mouth across my outside wall. It was three yards from the door, which was wide open. "They're gone?"

White Feather fingered the silver ring I had designed for him. It contained pieces of my own jewelry, including turquoise originally a part of my grandmother's bracelet. "The silver in the ring froze as cold as ice right before I heard you scream. Only you weren't there. What happened here?" His green eyes met my whiskey brown ones, flashing shades of the forest, winds that wanted to rip into something. His entire body was taut and ready for a fight, but the threat was gone.

"What happened here?" I repeated dumbly, shock immobilizing my brain.

He released a huge breath of air, gathered me into a fierce embrace and squeezed. "I was hoping you could tell *me*."

Chapter 3

Wintertime in Santa Fe is often blessed with pockets of warm days, especially when the sun stretches across cloudless skies and gently warms the rocky desert. Even on a cold, crisp day you might find heat rising in a sun-filled canyon or bouncing off an adobe wall. Mother Earth could be cold and fierce, but the warm desert heartbeat was never far away.

The safety of White Feather's arms was like that heat; steadying, a bit heady, a lot magic. I clutched the dark curls at the base of his neck, letting his presence calm me. His normally combed hair stood on end. The long-sleeved black shirt he wore as a jacket over a tucked in t-shirt was soaking wet.

My own arms, matching the color of his Native American tinged with Hispanic gold, were bare. Only goosebumps covered them against the air swirling through the open door and the hole in the wall. My thick fleece sweatpants, when dry, were cozy enough to double as pjs. I often worked late in the lab and was too lazy to change.

The desert night snapped at us, threatening icicles for anyone dumb enough to walk around bathed in holy water. "We should go in the lab," I whispered.

White Feather gave the living room another quick inspection using the cold wind to ensure the danger was past. I couldn't read his magic, but as he stirred the breeze, the chill of outside air mixed with the last of the inside warmth. A paper towel fluttered from the counter to the kitchen floor.

Finding no vampires waiting to pounce, White Feather strode to the front door and shoved one of the kitchen chairs under the doorknob. The top still sagged because of the destroyed hinge.

"Patrick snapped the door off the frame," I said. A bit unsteadily, I approached the fireplace and hung the crucifix back over the chimney. It was a nearly useless gesture, a lot like shutting the barn door after a bull had ripped through.

My hands shook, but my rings, all of them this time, were quiet. I pulled my long black hair away from my face, but had nothing to fasten it with. White Feather hustled me in front of him and together we ducked into the lab and bolted the door.

Between deep breaths, I told White Feather about the rogue vamp making himself at home.

"That's it. You're moving in with me," he said flatly.

I pictured White Feather's house in its current state of almost-but-not-quite closed to the elements. It hadn't been completely rebuilt after the incident with a malicious tornado. We had been working hard on it, but in the meantime, he stayed at my place a lot. We hadn't talked about any permanent changes. Every time he hinted at me moving, I scuttled away from the topic. "Patrick took care of the vamp. I'm pretty sure he killed him. No one, not even the vamps, wants anything running around that has been infected with Sheila's experiments."

"You saw him kill the thing? No wonder I heard you screaming from miles away. I didn't know a vampire would go so far as to stake another vamp."

I shuddered. "I don't know how he did it. I was in here getting a stake."

The muscles under his shirt rippled as he reached for me. "So the vamp could still be around. Along with Zandy." His eyes flashed as he evaluated the situation and found nothing to like.

I shrugged. When I swallowed, my throat hurt. "It's not Zandy or the vamp that I'm scared of at the moment."

White Feather growled a half question.

"Patrick didn't pull the vamp through my wall from outside. I had to invite Patrick inside so he could dispose of the vamp."

White Feather's wind wrapped around me. "Why are we still standing here?" he yelled.

Air puffed out my lips, a half laugh. "My lab is practically a separate structure from the house. I couldn't afford to do the whole house with some of the added protections in the lab. The room is right up against the adobe, but I'm pretty sure Patrick can't get in here. The invite doesn't include the lab, just like it doesn't when I invite most people in my house."

His eyes darted to the outside door. It was closed and locked, as was the inside door. He weighed my words, and then rubbed his jaw as if it hurt as much as my neck and shoulders. "You're moving in with me." He hadn't been all that comfortable half living in my place, even though my home had walls and a roof and his place didn't. He might also be growing tired of waiting for me to stop avoiding the discussion about where we'd live permanently.

Not one to over-argue in the face of logic and a vampire who could step inside my parlor anytime he wanted, I didn't scream out my fears of losing everything I had worked so hard for, of not knowing how to be part of him and still keep me at the same time. Instead, I nodded. "I should probably move in with you, except for when I'm here, working in the lab." It was a bit of a hedge, but far enough over the cliff that I hyperventilated.

Green rolled across his eyes right before he crushed my lips underneath his. He tasted of the rich sage desert, his lips warm and very welcome. Every part of him was breathing, *living* male.

The lab was really not the place for this sort of thing, but coming off fear and tension, I gave as good as I got, grateful he had arrived, even if I didn't understand how he'd known about the danger. We'd never had that kind of connection before. Just like normals, we relied on a phone for long distance communication.

White Feather did a thorough job of making sure all of me was intact before finally letting some air between us.

I gasped, "How did you know I was in trouble?"

His hands rested underneath my wet t-shirt, heating me all the way to the core. "You called me. It was as if I searched with the wind, only this time the wind came to me."

I lifted my hand from his chest, the one with the diamond ring. He had given it to me only a month earlier. It was my wedding ring, although we hadn't officially gotten married via regular channels, a point my mother harped on. "Interesting. Mother Earth was definitely warning me, but this time was different. There was a sense of you—and your wind power."

"Worked for me."

"I wonder what we can do with it if we really try?"

"Let's not test it too soon. It was bad enough that I was halfway across Santa Fe at a robbery scene inspecting a dead body when the wind started screaming at me."

My mouth dropped open. "What?"

"This hasn't been my best night. Grab some things to take to my place. We'll stop by Gordon's latest case since I wasn't finished. You taught me enough about auras to trace who walked where, but as long as you're coming along, it won't hurt to have your expertise."

I pulled at my wet shirt. "I need to grab some clothes and...things." Panic fluttered in my chest. I wanted my entire lab with me, not just a piece or two. This was my *home*. Sure, it was smaller than White Feather's place, but we could live here...well, not right now we couldn't. "I can still come back here and work if I need to."

White Feather must have sensed the insecurity in my words, but he guessed wrong about the reason. "I'll be right next to you while you pack some clothes. If Patrick or any other vamp is stupid enough to show up, we'll be ready."

Now probably wasn't the right time to tell him I didn't want to give up my home and move in with him. Especially since I was the one who had sealed the deal by inviting a vamp into my house.

Feeling the tension lodge deeper in my shoulders, I moved to bundle up a few of the basic necessities from the lab.

Chapter 4

When I was sixteen, I began selling spells. At seventeen I brokered the deal to buy the property where my house currently stood. It was a trade for removing a nasty curse from a very desperate and wealthy individual. My parents hadn't taken my witching business seriously, which was a huge advantage in getting started without interference. It was over a year before they realized I was well on my way to rebuilding the house on the property. The first house had burned to the ground after my inexperience with tainted gold loosed an evil spirit.

I'd been doing my own thing for the better part of ten years.

Loving someone and living with them day in and day out were two different things. The love part was easy. I was head over heels. Giving up my freedom was a lot scarier. And I didn't mean dating freedom.

White Feather not only helped his brother Gordon with undercover work, he was a consultant on various engineering projects, usually projects involving wind energy. He worked from home frequently. So did I.

White Feather had more or less planned for the working from home thing. With his house torn in half, it wasn't difficult to add a lab for me. The problem was that the lab wasn't done. And "moving in with White Feather someday soon" was not the same as "moving in with White Feather right this second."

It wasn't that I wasn't committed to White Feather, it was that...what if he decided he didn't like me after he knew all my weird quirks? I wasn't a great cook. I was neat as a pin in the lab because it was necessary; you don't want stray ingredients sneaking into a spell, and you must be able to locate items quickly in an emergency. The rest of my house collected dust as though dirt were a fine wine that needed to be aged. The kitchen was almost always clean, but that was mostly because I didn't cook often. Laundry was done under the duress of washing it or buying clean clothes every month.

I packed items from my lab halfheartedly, unsure what to take. My ears listened for a vamp, which was silly. If Patrick decided to return and didn't want me to hear him, he would be quieter than a whisper. "Do you think we could cover that hole in the living room? And fix the front door?"

"Good idea." White Feather set aside the box I had just handed him.

We stared at the closed lab door. Then we looked at each other. He wouldn't allow me do it, and I wasn't about to sit in here packing like a good wife while he did it.

"I have some plywood." At the wood stack, I grabbed up a long piece of sharp willow instead of the flat plywood. "The ash, at least I think it is ash, is in the hallway."

We moved together, a team.

The living room was quiet. And cold. Morning was a long way off, but with no vamps in sight, we had time to secure the place. I picked up the discarded piece of ash on my way back to retrieve the plywood. "Let's get this done."

* * *

By the time we left, I had worked up a sweat and felt a sense of satisfaction from sharing chores with White Feather. It helped my mood that we headed to the robbery site rather than driving straight to his place. Working a case was just another job.

I asked, "What's the deal with this robbery?"

"No witnesses, but a bystander—or more likely one of the perps—was killed inside the jewelry store."

"Shot?"

He shook his head. "ME said the cause of death mimicked a strangulation, but her neck is intact. There are pinpoint hemorrhages in the eyes and more hemorrhages across the chest and at least one arm. The robbery was called in about nine o'clock when the shop owner stopped by to stash some new inventory in the safe. Everything on the street was already closed, thus no witnesses."

"Hmm. That late at night doesn't fit innocent window shopper."

"Especially since the dead lady was inside the store."

Santa Fe had numerous art galleries and high-end design stores all over the city. The most popular and successful were in the plaza area, of course. The older galleries had learned to bring in popular local commissions and stayed in business for years. New ones popped up in homes redesigned as stores and came and went with the seasons or fads.

White Feather pulled in front of a white-washed building four or five blocks from the plaza. There were no restaurants on the street, and nothing opened late. "Piercing Hoops," I read. The building had crime scene tape strung across the front, but the police personnel were gone. "Looks like you missed most of the fun."

"Yeah. Too bad." White Feather opened his door. "Everything taken was gold or silver, except for a couple of nicer pieces that had little precious metal, but must have caught the eyes of the perps."

"Sounds planned, except they probably lost one of their own. Why were you called in?"

"Because it's the second robbery in two weeks where it looks like one of the perps died of the same symptoms."

"Hmm." The windows were intact, and the door was locked, but White Feather knew where Gordon had hidden a key for him. He unlocked the door, let his wind search ahead, then found the light switch. He motioned me inside.

Before stepping forward, I took a deep breath. The air smelled of White Feather; soap, shaving cream, and a touch of mountain forest tinged with mesquite that was his wind magic. The second breath wasn't so nice. The odor of dead body was a stink of loose bowels. At least there was no blood. I had my witching fork ready.

White Feather pointed to where the body had been, but it was pretty obvious.

Wrinkling my nose, I rolled the fork in the essence, and let it lead me where it would. To my surprise, it led right back outside to the curb.

I traced it twice, getting a stronger pull right near the door, but otherwise the strongest spot was where the woman had fallen.

"That's exactly what I found," White Feather said with satisfaction. "The perps pulled up to the curb, stood at the door until the locks were picked, and went inside. This lady never even made it to a jewelry case before collapsing."

"How did the alarm get disabled?" I inspected the small space, noting that the paintings hadn't been of interest to the thieves. "And what about the cameras?"

"That's where the robbery takes another unusual turn. The door doesn't show any signs of being picked. The alarm appears to have been turned off right before the robbery. Same with the cameras. One of the technicians with Gordon said it was possible a strong electromagnetic source interfered with the camera signals, but that wouldn't have disabled the alarm. That had to be done manually."

I stood under one of the cameras and held the witching fork up. Nothing. "Where is the switch for the camera and alarms?"

"There's an emergency alarm button by the register. The cameras and the overall alarm settings are controlled from a computer in the office."

I waved the fork over the counter and the alarm button, but there was nary a twitch.

The office was nothing more than a glorified closet behind the counter.

As I poked my head through the door, White Feather said, "The alarm was easy to disable. Turn around, and you'll see the alarm control right next to the light switch. The code to set or disarm it is written underneath. The owner figured if you were inside the office, the alarm had already gone off or you were one of the employees.

"Shutting down the cameras was done easily from the computer. The digital recording should have shown the first person who entered and came back to the office to shut off the alarm, but the recording doesn't show lights or people. It was simply turned off and never turned back on," White Feather said.

At the desk, the fork twitched ever so slightly. "She was in here?" The fork definitely twitched on the keyboard. I moved the fork around, but had to crouch to pick up the signal on the floor. Even then it was weak.

"I didn't find any aura in there." White Feather leaned over the counter. If he tried to join me back here, we'd trip over one another.

I expected the trail to lead me back to the body, but once I reached the counter, it went around one side and then faded. "Can you enhance this with your wind?" He had strengthened a witching fork for me before, but that was to make it search further out. This time we needed the opposite. "Maybe if you create one of those air pockets of blank air around the fork so that it stays focused on this narrow trail?"

He lifted one eyebrow. "Those bubbles are hard to form and hold, you know. I've never done one that wasn't around myself."

The bubble trick was one he'd learned for survival. Attaching it to something else, especially without life and death as a motivation, might take some doing. I smiled. "Aw, come on. Just move the bubble in front of you. Put it around the fork."

He grumbled something that sounded like, "Most guys only have to come up with wine and roses." Then louder, he said, "Gimme the fork."

When he handed it back to me, I could tell no difference, except it smelled of his magic.

He stepped back and watched me work, his eyes hooded as though he were still concentrating. I left him to do his thing and did mine.

Holding the fork near the ground, I duck-walked behind the signal halfway to the door before it completely stopped right in the middle of the store. Searching from my position, I noticed a nearly one-inch gap at the bottom of the entrance door. "Looks like the rubber weatherstripping is missing from under the door."

White Feather leaned down to look. "Or wasn't ever there."

Running the fork along the bottom of the door yielded another light tug that I was sure would return directly to the body, but with White Feather's bubble keeping it focused, this line went around the jewelry counter on the other side and into the office. "In and out and then it stops." I followed it twice. "But this weak line never goes to the body. Odd. The fork is set to the body. It's like it's following something that came from the body, but never went back there."

I wandered throughout the store, letting the witch fork hover. There wasn't any sign of aura near the jewelry cases. They had been smashed open and looted hurriedly. "Was she a witch? What was her name?"

"Alicia Romero. No idea if she was or not."

"Doesn't ring a bell. It's almost as if the dead lady magically pushed an object into the office and used it to turn the alarm off. She didn't walk back there. The signal isn't strong enough. But whatever went into the office didn't return to her." I didn't like where my thoughts were taking me. The pattern almost resembled someone controlling a familiar.

"Maybe one of the other perps picked up whatever it was and carried it out. With that weak signal, and all the people investigating the scene walking through here, the trail might have been obliterated."

I shrugged. "Maybe you should have Lynx stop by here."

"Why?"

"His nose." Lynx wouldn't be pleased about being asked, because his birthright and past were sore spots. "Lynx can tell us if the victim was a shifter. And if she wasn't, he could probably tell us if they brought in an animal that the others took home with them, some kind of familiar."

"A familiar." His eyes narrowed as he considered the idea.

"You should also ask Gordon for a picture of the dead woman, too. I can show it to Mat." Many witches sold on consignment through Mat's shop to prevent broadcasting to the world who and what they were. Mat might recognize the face, but not the name, because most witches didn't use their real name.

"Photos won't be pretty."

"I don't imagine so."

He switched off the lights, and it was time to go. Home. The new one, not the old one. I was too tired to fret about it.

Chapter 5

Waking up next to White Feather did a lot to make staying at his place worth it. He took his time saying good morning, persuading me that I was welcome. The bedroom was a safe haven in his home; one of the few rooms in his house that was completely intact. Computer terminals on his hand-carved desk monitored the power-generating reeds and windmills that had been rebuilt along the edge of his property.

The purely masculine ambiance was very different from the decor of my own bedroom, but the combination of hand-worked wood married to his engineering background was a comfortable blend of magics.

While White Feather showered, I stretched lazily. My eyes couldn't help but drift to the dark, gnarled mesquite dresser that was his connection to his heritage and far more than a gorgeous work of art. White Feather was a guardian of the sacred place hidden behind the dresser. His grandfather's ghost still kept guard too, but I had never seen him.

The place wasn't home, but I could probably get used to it. I had better, because returning to my place wasn't in the cards, at least not right now.

When White Feather was finished showering, I took my turn before joining him in the kitchen. The dining area, what was left of it, had been shut off from the elements with plywood and plastic sheeting. It didn't hurt my feelings that I was still close enough to guest status that White Feather started frying bacon for breakfast while I sipped hot breakfast tea spiked generously with half and half.

I never bought half and half, but men didn't concern themselves with things like "calories" and "healthy." If I hadn't already been in love, the morning activities and breakfast would have sealed the deal.

As he grated cheese for omelets, he said, "Don't forget we're having dinner at my mom's house tonight. She's really looking forward to meeting you." He smiled at me over his shoulder.

"Uh-huh." I hadn't forgotten, despite filing it waaaay in the back of my mind where it wouldn't make me nervous. I decided to forgo the wonderful view that was White Feather cooking and bring in the rest of my luggage.

I slipped off the bar stool and strolled out to the car. We had left several bags in the trunk and backseat, rather than haul everything in last night. I extracted two suitcases before carefully rescuing my little pear cactus. In the old days, the placement of the cactus on my own porch signaled Lynx when a business offer was in the making. These days, he had a cell phone, but old habits died hard. I wanted the cactus even if Lynx wouldn't know to look for it here.

I placed it gently on the porch in the same spot that on my porch meant "meet needed."

"Breakfast," White Feather said from the doorway.

I jumped, stuck in a time-warp as the prickly shrub brought to mind memories of a scrawny kid anxious to prove he could do any job, any time, better than any of the competition. "Coming."

White Feather picked up one of the suitcases. "You'll need a few more trips back and forth to your place."

The sound of a vehicle distracted me from answering.

My buddy Lynx managed to outsmart me again. That or his nose for food was even better than I suspected. He parked and sauntered up the walkway.

"Unbelievable," I muttered. "How did he know I was here?"

"Maybe because you belong here?" White Feather suggested.

Lynx cocked his head in a way that told me he was listening intently to his surroundings, but his nose didn't twitch, not in the least. His black hair hung in small braids, almost cornrows. It was a look he could pull off well. He was probably mostly Hispanic, but his skin was dark enough, you could never be certain of his exact heritage. Like the shifter he was, he chose to highlight some physical aspects more than others depending on his mood—or the job.

Since food had somehow become a standard part of the payment package, as we trooped inside I said, "Heavy on the bacon, easy on the eggs."

Lynx grinned. "Hold the OJ."

"If White Feather has green chiles, I'm putting some in your eggs." The typical banter made me feel more at ease as we arrived in the kitchen. This wasn't my home, but I'd just pretended it was. If Lynx hadn't been here, I'd never have had the guts to take over White Feather's kitchen, but no way did I dare look hesitant in front of Lynx. Letting him know I was off-balance was akin to handing him a weapon. He might use it on a mutual enemy or he might find a less beneficial way to wield it.

White Feather said, "I don't have any green chile unless you count cans."

"Ick."

"No way," was Lynx's contribution. Since he made a big show of avoiding all vegetables he would have said that regardless of the freshness of the chiles.

I busied myself with the bacon. Lynx stood next to me as if we were in my kitchen, something he had done a hundred times before. He watched over the bacon while I dished up the cheese omelet. Both of us stole a glance or two at White Feather, but he was busy tinkering with rebuilding his coffee train set. It was an awesome invention; a train designed to deliver coffee to a roaster, grinder and then the brewer.

"We have a job for you," White Feather said to Lynx.

"That train looks too uphill to me," Lynx replied.

I jabbed him in the arm. "Not the train, dummy."

Intent on his project, White Feather allowed himself to be distracted from the job discussion. "I decided to improve the old design. I'm thinking of putting the roaster below the counter, but I'll have to vent it outside and put in a serious fan. It generates a lot of heat and smoke when roasting the beans."

The old train system, powered entirely by a miniature windmill, had been destroyed by the tornado. White Feather had given me one of the original cars. It would probably make the magic of the new one stronger if I let him use it in the new design, but he had carved it himself so I was selfishly keeping it.

"Don't matter to me where you put it," Lynx said. "I don't drink coffee, but keeping the smoke out of the house is a good idea." He grinned at my eye-roll.

"We need you to help investigate a robbery," White Feather clarified as he opened a small jar of wood stain. "Use your—"

I broke in because Lynx could be very sensitive about his skills, especially any open reference to his bobcat skills rather than his human ones. "Check the scene. Tell us what you can. Lady died there. She might have been a shifter. Or there might have been one there, if not her."

"Might need to examine the body after you check the crime scene." White Feather dabbed stain on a tiny chipped section of the burl wood that formed the base of the mountain scenery. "You up for the job?"

Lynx did what he always did. He carried his food to the bar that ran between the kitchen and living room and started eating. "Usual rate. Tell me the location. I'll go tonight."

"We can do this today," I said. "White Feather has a key."

"Why you always want to work in daylight? Better to work at night."

"We can be there *legally*," I pointed out. "Which means we can get it done faster before the smell...evidence gets trampled." For all my sensitivity, I could blow it with the best of them.

Lynx cut his eyes to me and missed a half-second of chewing, but then he said, "I can do it after one-thirty. Got business before that."

I didn't ask.

White Feather frowned. "The contractors are coming at noon to bake more adobe bricks. But there's no reason you two can't take a look without me."

"Do you have enough spelled chicken wire mesh for the bricks and wall?" I had spelled several rolls with a diluted mix of silver and copper.

"Plenty. Your dad prepared more special ashes for the bricks, but I want to ensure the bricks are mixed and baked properly."

"Okay." It was important that we both had a hand in the building and design. You could buy spells or hire out work, but you couldn't impart that extra special essence without doing at least some of the physical labor yourself. Even if I wasn't moving here, I'd make sure he had the best protection a witch could spell.

White Feather added, "I've decided to double up on the adobe on the inside wall between your lab and the main house like you did at your house. Not a bad idea to keep things separated."

The reminder of my latest disaster set me to grumbling under my breath.

"I had no idea at the time that it would be useful for keeping a vamp out."

Lynx perked up his ears, not that he was in danger of missing a single word.

"You guys check the jewelry store, and if you don't pick up anything useful, we can arrange a visit to the morgue. The lady from the first break-in has already been autopsied. The one from last night hasn't."

Bodies and their discussion didn't bother Lynx. He never missed a bite. I wanted to ask White Feather more questions about the house rebuilding, but I didn't want Lynx to know how much I didn't know. I pressed my lips together and went back to the car to haul out the last of my bags.

Chapter 6

Since everyone else had plans for the next few hours, it was a good time to visit my best friend, Matilda. She needed to know about the rogue vamp and my run-in with Patrick. Mat was also the most likely person in the entire city to know if either of the dead women at the crime scenes were witches.

We had been best friends since the day we met in grade school. She was everything I was not; flamboyant, outgoing, a redhead with green eyes, and a witch who was more than happy to do business out in the open.

Her shop was the place to be and be seen. Only I didn't want to be seen, even though we were best friends. She was always intermittently busy, and today the place had no less than three women shoppers and Jim, Mat's boyfriend, packed inside the small store.

Getting personal time with that many customers around wasn't happening. Opportunity was slim even for Jim, apparently. As soon as he recognized me, he sauntered over to chat.

"Hard to get in a word edgewise in such a popular place." Jim was clean-shaven and almost as good-looking as White Feather, but he was shorter and stockier. With dark sunglasses, his swarthy Hispanic looks and confident swagger, he could easily make a living as a tough guy in movies. His blue jeans and tucked in t-shirt were bad-boy tight. A nice package that Mat was having trouble keeping her eyes off of. Probably her hands too.

I grinned. It was nice to see Mat so blissfully focused on a guy. We witches had a hard time finding people who accepted our quirks.

"Business is good," I said. "Maybe I should come back later." If he hadn't had a chance to chat with her yet, I wasn't next in line.

"Might clear in a few minutes. I'm on my way out. We just grabbed coffee and dessert at the new place down the street for an early lunch break." He kept his voice down, but the shop was small. "I didn't have a chance to tell her I won't get off work until late, but I'll see her tomorrow morning. If you talk to her, let her know for me, would you?"

"Sure."

He walked backwards out of the shop, purposely pausing to entice Mat to glance his way.

Flirt.

The three ladies perusing items seemed determined to giggle over every spell in the place. They were well-heeled, dressed in tailored pants and nice sweaters similar to outfits my sister Kas often wore. They were dolled up as if they had just spent the day at a spa luxuriating in a full makeover from head to toe.

Rather than hover in my low class jeans and sneakers, I sidled to the back of the shop where a curtain of beads separated the shop from Mat's living room. She always invited me to take cover rather than stand around like an aimless waif.

Before it could slip my mind, I wrote her a note with Jim's message.

Another minute or two and the cash register slammed shut on a stream of giggles and a purchase. Mat waited a few seconds before she appeared in the doorway. Her flaming red curls were perfectly coiffed into a french twist. Since dating Jim, some of her flamboyance had been replaced with elegance.

"The gods are smiling on me," she said. "There's a fabulous new bakery up the street and right next to it a new nail salon. I can close shop for fifteen, but let me check to see if more people are coming."

I waved my hand. "Don't bother." I gave her a succinct rundown on the vamp invasion, completely ignoring her gasps. When I finished the story, rather than dwell on it, I slid on to the next item on my list. "I really came by to see if you know any witches by the name of Alicia Romero or Dana Clark." White Feather had written the names down. I handed her the scrap of paper.

She waited for more information, but when none was forthcoming, she rolled her eyes. "Okay, so I can find you at White Feather's if I need you. It will surprise you to know that is exactly where I would have looked if you weren't at home. As for Patrick," she shook her head. "Wow."

"There's no point in hashing it to death," I grumbled.

"Given that he's already dead, agreed."

"Very funny. Do you know either of the names?"

"Neither rings a bell, but if you watch the front for me, I'll check my records. I assume this has nothing to do with the vamps."

We traded places at the doorway. "Nope. I'll get a picture of the ladies in case they were using alternative names for their witching business."

"Last time you had me look up a witch, she was a ghost. You're not still getting such visitors, are you?" Her joke fell into an awkward silence. She glanced up at me from her spot leaning over the computer.

I sighed. "Not yet, but these two are in that realm."

"You're a real breath of fresh air today, aren't you?"

I kept one eye on her and one on the door. She worked at the computer and talked. "You should visit the bakery up the street. Jim and I ate breakfast there this morning. *Heavenly* cinnamon rolls. At noon they have sandwiches and desserts. It's a total sin factory. Oh, and the coffee. I love coffee."

I grinned. Jim had mentioned the place, but she called it breakfast, not lunch, so things were obviously going really well between them. "Do they have tea?"

She straightened up from the desk. "Nothing under those names. If you get a line on what kind of spells they might have sold, I might be able to help. Witches don't use their real names most of the time, but they all have signature spells." Without missing a beat, she switched back to food. "Yes, Sweet Puffs has about forty kinds of tea and cakes to compliment each blend. The place is upscale, but the prices are decent, if just barely. With the nail shop starting up right next door, business has been booming for me. The ladies get their nails done, have a bite to eat and gosh, so long as they are out having a good time, here I am!" Mat beamed, her green eyes sparkling.

"And you just happen to have a spell or two that will make them even more irresistible."

"If only I had space for the ladies to try on clothes. I could carry some awesome negligees or sexy bras to go with the spells. They buffed up the outside, might as well drape themselves in silk...tsk." She joined me in the front. "There's just no room for it in the shop."

I laughed. "How about shoes? Women like to buy shoes."

"Too much inventory and no place to sit."

"What about spell sachets? Cute little ones with something on them to match the nail designs. All three of the ladies had flowers painted on their fingernails and toes. You could coordinate with the nail artist and put out little purses to match their nails."

Mat put a hand to her mouth, but didn't quite trap a squeal. "That is brilliant! I've gotten to know Tam, the owner, and you should see her nail work. The designs are exquisite! I've seen stars, cats and some florals. If I find someone to embroider matching designs on the outside of spell packets, they'll sell like hotcakes!" She clapped her hands. "I'll make the pouches big enough so that after they've used the spell, the pouches can double as cell phone cases."

"Works for me." I blew her a kiss on my way out.

She was busy scribbling notes about her plans, but at the last second she paused and called after me. "Be careful, Adriel. Patrick's a good guy, but be careful."

"No one is more careful than me where vamps are concerned." I'd moved out of my house. There wasn't much else I could do.

Since it wasn't time to meet Lynx, it seemed like the perfect opportunity to check out Sweet Puffs. I didn't deserve it; breakfast had been plenty filling even though we split it three ways.

I passed Tam's Spa and Nails without looking in. The windows were artfully decorated to showcase the intricate nail designs available inside. Unlike some places, the clients weren't on display. The painted windows were tinted for privacy, which was a nice touch if you were the type to have time to get your nails done. To say it wasn't my cup of tea would be an understatement.

I glanced at my hands, happy to see my nails weren't chipped or broken. Keeping them short when you're an earth witch is almost mandatory.

Once inside Sweet Puffs, I wasted approximately a nanosecond before zeroing in on the chocolate eclairs. Sure, there were probably other goodies worth considering, but what if they ran out while I dithered? The eclair was large enough for two people, maybe three. Hmm. Well, I was meeting with Lynx later, so leftovers weren't an issue.

Normally I'd sit by the door or windows, but a young Asian guy was painting fabulous-looking desserts on the glass. Luckily, there were plastic tables and chairs outside on the sidewalk, so I helped myself to complimentary hot tea and nabbed a seat. It was hard not to drool on my eclair.

I people-watched, noting that most of the ladies went from either the bakery to the nail salon or vice-versa. The kid painting the windows handed out a business card or two, but it wasn't until he came outside to check the finished design that I realized the cards were actually for the nail salon, not his own work.

"Nice job," I said.

"Thanks. I did my mom's too." He pointed to the nail salon and offered me one of the cards.

I had a thing about business cards lately, so made sure my hands were full of tea and fork. "Oh, thanks. You'd better set it down on the table. My hands are a bit messy." I made a big show of reaching for my napkin. "I do a lot of gardening so getting my nails done is—" His paint spattered hands inspired me. "Makes about as much sense as you getting a manicure before painting window designs."

He grinned. "Do you think I need more whipped cream on the mocha?"

He was hard to peg age-wise, but he was probably still in high school. His jeans were dotted with fashion designed holes. He showed his good taste in music with a gray tee depicting a guitar with the words Dire Straits underneath.

I studied the painting in question. "Nope. Just a few sprinkles of chocolate."

His scant eyebrows lifted in consternation. "You're right!"

"Never forget the chocolate. It will serve you well in life with food—and women," I told him with a wink.

"Here." He retrieved the card from the table and turned it over. Using a charcoal pencil from his stash, he drew two Chinese characters on the back. "Give this to my mom, Tam, at the shop." He spared a covert glance at the other patrons. "This is for the good stuff in the back. She doesn't advertise the massages and hair styling because she doesn't want to hire more people for the front. It's only for her special clients."

"Oh, well. You don't owe me anything, and really I can't accept anything." Implied in there was the spoken spell to ensure any spell on the card didn't attach itself to me. Reminding the kid about chocolate sprinkles wasn't worth special treatment. Of course, I was overly paranoid. I flipped the card and saw nothing but the address embedded in a trail of delicate flowers.

"Trust me, no one is better with hair than my mom. She's as good as Dad is with the desserts." The kid gave me another shy smile and hurried back inside to add sprinkles to his mocha.

What a combo. The two shops were the ultimate in Mom and Pop retailers. I studied the card, but the Chinese symbols meant nothing to me. The only way to find out if it was an innocent instruction was to research it or visit Tam's nail salon and see what happened. Admittedly, I was curious about Mat's new neighbor.

Hmm. Maybe the card was already insinuating its magic. Or maybe I was badly in need of a decent haircut, especially since I was meeting White Feather's family tonight.

I muttered another spell and tested the card with my silver, but if there was magical residue, it was dormant. I had refused the card and protected myself, but I didn't pick it up anyway.

I folded the cover on the eclair take-out box and scooted inside Sweet Puffs for a paper sack. At the counter, there were more cards for the nail salon, along with cards for the bakery.

Still curious, I wandered over to the nail salon for a peek inside.

Like most salons it contained a few neatly organized stations. Two women clients were buried under hot face towels while their feet soaked in bubbly baths. There was one male employee, but the rest were women. A check-out counter ran halfway across the front. The customer area stopped near the back with silk curtains protecting a doorway into an even more private area. The store was much like Mat's; very clean and not overly heated for a winter Santa Fe day. Surprisingly it smelled more of herbal tea than nail polish.

"Can I help you?" A short Asian woman appeared from behind the curtains. She had no discernible accent and no wrinkles either.

My half smile was hesitant. "I met your son next door. He said you do hair. He left me his card, well, your card—"

"That Kevin." She bustled forward. At five-six and a half when I stretched, I still beat her by six inches, easily. My hair was encased in its standard ponytail, halfway down my back.

"You need something special? I don't like highlights, not on Asians or Hispanics. Oh, they can be done well, but you have the dark hair. You want highlights, they should be silver."

I shook my head. "I was thinking more of a trim. Well, really, I'm a friend of Mat's from up the street and she told me—"

"Matilda! The red-haired mystic? Yes, yes, sweet girl. Beautiful. You come back here with me. You have the mystic eyes yourself, yes." She swarmed ahead, moving aside the curtain.

I didn't appreciate it when people noticed the green streak of color in my left eye. It wasn't usually noticeable in inside lighting against the whiskey brown, but it wasn't ever entirely hidden either.

I hesitated, but she said, "You like her new French twist, yes? Very elegant. She has the big hair, but those green eyes, they don't need all that hair teased. She can do many styles."

Mat's new hairdo was awesome. I had attributed her quieter, more elegant styles to Jim's positive influence, not a new stylist. The fact that she used Tam's salon put me at ease. Mat would have carefully checked Tam out before letting her touch her hair.

My silver certainly wasn't complaining about Tam either. "Mat's French twist is fabulous," I said, trailing behind Tam to the back. "But uhm. I'm not the French bun type, I don't think."

"Of course not. Come in, come in. You need some softness around your face. This hair needs a bit of shape, some feathers of light."

The back room was subdued. A massage table filled one corner, leaving room for a sink and a black leather beauty chair on the other side.

In no time, I was shampooed and smelling of grapefruit and tangerine.

Installed in the beauty chair, it didn't seem possible that she would be able to reach the top of my head, but she began combing and snipping and fluffing.

"Kevin is doing a good job next door? That boy, he loves to talk." She pattered on, not giving me time to answer. "With his skill he could do nails, but you know he won't have anything to do with woman's work. Okay, okay, but what will he do with his life? He loves to draw, like me."

In less than fifteen minutes, I went from plain ponytail to a completely unrecognizable woman. The layers even curled on their own at the ends, a bit like White Feather's adorable waves at the base of his neck. "Uhm. Is this easy to take care of? If I want it to look like this again?"

She handed me the mirror and spun me to inspect the back. The layers made my hair...bouncy. I wasn't sure about bouncy, but she said, "Long enough for ponytail. You wash and let dry, it will look like this. Those bangs will need trimming every four weeks. You come here, I do it for you."

I paid her, tipped her generously and left, almost forgetting my eclair. I don't know what magic she used to make me put a haircut above an eclair, but her son was right. She had some kind of talent.

On the way out, I waved at Kevin. He was outside studying his design from across the street.

He raised his hand in a thumbs up. Feeling ridiculous, I blushed and hurried to White Feather's car.

Chapter 7

The jewelry store showed more evidence of wear during daylight hours than had been obvious at night, but it was a well-cared-for building with clean windows and new signs, including the closed sign that now hung in the door. Someone, probably the owner, had taped a note underneath that said, "Closed Until Further Notice."

Lynx was waiting and, much to my surprise, hadn't driven his car. I knew better than to ask questions. If he noticed my new hairstyle, he didn't comment, but he did tilt his head sideways and stare for an extra second or two before saying, "Got a bead on a new client. Wants a matched set of packets so that someone with one of the packets can find the other one."

"Doable. Depending on how personalized the client wants it, I'll need some specific personal items."

"You take the job, I already have the items."

I rolled my eyes at his sly grin and named my price. He handed me a silk bag. "I haven't touched anything inside. No contamination."

Lynx didn't miss a trick.

I stowed the bag in the car before turning to the business at hand.

After unlocking the jewelry store, I provided Lynx with the same rundown White Feather had provided me. I didn't tell Lynx how to do his job because he didn't like to be reminded that he was a shifter. There had always been a large part of him pretending he was a normal. Knowledge misused was dangerous for him, but it was more than that. He was self-conscious because his mother had abandoned him, and he carried a completely misplaced sense of shame and guilt. Today that attitude was a badge, a sudden scowl across his features as he followed me inside.

"There's a lot of aura in this spot where they found the body," I said. "But the other thing that triggered the fork is only near the floor. Barely discernible, whatever it is." I found the pattern with the fork and showed him the trail. He could have put his nose down and followed it without me, but this way, he was crouched next to me and watching the fork, not using his animal talents that, accept it or not, were a part of him.

"We could have done this at night," he complained. Without witnesses, he would have broken in, done his thing and earned his paycheck without my interference.

I strolled into the office without glancing back. "We found the trails, but that one in particular is very faint. Had to use a special spell to trace it." The last was to remind him that I wasn't exactly normal myself. My back was also to him, and I kept it that way. "Goes in here, touches the alarm, the computer, and then back out."

"Not a shifter," he said, but his words were slow, thoughtful, as though he hadn't quite made up his mind about the smell.

I faced him cautiously. "But?"

"There's a funny smell where she died. It matches the trail that is away from the body. The scent isn't all human, but it's bloody."

My guts clenched.

"She stinks human. But the other smell is on her, whatever it is, and it doesn't smell human, but it still has her scent."

"Animal? Something small?" I pointed to the doorway where the bottom of the door gaped. "Mouse? Bat? Roach?"

He glanced at the opening. "Bats don't need to crawl."

"But?"

"Kinda has a smell, like earth. Dry earth, not the smell of oil or fur." He frowned. "Reminds me of something. There's human all over it though. And some other smell. Not an herb. It's a chemical. Stinks almost like that dye White Feather was using this morning. But it's not paint. Don't know what it is."

"Magic," I declared.

He shook his head. "Some of that too, but not like yours."

I frowned. "I don't crawl around jewelry stores stealing."

"Don't get your sage on fire," he said. "Not a shifter. But maybe if I see the body I can tell what that other smell is."

"We are not visiting a morgue at night," I said.

He shrugged. "I'm not showing up there in the day. People be there." He headed for the door.

He had a point. Standing around smelling a dead body with strangers watching would not be smart. "Okay, okay. You do the job your way. Since you didn't drive, can you come back to my place with me so I can get my car? You can drive White—I'll drive White Feather's Prius, and you can drive my car back to White Feather's house." White Feather's car was new, while my Civic had forgotten what better days looked like. I didn't want anything bad to happen to White Feather's car. Then again, Lynx's car was an almost new Mustang, a spiffy vehicle he kept in showroom condition.

For twenty-seven years old, how had I gone through two houses and never owned a brand new car? And Lynx worked for me. Shouldn't I have a nicer car than he did? Or at least a house without vampires???

I refused to think about it, but I was still older and supposedly more responsible, so I would drive White Feather's car.

On the way to my place I spilled the full details of Patrick's home invasion. "So if you find yourself on the run from him, my house isn't safe." Patrick and Lynx did business when necessary, but it was more a truce of mutual respect than a friendship.

"Whoa. How you gonna keep him out?"

My fingers tightened on the steering wheel. "My lab is safe, I think. It's very nearly a different structure and only shares a roof. I don't know if his spawn can get in too, or just him."

Lynx gazed at me in his non-blinking cat way. He didn't do it often, but now and then, his brain chewed on something so hard, he'd stare with such intensity, I'd swear he was trying to pull information directly from my brain. He was half cat; maybe he could do that. Who knew the real limitations of cats, especially half human ones?

"I'd chop the roof between the lab and the house just to be certain." He made two fangs with his fingers. "'Trick's cool, but how you gonna sleep on a chance like that? You movin' in with White Feather? Permanently?"

If I clutched the steering wheel any harder it would break off under my hands. "It looks that way, doesn't it?"

Lynx was no dummy. He noticed the tension. His stare wasn't as intense this time, but the wheels turned in his brain. Without saying anything more, he faced the window.

My grip relaxed in relief. I didn't want to talk about it. Thank God cats weren't big on wasting time on conversation.

It was still a beautiful sunny day with at least five hours before sunset. I conned Lynx into helping me load stuff into both cars. I didn't need the furniture. White Feather owned nicer stuff anyway. I wanted the lab burners, tables, jars, and the things that were in my safe places throughout the house.

Lynx didn't need to know about the secret stashes, so I had him load heavy things like my research books, the rocks with important spell qualities and the rest of the wood pile.

After sorting and boxing supplies and clothing, I opted to take only a few clothes and half of the lab supplies.

It was good that Lynx was helping. If he hadn't been with me, I might have wasted time wandering from room to room getting maudlin.

Once the vehicles were packed full, I handed over the keys to the Honda. He knew the way.

We would have headed out except the phone rang.

It was White Feather. "Is Lynx still with you?" he asked without so much as a polite greeting.

"Yes, why?"

"Another hit and another loss from their team. Body is cold, but if he can pick anything up, now would be the best time. The crew is done. Gordon has the place secured and can give us fifteen or twenty minutes undisturbed. You think he'll be game?"

I looked at Lynx. His hearing was good enough to pick up the conversation.

Lynx shrugged. "I'm on the clock. You want me to pack clothes for the dime or inspect dead bodies, it's all the same to me."

My wardrobe was nothing special, but comparing it to a dead body earned him my best scowl. "Yeah, he's good. Where is it?"

White Feather rattled off the address. "Near as we can tell, the robbery occurred at noon. I'll wait for you here, but hurry. And bring a witching fork. That bubble trick doesn't work all that well without a focal point."

The only good news was that I didn't have to pack the willow sticks. A quarter of my lab was already in his car.

Chapter 8

Lynx took my car, and I drove White Feather's. The Prius had a GPS. Lynx didn't need one, because the kid had walked, run and lived just about everywhere in Santa Fe, but he followed me anyway. The GPS led us perilously close to the jewelry store we had left a couple of hours ago to a house near the Santa Fe River Park, off Alameda.

The location was further than most people would want to walk to visit the plaza, but the park was a long, straight patch of trees running east-west and led there eventually. There were many nearby galleries, churches and eateries reachable on foot. The house in question was adobe, but the older houses in Santa Fe were all adobe. New buildings were required to be, thus only a few houses before the law took effect were made of other materials.

River Park was dormant now, with packed dirt and bare trees hoping for snow. The brush was all yellows and browns; Mother Earth was quiet, resting.

White Feather waited on the porch. It was decorated with colorful pots; a ceramic goat, sheep and a dragon. The cement was swept clean, but bits of earth clung to the corners and a light dusting of desert sand weighed on the ceramics.

Lynx beat me to the landing because I was hunting for willow sticks in the very overstuffed car. There were only five or so left in my stash. Rather than re-use them, I either burned them or buried them securely under sand and stone in my backyard. If White Feather kept finding dead bodies, I'd need to harvest more willow.

Lynx crouched by the steps, inspecting the area with all his senses. With as many police as had probably been through here, sorting auras and smells wasn't going to be easy.

When he finished, I followed.

White Feather gave my fingers a squeeze. "Work fast. Gordon is pushing the timing to remove the body. Don't get your aura or fingerprints on the body."

"As if I want to touch it," I muttered, following Lynx through the plain, but heavy wooden door. Lynx hovered just inside, staring and breathing slowly. The place reeked of bodily functions, but this time...I sniffed. "Blood?"

White Feather indicated the female sprawled on the living room carpet. "This one has the same under-the-skin hemorrhaging, but worse. Blood leaked from her nose and eyes and even her skin hemorrhaged."

Tiny blood droplets oozed from her arms as if she had rammed up against the smallest holes on a cheese grater, leaving pricks across her skin. Her mouth gaped opened in a silent scream. Thankfully her badly dyed hair covered most of her face.

The living room was quite modern with a big screen tv, leather recliners, and a nice fireplace. An incredibly detailed backdrop of the eastern mountains along Santa Fe was painted across one open wall. Anyone watching tv would have the illusion that the Sangre de Cristo mountains were hovering outside a large picture window.

The only glaring clutter in the room was the body.

Lynx floated across the room, careful where he put his feet. "She was leaking stuff from the door on in. Probably dead before she was dragged inside." He leaned over, edged closer, and then finally crouched down.

I got busy with the witching fork.

Lynx said, "Same smell as the other place. Stronger. It smells like a ballpoint pen, you know, when you bust one open. Or paint, but not that exactly." He finally crouched and pointed to her arm. "It's really strong here." Her arm was bright red from burst capillaries all down her forearm. Pricks of blood oozed through the skin across the lower part of her arm and hand. The pink on the back of her hand formed a pattern of bloody fingers reaching across the tops of each of her own fingers.

I rolled the willow fork through the air above the pattern, returned to the entryway and started the hunt.

Lynx and White Feather paced me as I worked my way through the house. White Feather had the bubble spell ready. We didn't pick up any extra twitching until we were in the back of the house in the kitchen.

Several of the drawers and one window caused the enhanced fork to vibrate.

White Feather pointed to a crack and a very small triangular piece of glass missing at the base of the window.

I stared at the hole. "Very small. Like the gap under the door at the jewelry store."

"What is it that gets in?" White Feather wondered.

"And why?" I shook my head. "What was taken?"

"Money, jewelry. The owners run a new bakery off the plaza, Cloud Puff or something like that. The couple usually deposits the money from each day directly in the bank, but Sunday the banks are closed so they bring it here and put it in a safe."

"Sweet Puffs? I ate there this morning! It's right near Mat's place."

"That's the place. The safe was accessed as though the perps had the combination. On Monday the bakery closes at three. Either the husband or wife comes home, retrieves the weekend money and then both days are banked. Apparently someone caught on to the routine. Whoever it was counted on them being busy at work through lunchtime. The bakery has only been open for about a month."

His phone rang, interrupting the conversation.

Lynx and I continued scanning the place. There was the faintest of twinges near the back door, but I couldn't be certain. "Lynx, give this spot a once over, would you? I want to recheck the living room."

White Feather snapped his phone shut. "They've got a name for the body. Donna Alderno was reported missing last night. Didn't return from her jog."

"Let me guess. She runs along Santa Fe River Park."

He nodded. "She waited tables from seven-thirty until two at Mangiano on Sunday. She left work, changed clothes at home, went jogging and never came back. Twenty-four years old, lived with her parents. Even though she wasn't missing long enough for the police to do much, the parents filed a missing person's report."

I hovered over the dead girl. "Out to jog and disappears. She ends up dead during a robbery the next day. If the robbery was today, she didn't need to disappear yesterday. Something doesn't fit here." Donna's hair was shoulder-length and dark brown except for the reddish-purple dye job along the top. She wore loose sweatpants and a short sleeved shirt. "It's cool out for short sleeves, but maybe not if you're jogging. Sun is still out at two, three, even four." Her arm, especially the right one, was flecked with blood. The pattern on her lower arm from where I stood looked almost like... "A snake?" I blinked and it was gone, but the swirls on her upper arm didn't lose the pattern. The capillaries formed a picture. "A rose on her upper arm? Or a bruise from being hit?"

White Feather's phone vibrated again. He glanced at it and then said, "Gordon's team is on its way back. Time to go. Lynx?"

Lynx had already appeared on silent feet.

"Her arm is a mess of bloody marks, but the lower part almost resembles a snake. Only it has an arm and finger looking digits on the end."

Lynx snapped his fingers. "Tattoo ink. That's what the smell is!"

White Feather had the front door opened. He herded us out, all three of us craning our necks to take a last look. "Tattoo?" I echoed.

"Yeah, and I think that thing on her lower arm is a lizard, not a snake."

Lynx didn't have tattoos. With his ability to shift back and forth, a tattoo might not even take. I wasn't dumb enough to ask how he knew so much about tattoo ink, but I substituted, "Since when do you hang out in tattoo parlors?"

He headed for my car. "I don't. But that stuff still smells for days after people get a tat. Stinks."

"Is the smell here the same as whatever you smelled in the jewelry gallery?"

"Could be, but there's magic all over everything. It's way stronger here, and there's fresh blood mixed in, but it's...like her blood isn't pure. And she's dead so the blood smells different anyway. I don't know what that is. But that ink smell is definitely tat ink. It stinks all along the trail like she walked the whole way bleeding. Thing is, the trail doesn't smell only human even though it has her smell. Maybe she carried something else and set it down? So it has her smell. But I don't know what it is. Has an earth smell with stuff mixed in."

"Let's get gone," White Feather said. "We'll meet you back at my place— our place."

I shoved the bag on the passenger side to the floor and crammed myself in the Prius. White Feather pulled away from the curb, swung around and parked on a side street. "I was planning on watching for Gordon in the rearview mirror, but that isn't possible with all the stuff you put in here." He grinned at me. "Is this everything?"

"Very funny. There's still a lot of equipment in the lab. Lynx has most of my clothes in my car."

White Feather rolled the window down, listening to the breeze. I shifted the bag under my feet off to one side. When an unmarked police car cruised up in front of the house, White Feather pulled away. An ambulance turned the corner as we eased past.

"I hope we learned something worthwhile," he muttered.

"It looks to me like the victims either carried a familiar in or controlled one to do reconnaissance and shut off the alarms. I don't know what it is though and neither does Lynx."

"Somehow I don't think reporting that to Gordon will help his case very much."

"Well, we now know that both victims had tattoos."

White Feather sighed and concentrated on his driving.

Chapter 9

I was nervous about meeting the rest of White Feather's family. It was strange to have been introduced to his ancestors before his living relatives, but we'd been too busy keeping ourselves alive and hidden from a rogue wind spirit to engage in normal social niceties. And like moving in with White Feather, I might have been putting it off.

Because of the latest dead body, we ran late on our promise to arrive at his mother's house at six. At least Tam had worked magic on my hair with the new style. No amount of fussing with it would improve on it, either.

White Feather waited impatiently as I sorted through my piles of luggage. It was six o'clock, and the evening was settling in below freezing. I dug out my purple ski jacket. Not that I skied, but I did hike in the winter, and it had been on an awesome sale.

Heels would dress up my jeans, but it was cold, and while first impressions were important, so was being able to run from danger. Okay, it was unlikely I'd have to run from any bad guys while eating dinner with White Feather and his family. My sneakers with the helium flight spell would definitely be overkill.

I went with the sneakers anyway because they were comfortable.

When the piles were pushed back into a semblance of unorganized, but out of the way mess, I stood to find White Feather watching me.

"You look good," he said. His eyes traveled across my face.

Feeling self-conscious, I brushed one of the newly trimmed bangs away from my cheek.

"I need a dressier coat." I fussed with the zipper, running it up and down. I didn't own a dress coat.

He smiled, his green eyes sparking with mischief. He touched a strand of my hair. "You're cute. Just the way you are."

Did that mean he realized I had a new haircut and approved? Was it important that he noticed? Cute was cute. I smiled. Good enough for me.

We headed out.

Like my parents, White Feather's mother lived in one of the older sections of Santa Fe. The short brown adobe house had an expansive front yard and a Spanish style middle section for gardening. In the old days, the center area might have been used for chickens, but White Feather's mother kept her chickens in the winter-dormant outer yard. A rolling coop was tucked around the side of the house.

Since the chickens had snuggled down for the evening, White Feather shut the door and latched it for her.

I waited while he rolled it around the back.

The only magic around me was that of family and a very content Mother Earth. This home was a happy little pocket of soil where vegetables had grown and trees waited for spring. The porch was swept clean of cobwebs and dirt, but the concrete steps were cracked, a somewhat obvious add-on or perhaps replacement for older wooden steps.

White Feather joined me on the porch. "Dad has been gone since Tara was five. Gordon and I keep an eye on things. Mom will be glad to meet you." His voice was filled with the guilt of a child who remembered his father every time he visited, and knew he could never fill the void.

I reached for his hand before realizing it would mean we'd end up walking in holding hands. Not that it mattered, but I wanted to make a positive first impression, not look like a clingy girlfriend.

White Feather ducked his head for a quick kiss.

My heart and face warmed. Resolutely, I stowed most of my nerves where they belonged, at least until he ushered me into the living room.

I stopped dead in my tracks. Three people waited off to the side, two of them seated at a long dining room table. The first person that registered was Mat's boyfriend, Jim. His smug, somewhat sheepish expression grinned at me as though he had just finished laughing—at my expense.

"You have got to be kidding me." The familiar golden skin, the handsome face...the resemblance to White Feather was there, although Jim was stockier, and his frank, honest eyes were obviously full of deceit. I grounded automatically, as though under attack. White Feather would have had to be dead magically to have missed the surge as I struggled to find my balance.

"What's wrong?" White Feather asked.

It might not be an outright attack, but as far as I was concerned, the threat was real enough.

Jim's smile widened at the shock on my face.

Tara giggled. She sat next to Jim, not resembling either brother. "Let me guess. My brother used a disguise on you, and you just figured it out."

I had no time for her. Tara was a smart-mouthed teen, struggling to train a talent that she should have discovered five or six years earlier. It had taken my mother, myself and a lot of danger to tease it out from behind her attitude problem.

She smirked. "Don't feel badly," she said, obviously hoping I would. "He fools lots of people. Smarter people—"

White Feather made a noise that was a cross between a growl and a grunt. He floated a breeze across the table that was hard enough to shift a napkin in front of her face.

Tara stiffened with surprise and her lips locked shut, something she had only recently learned to do, but should have conquered when she was seven years old instead of eighteen.

"You played your part well," I snapped. White Feather and I had met when he was operating undercover on a case for his cop brother, Gordon, the idiot sitting at the dinner table. I had never met him, not as Gordon. When I met Jim in Matilda's shop, he was playing a successful engineer. I hadn't known he was Gordon because he had completely failed to mention that he was a cop, related to White Feather, or was anyone but a doting boyfriend.

I had never made the connection. I was willing to bet my best friend hadn't made the connection either, because she would have mentioned it.

Gordon, aka Jim, shrugged and gave a quiet, assured laugh. "No harm done."

It was bad enough that he had chosen to spring his identity on me in front of a family gathering. Hurting for my friend over his deceit only made me escalate to furious that much faster. Mat didn't know he was a cop. If he was using her to gain inside information into the magical underground, she was going to hit him with a spell that might blow up half the plaza.

He was lucky I wasn't carrying any spells with firepower. Witches had a hard enough time trusting men; on top of the usual scum who discarded women carelessly, there were groupies, naysayers, and the worst of all, those who "wanted to see what it was like to be with a witch." From Gordon's smug attitude, it appeared that he was in a race to lock in a spot on the lowest part of the totem pole.

White Feather squeezed my fingers, his own tension ratcheting a notch. "Gordon, what are you up to now?" He switched his attention to me. "You haven't met Gordon yet?"

I shook my head. "No, I only met Jim. Mat's *boyfriend*, the impressive and successful engineer who has been spending a lot of time with her."

"We've been at enough crime scenes...but I guess we've never actually run into him." Light dawned on White Feather's face as he sorted through the times I had had the opportunity to meet Gordon face-to-face. But it had never happened, and maybe someone in this room had been actively avoiding it.

Well, here went positive first impressions. I swallowed my desire to throw a firecracker spell in Gordon's lap and said, "Twenty-four hours. If you don't tell her, I will."

That wiped the smile off his face. His eyes turned a darker brown, and he sat up straighter. "It's none of your business."

"She's my best friend. I guarantee you it's better if you let her down easy because when I tell her, I won't sugar coat that you aren't who you've been pretending to be."

A breeze swirled in the air, a warning from White Feather. I tore my anger away from Gordon, my muscles clenched for a fight. If White Feather sided with his brother, I didn't even have a home to escape to, not in the middle of vampire hours. But I wasn't going to stand here and watch some guy smirk his way through dinner at the way he'd put one over on my best friend. I couldn't blame White Feather for standing by his family, but what about Mat? She was as close to me as family, closer if you considered that my sister Kas and I barely spoke.

Before I could defend my decision, White Feather said, "Wait a minute. Mat doesn't know him as Gordon?"

My finger jabbed the air in the direction of the dinner table. "I didn't know him as Gordon either. If Mat had known, she'd have mentioned it. So far as she knows, he's Jim. Not a cop. Not your brother. Just a guy who *cared*."

"Hey, I do care!"

I whirled back to him. "Not enough to be honest with her," I snarled.

White Feather tugged on my hand, probably to prevent me from launching myself over the table. "Gordon, are you out of your mind? You've been dating a witch for how long? And you didn't tell her you were a cop? You *lied* about who you are to your girlfriend?"

Gordon's eyes narrowed, but before he could respond, White Feather turned to me and said, "You might want to give him forty-eight hours. After we eat, he'll have time to check in with work. If I were in his shoes, I'd clear my schedule."

"Hey, whose side are you on, anyway? You know my job! Some of us don't get to entice chicks with fancy magic. You could at least stand by your own brother here. I'll tell Mat when I'm ready."

My fingers cramped when White Feather's grip tightened on mine. The ring on my left hand warmed even as the air swirled around it. "In case there was ever any doubt." White Feather held up our linked hands. "Adriel's mine. My family. Do what you have to do any way you see fit with your relationships, but mine is for life. Be happy she's giving you twenty-four hours instead of marching over there right now, because if that's what she decides to do, I'm going with her."

I sucked in a breath and let it out slowly. As introductions went, that was putting the cards on the table. I had expected "This is Adriel," or "Adriel, the witch I told you about." My heart was beating fast, but his words tripped it with relief. A small spark of giddiness spread through me that was its own kind of magic. I tamped down on my anger, letting some of it drain into Mother Earth.

White Feather didn't bother to employ a similar trick with the wind, at least not until his mother stepped away from the entrance to the kitchen, breaking the stare between the brothers.

"Welcome to the family," she said. "I hope you like enchiladas, and I hope you like things hot. This family doesn't do cold chile or cold anything else." She set down a bread basket and approached us. When she clasped my free hand, she felt the ring White Feather had given me.

The diamond sparkled up at her. She smiled and winked at White Feather. She released my hand and hugged White Feather. Her black hair, mostly gray on the top, wound down her back in a single braid that was still black on the latter third.

White Feather had to lean way over to embrace his mother.

As soon as she stepped back she said to me, "Ignore any food you don't like and eat what you do. My son tells me you are of the earth." She inhaled deeply as though she might be able to smell me. "That is good."

She touched my arm and guided me to a chair, leaving White Feather to follow. "Sage bread for appetizer?"

My hand might have been a bit shaky from residual anger as I helped myself to a slice from the woven basket.

There was a long silence before Tara finally broke it with her own concerns. "How is Lynx?"

I chewed on a bite of warm bread. Even in my current state my taste buds declared the bread a slice of heaven. "Lynx? He's fine. I'll tell him you asked after him."

Her face blanched. "I don't think it will do much good. I have about as much luck with relationships as Gordon."

Gordon didn't have his head down, not exactly, but he was intent on buttering his bread. His intense concentration was warranted even without the family spat. The bread tasted of baking in a stone oven; crisp crust, wonderfully soft center. I followed his example and focused on eating. It wasn't hard to compliment the blue corn enchiladas or the cheesy pan-sauteed zucchini.

For the rest of the evening we all behaved, but the event could only be considered a qualified success. No one died and there were no actual fist fights. I didn't set off any spells, and if Gordon had any, he kept them quiescent.

I fully intended to follow through with my threat to tell Mat, and everyone knew it. That fact kept Gordon appropriately preoccupied. Before we left, I would have suggested Gordon have fire engines in the area to put out the fire that was likely to ignite across his head when he told Mat, but Tara distracted me when she handed me a note.

"For Lynx," she whispered. "I spelled it. You won't be able to read it."

"Do you want me to try?"

She started to reply and then stopped, warring with her desire to know if I could beat her magic.

I laughed. "Don't worry. I won't."

White Feather's mother hugged us both and sent us home with leftovers.

On the way back to White Feather's house, he asked, "Were you ever mad that when we met, I pretended to be someone else?"

"We weren't dating. We were business associates protecting our identity, and we both used disguises. We both knew they were disguises. Your brother met Mat in a social context and kept it that way. What is he trying to hide?"

White Feather was silent for a while. "A lot of women don't like cops."

"And a lot of them do."

"Some women don't like...warlocks. He might have done it to protect me. Or hide it from her. He's done that before."

"Mat is a witch. She's an *obvious*, never even been in the closet, witch. She's met you. What's to hide?"

He chewed on that for a while. When we pulled into his driveway he said, "If he's been using her to investigate some case or other, I might have to kick his ass myself."

"You can get in line, but if that's what he was doing, after Mat gets done with him, there's isn't going to be much left to kick." And if she didn't finish the job for some reason, I would.

Chapter 10

Pounding on the front door early the next morning—very early—had me rolling across the expanse of the king bed, reaching blindly for my silver dagger. White Feather jumped into his pants before I found my weapon.

His ability to explore with wind filled in the cracks between the knocking. "It's your dad," he sputtered.

It took a moment to register. "Moonlight madness!" I relaxed my grip on the sheath and sat back on the bed, blinking blearily.

White Feather finished pulling on a tee shirt, and only then noticed my stupor. "Isn't there an emergency?"

I hadn't even started searching for my clothes. Around a yawn, I shook my head. "Not necessarily. Dad gets up early."

"And visits? It's 5 a.m.!"

My brain was too befuddled to explain. I nabbed a sweater and jeans from the pile on the floor and stumbled along behind White Feather to the front door.

It was an effort to discern which of the two very large men at our front door was Dad. "Dad, it's five in the morning!" It was also freezing out. "Come in. Or let me get my coat. Is Mom okay?"

White Feather retreated behind me, allowing everyone to crowd into the foyer.

Dad eyed me up and down. "You still in bed? How do you expect to finish building this house if you're sleeping in?" He subjected White Feather to a snort of disdain before turning to the man with him, a guy almost as bearlike in size as Dad. The main difference between them was that Dad had a head of short black hair turning silver, and the friend was blessed with a brown beard and a crown of curly brown hair that hung almost to his shoulders.

I stifled a groan. White Feather was going to disown me. I knew moving in with him was a bad idea. I had mistakenly worried about my own bad habits and hadn't even considered those of my *family*.

The barrel of a man next to my father held out a rough palm. "Mason," he said.

I shook his hand. "Adriel, and this is White Feather."

"No," he said, ducking his head shyly. "I'm a mason. Your dad says you need some building done."

I blinked fully awake, my suspicions rising.

Dad did nothing to alleviate my concerns when he asked, "Have you at least put on the coffee? It's a little cool in here too. I'll start a fire." Dad had a habit of taking in strays—dogs, horses, and yes, people.

It would be rude to ask if he had found this mason under a bridge, but it was entirely possible. I sighed. "Yeah, sure, the coffee is about to brew."

White Feather was already in the kitchen by the time I turned around.

Since the coffee train wasn't yet in operation, he made coffee the old fashioned way, in a plain glass coffee pot.

Dad lumbered to the living room fireplace and ignited the logs. It wasn't even the effort of striking a match for him, although his arm muscles bulged slightly as he changed his internal energy to fire and directed it at the kindling.

The mason stood with his hands in his pockets, staring down at the floor. "Looks like you need a wall finished up in the kitchen. I can do it. Take me a day or so."

Dad said, "Do you want me to cook breakfast or—"

"Dad!" I blushed furiously and beat him to the fridge only because it wasn't his kitchen so he stayed in the living room on the other side of the bar.

"Can't expect a man to erect walls on an empty stomach."

White Feather did not look my way, not once. He lined up coffee cups, found the bag of sugar and retrieved the half and half. Completely mortified, I scrambled eggs. There was no way to trick Dad into leaving. If I told him we didn't need help, he'd be hurt. If I tried any of the lame excuses that came to mind, he'd just ignore me and buckle down to the tasks of his choice.

It's hard to protect yourself from family when they show up in the middle of the night. My defenses were down.

"I'll check on the supplies," Dad said. "See how the bricks are coming along. We'll be back in time to eat." He nodded at the mason, a man whose name we still didn't know, and headed down the hallway. They disappeared between sheets of plywood where the hallway abruptly met the great outdoors.

I apologized to White Feather. "I'm really sorry. Dad has this way—"

White Feather plucked the fork for the eggs from my madly waving hand. He chuckled, almost silently. Either he was hysterical from the rude awakening, or he was amused at my complete inability to manage the situation.

"He seems to enjoy getting his way," White Feather said around his amusement. "And he checks on you often. Is there enough light for him to inspect whatever it is he is inspecting?"

It was November and pitch dark this early. "He'll start a fire if he has to. Just a small torch, he'll call it. But he can do sparks of light too." Dad's talent was that of fire, a flame he could ignite, control or extinguish by channeling his internal passion for life. He made it appear simple, but it was a silent workout. His muscles paid the price, flexing and burning up energy as he fueled the fire with his magic.

White Feather grinned down at me. "He seems eager to make sure you have a decent place to live."

I didn't see the humor. "I have a house." But I didn't, not anymore. Dad didn't even know about my recent run-in with the vamps. My parents weren't thrilled that we hadn't been married conventionally, but they did respect my choice, if only because White Feather had proven himself when he endangered himself to rescue me. Saving my life held some sway when it came to my family. "Moonlight madness, you don't know what you've gotten yourself into," I muttered.

"We do need the walls up as soon as possible."

"It could be worse," I muttered.

"Oh?"

"He didn't bring Kas and her husband to install the toilet and other plumbing!"

White Feather shook his head and grinned. "There's always tomorrow morning."

By the time we finished breakfast, we learned that the mason's name was Tracy. He was a drifter who had been a trucker, a guitar-picker and had been hired at the hardware store off the books when Dad heard about a guy with a "talent for brick work."

I had to recite spell ingredients in my head to refrain from blurting out random curses. The guy who ran the hardware store was my cousin Manny. And he knew Dad and his penchant for strays. Kept an eye out as it were.

As soon as White Feather offered to show Tracy around in preparation for the day's work, I walked Dad to his truck, fully intending to lay down the rules of engagement. They included a seven o'clock curfew—no showing up earlier.

Dad strolled out, extolling the virtues of his latest find. "He seems like a good fellow. Doesn't drink and doesn't smoke. I'll be back to pick him up this evening. He's staying with cousin Manny."

"Dad—"

"I was right impressed with the workmanship your White Feather has done so far on the house. It's quality." He smothered me in one of his big hugs, his favorite technique for preventing me from getting in a word edgewise. I dug my feet in.

"Dad, you let White Feather build this house how he wants it."

"To be sure. To be sure."

He hopped in his truck, but then rolled down the window. "Tracy has something. It's of the earth. Your mother couldn't tell either."

"He's an earth witch?"

"No, not like you, but something. I don't think he knows what it is or what to do with it. It's kept him from finding a place. He thinks in a nice straight line, but life isn't ever that simple. You help him if you see it, you hear?"

"Dad—" It wasn't that I minded helping. But it was different now than when I was on my own. I'd never had to worry about anyone else being impacted by family strays, wild-haired ideas or relatives that weren't quite normal. It was bad enough that my parents had never stopped nagging me about helping my sister Kas find a talent or at least passion in life.

"You'll give him a nudge in the right direction." Dad smiled, his eyes sparking. "You take after me that way."

He put the truck in gear, leaving me sputtering as he drove off into the cold dawn. "I do not," I told the empty driveway. I loved my parents, but I wasn't anything like either of them. I'd worked hard to be my own person, my own witch with my own talents. I certainly didn't go around hiring strays who had odd talents that didn't fit into normal society.

"Moonlight madness! Lynx better run some background on this guy," I muttered on my way back inside. "And if this Tracy dude messes anything up I'll—well, I won't let Dad fix it. I'll have to do it myself. And White Feather better not kick me out over this. I am *not* moving back in with Mom and Dad because of a little thing like a vampire."

I stomped out back to find White Feather, wondering how in the world to explain it all.

Chapter 11

The sun was not yet up, but there were hints of morning light. The smell of frigid night air resting against Mother Earth was already drifting, letting bits of desert dance with the scent of smoke swirling out of White Feather's fireplace. When the sun finally did flash its way across the morning, it would be lighting the stage of a beautiful backdrop.

White Feather and Tracy dumped bricks around the outside wall. Tracy appeared to know his way around the tools and supplies without any encouragement. I considered pulling White Feather aside, but there really was nothing to say that would change anything, not at the moment.

Maybe I should just tackle some of my own tasks and let this Tracy situation either work itself out or not. "I'm headed to my house to complete some spells in my lab. I'll stop by Mat's on the way home and check on her."

"She might need a shoulder to cry on?" White Feather guessed.

"A shoulder?" I shook my head. "I thought I'd try to talk her out of cursing him for life since we're practically relatives and all."

"Practically?" His eyes narrowed. "You're having difficulty accepting all the ramifications of this marriage thing, aren't you?"

Admittedly, issues did seem to be presenting themselves with terrifying speed, but I wasn't going down without a fight, especially for the easy problems like his lying, conniving brother. "In Jim's case, I figure it's not too late to disown him. That way I won't be caught in a cross-curse."

"Mm-hmm." He reeled me in for a kiss. "Do not let her kill him. He's a pain in the ass, but I don't want to have to console my mother over the loss."

"I'll do what I can, but he got himself into this mess."

I left them to their work and headed out to do mine.

* * *

The lab was home sweet home. I was behind on at least three client spells because of the vamp invasion, but as excuses went, the clients were better off not knowing about any vamp visits. Two of the spells were for previous clients who needed renewals of protective charms. I hammered them out in less than an hour.

Lynx's new client required a more intricate spell. It was rare to get an order from a client who not only believed in witchcraft, but knew enough about it to request such a complicated spell. "Matched set" spells were magical elements split in two that would allow either half to be "found" using the other half of the spell.

Because I had already moved most of my dried herbs to White Feather's house, I selected juniper bark and berries from a single tree out back. The client had also provided two birthstones, a red garnet and an amethyst. I cleaved them in two and split the results across each packet.

Wisely, the client had also sent hair for each set, which I snipped in half before sealing the strands in silver to protect them.

If the client knew the best ingredients for a finding spell, why hadn't she completed the magic herself? Or had Lynx had a heavy hand in advising the client what to send?

A witching fork would be necessary to locate the matching packet, but the client could always hire a witch for that part too. It was quite possible that I'd be the witch hired should finding the packet become necessary.

Once business was out of the way, I turned to my own experiments, many of which needed finessing. Today I wanted to mimic White Feather's ability to extract information from the air, only in my case I intended to gather data from Mother Earth. So far my attempts resembled warfare rather than reconnaissance, but I had a new idea.

After being stuck in the eye of a killer storm, I realized my affinity to silver didn't require that I be in actual contact with the metal to push or pull from it. Silver was an electrical current for me; it provided a ground and energy. I could feel it across a room. Of course, its ability to communicate information was in doubt, but one step at a time.

I arranged multiple caches of silver around the lab. Sensing them was no effort at all. Pulling them to me...I could certainly feel them, nudge them around, and if I needed to...yes! "If they were round, they'd roll easily. Or arrows would be good. Wait. How did I get back to warfare? Beads would be better."

Melting silver into balls was child's play. While the balls cooled, I grabbed a quick lunch, but the rewarmed pasta was on the stale side. Seemed to me that there had been a few more items in the cupboards. I checked the spot where I normally kept animal crackers.

Nothing but dust. Hmm. Lynx had been helping me pack.

Well, I'd been eating more than my share of fattening foods lately anyway.

I tossed the remaining pasta in the garbage disposal and returned to the lab.

The silver beads weren't perfectly round, but there would be time to perfect them later. Not having a complete handle on anything other than sensing, I rested my hand on the table a few inches from the first ball. I grounded to the bead, purposely reaching for it, knowing it was there.

It rolled right to my finger as if yanked by a magnetic force. "Awesome!"

I pushed the round blob of silver while pulling another one towards me. The two hit each other rather harder than expected. One flew off the table and slammed into the potted aloe vera sitting high in the lab window.

I didn't need magic to tell me to duck away from the ricocheting missile.

Good thing I hadn't taken the plant to White Feather's or I'd need to replace the window. "Wow."

Okay, I hadn't really figured out how to use this technique to gather information, but I was progressing fine on the warfare part.

I sighed and took a moment to rethink. "My door is lined with silver. If Dad knocked...how can I read the aura?" Dad's aura was very familiar to me. And silver recognized auras...I played around with shapes and various properties. Strangely, one of the easiest things to do was push or pull the silver. Excited by the possibilities, I designed larger beads.

I was nearly finished stringing the beads onto a bracelet when the phone rang. Normally I'd ignore the interruption, but the silver needed to cool more anyway.

I scooted to the kitchen. "Hello?"

"A fire hydrant burst on Matilda's block, maybe four shops up from hers," White Feather said without preamble. "Something about the sidewalk erupting from underneath due to sudden unexplained water pressure rising. It's probably coincidence, but Mat hasn't called you, has she?"

My backpack containing my cell phone, one that I almost never remembered to turn on, was in the lab. "Noooo."

"I haven't heard from Gordon. She wouldn't really blow up a city sidewalk to douse my brother, would she?" When I didn't answer immediately, he asked, "She's that strong of a water witch?"

He couldn't see me nodding frantically. "She's that strong. Not that she was likely trying to spray your brother. But when she's mad, you do not want to be downstream of her. Aztec curses, you do not want to be upstream of her either. In high school she hosed down a guy with some nasty toilet water because he groped her."

"That's not the same thing as a water line."

"White Feather, we were in the *classroom*. The toilet was down the hall. She flooded four rooms, drew out a stream of water from the mess and nearly blasted the guy through the window. I'd better go talk to her. If you see a storm brewing with a lot of clouds, shut the windmills down."

"She calls storms too?"

"Not that I know of. But she's a water witch. And she had fallen hard for your brother."

"Call me if—" he paused. "I'm of no help with this one, am I?"

"No. I'll call you later though."

I grabbed my backpack and left the house at a run.

Chapter 12

The street in front of Mat's shop was indeed flooded. Since I never parked on her street, my only concern was staying out of the rush of water and avoiding the hordes of onlookers as I made my way to her door. A few children tugged against parental restraints, anxious to play in the water, but the temperature hadn't topped sixty today. It was closing in on four-thirty, which was still warm enough with a jacket, but it wouldn't be cozy warm when sopping wet.

A fire hydrant at the end of the street had blown. Men, mostly firemen, were toiling away or shouting random suggestions.

Kevin, from the bakery up the street, was standing outside Mat's shop. The other Asian guy who worked in Tam's shop was also there. He was slightly taller than Kevin and older. His longish, baggy khaki shorts left plenty of bare leg exposed to the cool afternoon. To make up for the cold, he had his hands stuffed deep in the pockets. His Birkenstock sandals were dry, an indication the two of them had found a way to cross the street without slogging through the water.

Kevin raised one hand in a weak wave as I walked up. "Hey, the hair looks good! You like it?"

I smiled. "I love it."

"Good thing you came the other day. She can't do hair today. They're shutting off the water. Mom sent us over here to see what caused the mess. This is Lee." From Lee's shorts, it was evident he had expected to be working in a nice warm nail salon all day.

We shook hands. "Adriel."

He turned my hand sideways to inspect my nails. "You decide to get your nails done, ask for me." He winked. "I'm better than the best, right Kevin? We'll personalize it."

"Uhm, thanks."

Mat's shop had remained ominously dim the whole while we exchanged pleasantries. Her windows were tinted so that no one could see in without some effort; the better to protect her customers from prying eyes. The water in the street was receding bit by bit. They must have shut off the main. "Looks like this could take a while." I stepped around them to enter Mat's shop, but the door was locked. Oh, that was a bad sign.

Kevin said, "Mom asked us to share some design ideas with her, but she's not open. Maybe she had some damage from the water or can't run her shop with it off."

"Maybe." My voice sounded stiff, even to me. "I'll stop back later. I know she's really thrilled about the idea of offering purses that match the nail patterns you do. I'll tell her you were here."

Kevin smiled, and held up a binder. "Yeah, we have a bunch of ideas. It'll be radical."

Lee gave me a nod and then faced the workers at the end of the street.

I was careful to make sure no one noticed me as I ducked into the convoluted set of alleyways that led to Mat's back door.

After tapping the secret knock and receiving no answer, I called out softly, "Mat? Are you in there? Are you okay?"

No answer. My worry escalated a notch. "I'm standing here until you at least let me know you're okay. You didn't drown yourself accidentally when you blasted Jim, did you?"

There was a long silence before a small wedge of wood slid to one side, creating a peephole. "When did you know?" Her voice was a cross between a hiss, squeaky tears and ice.

"I gave him twenty-four hours to tell you himself." It pained me to admit it. I should have called her right away, dammit. "White Feather said to make it forty-eight so Jim could schedule around his job."

The window slammed shut, but the door didn't open. I kept talking. "I met Gordon last night when White Feather invited me to meet his family. He's the Gordon I've mentioned before—White Feather's cop brother. I had no idea it was Jim. Mat, you know I'd never keep anything like that from you."

No response.

"Did you know the street is flooded out front? No, no, you probably had no idea." Of course she knew. "I'll bring you a few gallons of drinking water tomorrow. Oh, and Kevin from the nail salon is out front of your shop, prepared to share his grand design ideas."

I stood there talking to the closed piece of wood for another ten minutes, feeling like a fool and a miserable one at that. The peephole, never mind the door, never budged.

Maybe I should have lit a firecracker in Jim's lap after all. At least that way he would have been visibly injured, and my friend would know I had taken action on her behalf.

Chapter 13

By the time I left Mat's it was zeroing in on five o'clock. Not evening, but close. I wanted my new bracelet and the other silver, but I'd abandoned it in the lab. The remaining tweaks could easily be finished at White Feather's house.

Clouds hung over the mountains, and as they were wont to do, they dipped lower into the valley as dark crept closer.

There was time to retrieve the bracelet, but barely.

Daylight teased me by fading in and out of the clouds as I drove. Of course, if Patrick was really after me, he could wait until I was out after dark and pounce on me anytime. He didn't have to invade my house and skulk behind the couch.

A small hint of sunbeam winked at me from the west and lit my path like a beacon from heaven as I rolled to a dusty stop in my own driveway. "I can't run scared from him the rest of my life." I had known inviting Patrick inside was a big mistake. Once invoked, how was I to rescind the invite? My desperate impulse made me a stranger in my own home, ready to run scared.

It took less than a minute to collect my bracelet and other paraphernalia.

I peeled open the front door to escape, but a warning tingle of heat across my turquoise informed me I was too late.

Apparently Patrick had decided he was my best friend and wanted me to meet all his closest buddies. He waited in the open, pretending to be polite by standing off the side of the porch. It wasn't dark, but the sun was very low in the sky. We both knew he could cross the threshold of my house despite the garlic, chile and silver around the door.

Hating him would be easy, but the knot in my stomach left room for nothing but fear. My feet ground to a halt even though I wanted to run back to the lab.

"What do you want?" I slammed the door behind me, pretending bravery. Probably a foolish display, but if he wanted to kill me, he would have already done it. His companion...I tried not to show my surprise, but failed.

"This is Joe," Patrick said. "He has a problem."

The porch light wouldn't snap on until darker dusk, but there was enough daylight left to discern that while Joe was a vampire, he was uncharacteristically dumpy. His fangs protruded at odd angles; an obscene invitation to any decent dentist. He had made an effort to tuck his plaid dress shirt into his black chinos, but it hung sloppily over a muffin-top belly.

What self-respecting vamp wore a wrinkled, flannel shirt like that?? What self-respecting live human would even be seen in it???

"Is he new?" I blurted out. Vampires always turned handsome after they died. It was either the blood they consumed or the death magic, but a guy could die looking like this balding, out-of-shape mess and normally he'd be transformed into an ageless, handsome...dead guy.

"Show her how charming you can be," Patrick commanded.

I yanked my eyes from Joe's chin to his forehead; anywhere but his watery eyes. "No, no." I backed up a step and hit adobe. I had no desire to succumb to vampire charm, diseased or not. My mouth dropped open when his bulbous nose reddened, either with embarrassment or because he was—had been—a heavy drinker in life. His face went blotchy and old pock-marks appeared.

I yelped.

"Indeed," Patrick intoned. He rocked on his heels, perhaps wanting to step away himself, but felt forced to hold his ground.

My eyes brushed past Patrick. He was a dangerous dude; the epitome of vamp and every inch the handsome Spanish aristocrat with his dark hair swept into an elegant braid. High-end leather lacing was woven through his hair, the kind that ordinarily might carry spells. With a vamp, who needed spells? He oozed power when he chose, which was most of the time.

Right now, he was at his most impatient, probably because he was dragging Joe around, and Joe seemed less than capable.

"Enough." He chopped a hand at Joe.

The old scars on Joe's face faded, but didn't disappear instantly, even though vampires supposedly could heal themselves. Gradually, like melting putty, his nose changed back to a pasty white. As he made a monumental effort, his teeth even receded.

"Wow," I said.

"Can you detect what is wrong with him?"

My eyes darted sideways towards Patrick again, but settled on his shoulder. "Are you—" I bit back "crazed" and settled for, "I'm not a healer."

Patrick's golden toned skin was nothing like Joe's unhealthy pallor, but it was as polished and unreal as a painting. "I realize healing isn't your specialty. But you can sense auras. We need to discern what illness or spell has attached itself to him."

I didn't ask why, I just started shaking my head. "I cannot."

"Yes, you can."

"So can every other witch then. Go ask one of them."

The hand again, chopping at my sentences. Maybe he did that so often because I refused to meet his eyes. "Some witches can, some can't. You've got a special ability with auras."

That was news to me. "No."

"Oh, for the love of—"

"No," I interrupted. "It's the same as touching someone, and I'm not going to do it."

"Are you sure your refusal to touch him isn't because of the spell?"

"What spell?" I asked cautiously.

"Obviously, he has some spell or curse that makes him repulsive. It affects a lot of what should now be his innate abilities. Is it the spell that makes touching him abhorrent?"

I wasn't certain Joe needed any spells to repulse me. Vampires didn't sweat, but Joe had a sheen across his skin as if he had been sweating for hours.

Against my conscious wishes, my thoughts churned. My stubborn brain was probably the only reason Patrick bothered to plague me with questions on a regular basis. "Curses and spells are entirely different," I said. "Does a spell work on a vampire?"

Patrick frowned, his impatience and disapproval swelling across the porch in a wave. "Why didn't you ask about curses being effective on a vampire?"

See, that was what I meant about Patrick and why he never stopped asking me questions. Even if I didn't know the answer, it might be hiding somewhere in the back of my brain. "A curse would work on a vamp because curses can pass through death if they are strong enough. But spells usually can't. Vampires exist due to magic, but it would require stronger magic to overcome that magic and make a spell stick."

"Why would a curse work?"

"Different kind of magic." I was fascinated despite the fact that Patrick was an annoyed vamp, and I was standing outside a house that offered me no protection from him. It had never consciously occurred to me until now that a vamp would be vulnerable to a curse.

As vamps are wont to do, he caught me peeking at him. His black eyes were cold, but without real malice. "That's why we're here, yes. I require a deeper understanding of this weakness."

It was never pleasant uncovering a person's Achilles heel. Socially, it was awkward. When that person was a vamp, well, it was even less comfortable. This was twice in a few days that I had discovered a vamp weakness. I wasn't stupid; Patrick could smear me across the tarmac on any given night. Sure, my protections might make it more difficult, but he had been around long enough to know more about witches than I knew about vampires. "Why me?"

Joe coughed, a phlegmy, disgusting sound. "I'll research it myself! Who needs your help anyway?" He shoved a finger against the bridge of his nose as if pushing up invisible glasses.

Patrick did the chopping thing with his hand, ignoring Joe and answering the question. "The choices are limited."

"Yeah, I can see where they would be." The two of them were asking me to closely examine the cause of something that was detrimental to vampire health. If I figured out what caused the weakness, it would give me a certain leverage over them—and that made me dangerous. "I can't help you."

Patrick sighed. "Can't or won't? We've been through the pay thing before."

"No, it's not the money."

"The situation has already been compromised," he said smoothly.

"Is that a threat?"

He laughed softly. "That's not the way I do business."

I wasn't buying his light and hearty. "If you recall, I don't do business *at all* with vamps. For the very reason that I like my skin and blood the way it is."

"That is unfortunate."

His answer was as ambiguous as always. That made me very angry. He had backed me into a corner. I could either help him or be on notice that I was now considered a threat because I had figured out that vamps were vulnerable to curses. But even if I helped him, I'd still be in that realm because I had stopped a vamp in my own living room.

"Would you touch me or my aura?" Patrick asked.

The very question made my skin crawl. My face did all the talking; there was no need to verbalize it. He tilted his head.

"Hmm. That is very interesting. So it is not just the curse. Can you spell a vampire?"

"I'd be more than happy to attempt to put a spell on you." He deserved my best and nastiest for cornering me. Unleashing a stream of silver crucifixes up his pant legs held delightful appeal at the moment.

"Could you do it?"

I glared at his chest, curling my lip. He was serious, treating me as an equal, a colleague. It was quite a drop down for most vampires. From the sneer on Joe's face, it was obvious he didn't consider me an equal, and he was so far from the top of the heap, he'd never set eyes on it.

I flexed my fingers and pretended to be thinking. I wanted Patrick to worry, to sweat it out, to maybe feel a fraction of the fear that I was living with.

"Well?"

I sighed. Even if he believed I could spell him, he'd still be the stronger, always. Much as I didn't like admitting it, him treating me as an equal was classy, because we were not equals and never would be. "No, I don't think I can spell you." I pushed away from the side of the house before my legs cramped from holding a half fighting position. "The only spells off the top of my head that would be effective on you—or any vamp—are blood spells. I don't do those. In any case, as I'm sure you're aware, those aren't true spells, they are compulsions."

He gave a curt nod. "And their effectiveness is limited."

"Somewhat. The spell, were it strong enough, would probably be effective on you, but wouldn't function as well as if you were human. I don't think you'd be as compelled to follow orders because your other instincts aren't the same. I doubt such a spell could compel you to kill. It might force you to answer a call, but not much beyond that."

"Into the daylight?" Joe asked worriedly, chewing on very chapped lips.

"Your instinct against daylight should win out. It could depend upon your internal strength, maybe how long you've been alive—er, I mean, uh, dead."

Patrick allowed a small grin of controlled amusement over my discomfort. "But we'd have to keep answering such a call."

"You'd keep *feeling* the compulsion, but I don't know if you'd actually be compelled to answer. Some vamps might find it easier to just align themselves and do the bidding of the blood spell than to fight the compulsion, but to actually spell complete compulsions—say to steal something and bring it back, those are difficult to maintain even on a live human." I paused. "Not impossible though."

"And so it might also be possible on a vampire?"

I shrugged. "Maybe, but you'd have to hide the spell behind a natural compulsion. With a vamp, if I wanted him to kill someone, for example, I'd create a spell that was an irresistible compulsion to drink the blood of a certain person and hope nature took its course before the compulsion spell ran out."

Joe gurgled his appreciation. "I bet I'd be good at blood spells." His crafty eyes traveled me up and down as if I were a tasty snack. "They sound delicious."

Patrick's form wavered just the tiniest bit, the monster closer to the surface. "She's talking about you being spelled, idiot, not you being capable of spelling anything!"

I swallowed my own retort. Joe might be the weakest vamp on the planet, but he could probably still take me down one-handed. His attitude made me want to shout blessings at him in a string of curses that would cure him, but good. Instead, I said, "Keep in mind that even using natural inclinations, that kind of spell doesn't work on all humans. They have to be extremely vulnerable to begin with, and without proper maintenance the spell would fail. Look, this is *really* not my area of expertise. Humans break free of that kind of spell all the time—or some of them flat out die from the fight."

Joe whined, "You keep saying humans, like we're not human."

Patrick and I both snorted.

Patrick then spread his hand in an eloquent apology. "A lot of things seem to have gone wrong on this one."

Joe sniffled. "Nothing I can't live with. I'm already better than I was before."

I really wanted them gone. To hurry the process, I gave Patrick what he came for, at least my best quick guess. "A curse can cross the lines to the dead. There's no natural protection even for a vamp. If it was a curse when you were alive that you carried over, it might lose some of its power crossing over, but death could actually strengthen it. Curses are strange things. They," I hesitated, but couldn't think of a better way to put it. "They have a life of their own."

"Can you get rid of it?"

My mind stopped. Gears whirled and thoughts moved, but nothing came out. "Wow. I don't think so."

"Can you *try*?"

"You don't understand," I said, to which Patrick nodded.

"That's the whole point of us coming here."

"A curse is…" I shrugged, holding out empty hands. "Getting rid of one that has crossed life boundaries…"

"Why?" Patrick put one foot on the porch step. I wanted to hold my ground, but it took a lot out of me and must have shown on my face. He stepped back, clenching his hands into fists. "Why is it so difficult? Explain!"

"I don't even know for sure that it is a curse!" I yelled. "I told you, I'm not about to touch his aura or even examine it from afar. But, well," I spun my new silver bracelet for reassurance while trying to sort through the curses I had dismantled before. "They're almost…a…they're like a *spirit*. They're sort of alive."

Patrick didn't like that answer. He swore, grabbed Joe's flabby arm and stomped away. There was nothing graceful about it. Joe stumbled twice.

"Think about it," Patrick said without facing me again. "Find a way around it. There must be one."

"Knowing too much about your weaknesses could get me killed, and we both know it."

The shadows shifted and when they were still, the vamps were gone.

I locked the door and stomped down the steps defiantly, but it was all bravado. I was halfway to my car when the next voice rippled out from other side of my house. I had the clasp undone on my new bracelet and was ready to throw silver before I realized it was Lynx.

"I want to buy your house." He must have waited in the shadows until he was certain the vamps were gone before speaking.

My breath was already gone, having fled in fear. His audacious suggestion had me sucking in air and spurting it out in a single horrified gasp. "What?!?"

"It's no good to you. You can't live in it with Patrick stopping by with his problems. You've moved in with White Feather. You don't need it."

I blinked rapidly as he sauntered over to my car, stopping at the outer edge of the porch light. "I don't want to sell my house." I'd never imagined selling my house. It was *mine*.

Lynx nodded. "Yeah, I figured you wouldn't be too happy about it. I been doing some research. Patrick could undo the welcome thing if he wanted, but did he do that? No. So you gotta sell it. Why not sell it to me?" His head was cocked in the way that meant he was listening for more than my answer. Lynx had always wanted a house. No, he'd always wanted a home. And if he had ever had a home, it's possible my house was the closest he'd ever come to it.

"If you sold it back to me, could he get in then?" I asked.

Lynx took the question seriously. "He'd be locked out if it was really mine before I sold it back." He gave me his cat smile. "But who says I'd want to sell it back to you?"

I frowned. "You're right. I can't symbolically give it to someone and have them give it back. I have to really move out. I have to…leave." And that was a sticking point. I gazed at the stucco exterior. I wouldn't be able to show up and walk in. It would be his, not mine. I'd have to remove the protections meant for me and me alone. Well, maybe not. Leaving them wouldn't actually hurt anything, but he was right. I had to sell it, not just move out thinking I could always come back someday.

Considering such an idea was ludicrous. I snatched the client spells out of my backpack and handed them over to him for delivery. I offered him a ride, but refused to discuss his stupid offer any further.

Chapter 14

By the time I pulled up to White Feather's, it was full dark. I could sense faint echoes of silver inside the house. They were so obvious, how had I ever missed them?

Standing on the walkway, I reached for the silver in White Feather's ring.

He was in the new lab area behind the kitchen. But how did I know that? Was it just my subconscious guessing the distance? Or was I completely off-base?

There was other silver in the house; some in the bedroom, at least two loop bracelets in the bathroom...hmm. The bracelet location was somewhat obvious because I'd left the bracelets there. Still, each bit of silver came with a sense of place that was more solid than the memory of where I'd left things.

White Feather must have heard me drive up. Or he sensed me with his wind the way I sensed he was walking closer through the silver in his ring. I laughed, hurrying to the door right as he opened it.

I threw my arms around his neck.

"Hey, I'm all dirty! I've been working all day and haven't showered yet!"

I loved the feel of him, so much stronger than me, all hard angles and muscles that touched me everywhere along the length of him. "Okay," I said and kissed him anyway.

"Mmm. Are you going to greet me like this every time you get home?" He backed inside, dragging me with him.

"Maybe. Wait until I tell you what I spelled today!" I followed him in, excited to have someone to share with. Mostly, I kept my advancements to myself; we witches were a secretive lot, but with White Feather it didn't matter. He wasn't competition.

I spilled out the quick rundown of my day, showing him the bracelet. I considered skimming over the vamp visit. Patrick was no more of a threat than usual except that my own house was no longer safe. Still, I wanted to discuss the weird vamp with White Feather. He might have different insights than me.

White Feather shut his eyes when I said, "Patrick stopped by, stayed politely outside and introduced me to a vamp who needed a curse removed. I told him to take his business elsewhere."

There was a breeze across my face, a subtle and instinctive check. "Two vamps stopped by."

"Not exactly." I described Joe in gory detail. "Ugliest vampire I've ever seen. Weirdest too."

"One healthy vamp and one with a bad case of baldness and heavy drinking. That had to make things perfectly safe."

"Yeah. Possibly. Probably not." White Feather apparently hadn't met any such vampires before either. "Never mind. Watch what I learned to do today." I extracted one bead from the bracelet and *pushed* it across the kitchen bar.

In my enthusiasm and due to lack of practice, I overestimated. The bead snapped across the room, hit the fridge and landed in the sink with a loud *ding*. Like a ball in a pinball machine, it spun along the sides before dropping into the disposal. "Whoops."

He raised an eyebrow at my feat. "That was impressive. Useful too if we can enter you in a pachinko tournament that uses silver balls."

"I can get it back. But I better stand closer."

He almost smiled. "The house isn't even put together yet. You better watch out for the windows with that trick."

"It's not perfect. But it works!"

He headed to the sink, retrieved my silver the old fashioned way and then washed the worst of the dust and dirt off his hands and arms. "You're okay?"

I sighed. "I don't like him showing up, but I'm fine. He's no more of a threat now than he ever was."

"He's not on my list of favorite visitors." He reached for the towel and changed the subject. "Tracy and I made unbelievable progress. Go check out your lab."

"Okay." I scooted down the hall, happy to put the conversation behind us. I knew I should have been more careful. Then again, it wasn't as though I'd entered my own home after Patrick had time to hide there. If he wanted to attack me at night, all he had to do was wait until I was out past dark.

Lynx claimed there was a way to reverse the invite. That didn't mean Patrick would allow it, but I'd still research it.

In the room that would become my new lab, not one, but two walls were up. Tracy was nowhere to be found. "You're using limestone for the walls?"

"There's an adobe layer on the outside wall, but this inner one is limestone butting up against the kitchen wall. Tracy is some kind of earth carver. I ordered in the limestone to use as a wall in my lab out back, but he started using it in here. And in a few short hours, he had two walls up."

"Earth carver." I frowned. "Dad said something about an earth affinity, but he didn't know what it was. Did you ask Tracy?"

"I mentioned he built walls quickly. He never said a word, but the stones kept flying. The adobe was the same way. He set the bricks as straight as though he'd carved them from a single rock."

I walked over and touched the wall. Solid. Humming. "It's happy."

"Happy?"

"It's all in alignment as if...there's mortar here, but it's all one piece. I suppose it could be because it all came from the same quarry. Whatever he did, it's positively a work of art."

"He was amazing to watch, I can tell you that."

I traced my fingers along the limestone. "I bet I can learn a thing or two from him."

"When you're not off figuring out how to shoot silver? Maybe we should use plexiglass in the windows in here."

I grinned. "Progress is progress. Have you eaten yet?" I checked my watch. "We better make sure Tracy eats before Dad shows up, or I'll never hear the end of it."

"Tracy's in the shower. If you warm up the food Mom sent home with us, I'll take my shower, and then we can eat."

White Feather's mom had sent us home with enough food for three days —until Tracy got a whiff of it. He ate more than Lynx on his hungriest days. The magic must have drained a lot out of him because he polished off half of a loaf of bread, all of the casserole, with the exception of the two pieces White Feather and I ate, and four glasses of milk.

A trip to the grocery store was in my very near future.

Chapter 15

First thing next morning, I hurried over to visit Mat. Surely by now she'd be ready to talk.

Her shop door was locked tight again, but this time there was a "Back in Fifteen" sign, one she displayed often. I frowned. Jim, aka Gordon, could be in there. If that was the case, I didn't want to be the next visitor.

As I turned away, there was a very loud *clank* from within the store. Before I could imagine what caused the noise, the sound of something else heavy and fragile shattered against the tile floor.

Not good. There were a lot of spells in there and any physical fight—or magical fight—would be a disaster. Been there, done that, and the results hadn't been pretty. Somewhere out there was a guy who still had petunias growing out of his arm as a result of mixed spells firing all at once.

I leaned in close to the door, struggling to peer inside. Not even shadows shifted within, but at least one deep voice or...was that a growl? Jim didn't growl, did he? And he wouldn't hurt her, right?

Sound didn't carry well enough through the glass, but it wasn't Mat making that noise. The high-pitched scream, however, was probably her. It rattled the windows and maybe even damaged the casing.

"Moonlight madness." It definitely wasn't in my best interest to visit, but I wasn't about to stroll away and hope for the best either. "Can't call the cops. He's probably already in there." For the second time in as many days, I ran for the alleyway. I didn't hide my tracks this time.

If the noise turned out to be a domestic dispute, I'd...well, Aztec Curses. If I weren't married to his brother, there would be no question. Between the two of us, we'd blast Jim into the next century. Of course, White Feather hadn't said I couldn't take action. He just said I had to leave Jim alive. There was a lot of room between alive and not alive.

I skidded around the corner, yelling to announce my entrance. "Mat? You okay in there?" My attention was on the open door, but I sidled close to the side of the building. I very nearly tripped over a pile of clothes strewn along the outside of the building.

Two more steps and Mat let out another screech. "Ruuuun—" Her voice cut off on a strangled gurgle.

"Mat!"

Reaching the door only made everything worse.

A coyote, shaggy blond and browns, larger and better fed than any wild animal, snapped wicked teeth in my direction. The beast was no better groomed than his wild cousins, and this one obviously had a lot less sense. No sane coyote would venture this far into town and attack two people.

"Zandy!" I cursed.

Saliva dripped as the coyote swung back around in time to dodge a piece of a broken chair aimed at his head. Jim jabbed with the chair leg again and then again. He was hunched against the living room wall with Matilda smashed partially behind him. The floor was wet, and the reek of sewage made me gag.

"You misbegotten mutt of an Aztec Curse!" I yelled.

Zandy turned his back on Jim to face me without a worry. From the lack of a real weapon in Jim's grip, Zandy's confidence was understandable. Zandy was dangerous enough as a coyote, and that was before his blood had been tainted with concoctions that, if he bit one of us, might make us wish we were dead.

I plucked a silver bead from my bracelet. Zandy snarled low and bunched to jump. No time for precision. I yanked the clasp of my new bracelet and *pushed* the silver hard. All of it.

"Choke and die!" I screamed.

The silver balls flew through the air. Several hit, singeing his fur. Sadly, the little missiles didn't stick. The welts may have hurt, but the silver bounced off Zandy as fast as they hit him.

The distraction of my attack allowed Jim to lean in and beat at Zandy. "Bastard!" The series of threats that followed were possibly more dangerous than the chair leg.

I called the rolling, ricocheting silver balls, spinning them relentlessly at the coyote.

Jim kept up his end of the attack until he suddenly stumbled and fell to his knees. He gave a hacking gasp and gagged.

The coyote stepped on a silver ball, yelped and dodged. I *pulled* silver and then *pushed* again. The ones that hit sizzled, but continued to bounce off. "Mayan moonlight sacrifices in a bloodbath!" I knew I should have gone with something pointy and sharp.

Matilda pounded on Jim's back. He heaved a breath and stopped gagging as suddenly as he had started.

Zandy coiled again. His growl was unnecessary showing off. I already knew he was gunning for me.

I *pushed* again, not even thinking about where or how. Balls zinged through the air, one of them scoring a lucky hit on Zandy's eye. It wasn't that my aim was improving, it was that I had no other option than to keep pounding him.

Zandy leaped anyway. The silver on my wrists flared, and the gold ring on my finger went hot. "Moonlight madness!" Now White Feather would be the one to find my dead body next to that of his brother.

I ducked and rolled. My momentum carried me further inside, while Zandy went over my head into the relatively cleaner alley.

Mat yelled, "Roll again!" No longer behind Jim, she gathered the water from the floor, her eyes an eerie transparent blue, a wave that you think you can see through, but can't. The water swelled into a black roll and spilled against the back of the door that Zandy had just leapt through.

She almost slammed it closed, but Zandy turned and jammed his canine self against the wood. Black water burst backwards from the force of his hit, mostly missing me.

I linked to Mother Earth in a desperate search for more silver. If Mat had a silver dagger...the first silver I sensed was in the kitchen, but I was too new at this to grasp any useful information.

Despite my concentration, the silver resisted me, clanging, but not moving to me. I took two steps towards the kitchen, but finally recognized the shape enough to realize its nature. "Great. I'll beat him to death with a spoon."

The only other silver sensation came from the shop. "Spells with silver?" The feel of it was odd, and I almost ignored it. But Zandy was behind me now so there was no point in standing in the open. I bolted for the front of the store and the silver. It didn't matter what the spell was set to do. If it had silver in it, that was good enough for me.

The jar was a beacon calling to me, but even after picking it up, I couldn't guess anything about it except its silver content.

Silver flakes? Maybe it would stick to his fur.

I didn't even have to return to the living room. Mat screamed an obscenity. Jim yelled something about a gun. I didn't wait. I pulled the stopper, pushed the silver, and physically threw the entire jar into the snarling jaws of a mad coyote.

I grounded hard, waiting to feel teeth lock onto my arm. My grandmother's bracelet was on my right wrist, held high, protecting my throat. I ducked sideways, but Zandy was already midflight.

He would have hit me too if Jim hadn't landed across his back, cutting short the launch. They hit the floor hard.

Zandy snarled, whined, sneezed. Both paws frantically rubbed at the liquid silver on his snout.

"Colloidal silver," I gasped. I didn't even need to keep directing it. The wet blob burned without bouncing off.

I clenched my fists with the effort of calling the silver beads from the living room. Several pinged off the wall; guiding them all through the doorway at once wasn't in my skill set yet. Those that beat the odds pelted the already injured coyote.

Jim scrambled to the right, putting some distance between he and Zandy.

I pushed and pulled carefully now. There were a lot of spells in this room. No sense in setting them off by accident.

Mat rolled through the doorway in one fluid motion. She spat a word, flung a spell and dove for the floor. I'm no idiot; I went down behind the counter the second she started flinging.

Zandy's fur ignited in a huge fireball. He barked an injured cry that changed to screaming yelps as he scrambled for the back door.

None of us made a move to stop him.

Chapter 16

Jim groaned first. Or maybe he was just the loudest. I raised myself on my elbows and dared peek around the side of the counter.

"Whaat—?" Jim moaned out.

"Did he scratch you?" I whispered. I owed Jim my life. Or my sanity. It wasn't a comfortable position to be in, given that my best friend hated him.

"Jim?" Either a rat was in the room or Mat had developed a higher pitch to her voice.

"What," he repeated weakly.

I decided to crawl over and see if he might live. Mat's phone rang. I touched the gold band on my hand, but it had cooled. White Feather was bound to be trying to reach me. I kissed the ring and hoped he'd know I was okay.

By the time I stumbled to Jim, Mat was patting his face and arms, searching for wounds. He stayed down, blinking and breathing.

"That stuff. What. Was that stuff?" he finally wheezed out.

"He's a shifter," I said. "Coyote."

His hand flopped weakly. "No. Stuff you were shooting. Buckshot? Lead pellets? Spelled?"

I frowned. "Silver."

"Spell? Will it kill me?"

Of course, he'd been hit. I'd been slapped with my own beads, multiple places. "Just silver. Shifters can't handle it. But the beads bounced off him for the most part. I was aiming for his eyes or hoping to stuff some down his throat, but I'm not that accurate yet."

He groaned. It was a magnificent cacophony, worthy of a passionate death throe. Quite overdone, really. Sure the pellets hurt. There was a large welt on my arm and possibly one on my forehead, but he was a cop. Surely he'd been hurt worse.

"Jim?" Matilda leaned in closer. "I don't see any scratches. Are you bleeding anywhere?"

He finally peeled one eyelid back, but he had eyes only for me. There was no sign of the smug individual from the dinner table. His brown eyes were regretful, worried and angry. "Your aim was off," he bellowed. "I swallowed the damn thing!"

Mat blinked and then switched her attention to me. When the tension left my shoulders in a puffed out breath, she said, "Unspelled?"

I nodded, unable to keep a smirk from my face. "But I'm definitely planning to change that. And add some arrowheads to my collection. Mat, did you know you don't have a single silver dagger in the place?"

She huffed. "I'm not like you. I generally don't *need* to carry around weapons."

"Yes, you do!" Jim and I yelled at the same time.

She startled back on her heels. "Well, I didn't before."

"What happened?" I demanded.

Her eyes slid to Jim. "We were having a discussion."

"A fight," Jim corrected. "And she opened the door to kick my ass out, only the damned coyote was there waiting. Luckily, I was avoiding the door, despite the fact that sewage was spewing from all the drains, or that thing would have had me for lunch."

Mat straightened her shoulders. "I told you there was nothing to talk about." Only from the way she was gazing at him now, maybe there were a few things worth discussing.

"I need to call White Feather." I started towards the living area, but stopped without turning around. "I owe you one, Jim. Gordon. Whoever you are." Mat would probably hate me, but he had tackled Zandy right before the coyote sank his teeth in me.

"White Feather would never forgive me if I let something happen to you," he growled.

"Neither would I," Mat said softly.

Okay, this was definitely the kind of thing I had been trying to avoid walking in on.

I stomped to the phone and called White Feather's cell. Of course he was on his way already.

I told him what had happened and assured him it was over.

He said, "I'll pick you up."

"What about my car?"

There was static on the line for a bit and then he said, "This truck will be madness to park that close to the plaza."

"Truck?" Neither of us owned a truck. Maybe he meant his jeep, although he was in the process of converting it from a gas guzzler to a vehicle that could run off stored energy from the windmills. "I'm fine. I'll drive myself home. No vamps this time."

His sigh was as expected as cold in the wintertime. "Zandy may as well be a vamp."

"I know. I'll meet you back at the house."

"You're fine?"

"Perfectly."

"What route are you taking back? When are you leaving? Zandy might come back."

"I'm leaving right this second. I'm going, I'm going."

When I hung up the phone, Mat had her hands on her hips, surveying the damage. "I think I'll invest in a silver dagger."

"And a spear. Zandy is infected with more than your average shifter."

She pushed her foot through a murky pile of sludge. "There was already some plaster missing from the side of the kitchen. Now it's wet. And smelly."

"Let me guess."

She held up her hand. "It wasn't the toilet. I kind of wish it was. Who knew the stuff that went down kitchen drains was this gross?"

I leaned over and picked up a silver bead. So long as I was down there, I called the rest to me. Unintentionally I felt the tingle of the ball that was inside Jim. "You okay here?" I asked, tilting my head to the front of the shop.

Her shoulders slumped. "Yeah."

"You tell Jim I said he can keep that silver bead, 'k?"

Despite her stress, she laughed. Right away, she stifled it with her hand. "I need to learn that trick of yours."

I shook my head. "It isn't perfected yet."

"Oh, it was perfect. Although the timing was off. I'd have liked to have done it without having to fight off a rabid coyote."

We hugged tight and I whispered, "I didn't know he was lying to you, Mat. And even still, he might not be all bad."

She nodded into my shoulder. "He said he started seeing me as a way to collect info on the underground, on us witches. But he swears that only lasted the first date. He saved me. And you. I wonder if he can fix my wall?"

I pulled back and surveyed the large missing chunk of plaster. My beads hadn't done that, but from the stray wood piece hanging from the side, it looked as though a broken chair had made solid contact. "Thanks to Dad, I know a guy who can help fix this up better than it was before the coyote."

"Really? It's awfully damaged."

"White Feather is waiting for me." I didn't tell her that he had picked up on the fact that I was in trouble. We didn't really understand what that magic was all about. "You okay here?"

She nodded. "Except for the mess that is my life and house, sure." She tried to smile. "You're better at this stuff than I am."

"Just think of it as another spell gone wrong," I advised.

"Yeah, but how do I know if there's anything worth salvaging?"

I didn't have an answer for that. On my way out, I noticed the pile of clothes that had been against the building was gone. Zandy had come in broad daylight, shifted, and was ready to ambush my friend. What I didn't know was why.

Chapter 17

When I arrived at White Feather's, Lynx was helping Tracy and White Feather unload Dad's red four-wheel drive truck. It was filled with the burners and exhaust hood from my lab. The cabinets and tables were already unloaded, sitting by the truck. The breath I let out sounded a little like "Aztec Curses," but I was still inside my car so no one heard. Half of me was annoyed about the stuff being moved without my permission, but the more reasonable side of me knew it was necessary. Still...

White Feather approached as I exited the car and gave me the once over. "We need to figure out how I can get to you faster, because knowing you're in trouble when I'm miles away isn't working." He closed his eyes. "I can't follow you around every second, and this time I was already *at* your place only you were not."

He was obviously conflicted, caught between anger and helplessness. Since my own feelings mirrored his, albeit for different reasons, it almost made up for his invasion of my privacy. "Maybe you could just send your wind magic like you did the first time." I eyed my stuff with a frown. He could have at least told me he was bringing my lab over.

"I sent my wind?"

"I think so."

"Would you know what to do with it?"

Now there was a problem. "Might take some practice. I see you've moved most of my lab." Voicing my irritation only made it build. I could drain anger into Mother Earth all I wanted; she was more than happy to accept energy, but when my emotions were out of control, I tended to draw power from her, rather than find a ground. And when I drew energy, it needed somewhere to land, such as a spell. Otherwise I was a fuse about to blow.

White Feather recognized the pending explosion. He gripped my arm. "I thought bringing all your supplies over here would mean no more of my heart jumping out of my chest to get to you. But you managed to find other trouble besides a rogue vamp."

"I didn't know Zandy was planning an ambush!"

Before we could escalate the argument, Lynx sauntered our way. No way would I air my personal problems in front of him. He'd already heard more than enough. My lips locked down in disgust.

"We moved your stuff without taking anything out of the cabinet," Lynx said, waving at the cupboards and drawers. "I told him the whole thing could explode anyway."

"Everything seems to have made it in one piece." Disappointment warred with common sense. I had spells on that cabinet to protect it and the contents, but this had to count as a failure.

Lynx said, "I wasn't gonna pick the locks, that's for sure." He crossed himself. "White Feather lifted most of it with his wind power. We just had to keep it from tipping over." His tone carried awe and respect. "I still don't know why it didn't explode."

"I'll have to see about fixing that. I never thought to protect it against someone taking the whole thing lock, stock and barrel. It's heavy and unwieldy."

White Feather's grin was a little too satisfied for my mood. "I didn't do anything that would set off any spells. Besides, your magic is attuned to mine, which is why I know when you're in trouble."

"Is that it?"

He frowned. "Maybe."

We walked to the cabinet. There were two spells that had activated, but one must not have worked because neither Lynx nor White Feather had mentioned burns. The delayed reaction spell had definitely been set off, so even if the initial burn hadn't taken, the later one would. "Lynx, you said you steadied it?" His hands would eventually blister from the delayed curse.

"Me and Tracy. Other than it heating up, it didn't do nothing."

"So you did feel heat from the first spell. But White Feather's wind must have cooled it." There were ways for me to concoct a stronger spell, not that my cabinet needed protection against White Feather. But his was not the only wind around, as we had experienced not that long ago. "Did you bring the holy water from my lab?"

Lynx shook his head and worriedly began inspecting his hands. "Why?"

"I used parsnip tops in a delay spell. Once your hands are exposed to sunlight for a short time, they will blister. The spell soaks through the skin." I scowled at his hands. "Never mind. Rather than rinse it off, maybe I can use another trick." I linked to earth and searched out the dust that would have transferred with the spell. Before I had learned to recognize silver from a distance, I'd never have tried to remove traces of a spell this way, but it was easier than expected. The particles were like little beacons. Calling them to me was easier than silver because they were lighter and attracted to me since I set them.

"Hey!" Lynx jumped back and rubbed his hands against his pants.

"Hold still," I muttered. "White Feather, you too."

I pulled, just like I did with the silver. The only difference was that this time, White Feather's wedding ring glowed for a couple of seconds before the dust went back to Mother Earth.

Lynx was more upset than White Feather. He peered at his hands, inspecting them for traces he hadn't seen. "Knew I should have stayed out of it. Witches," Lynx grumbled. "I ain't gonna move anymore of your stuff."

His snarky attitude reminded me of Tara, which reminded me of something else. I snapped my fingers. "I have a note for you from Tara. I meant to deliver it to you, but it's been warmer out, and it's in my heavier jacket." I didn't give him time to complain. I left him arguing with White Feather about how to transport the cabinet into the new lab without Lynx having to touch it. If they were paranoid about any remaining bits of the spell, well, they both should have known better than to mess with my belongings.

In the hallway I met Tracy on his way back outside. I reached for the curse particles without bothering to tell him, but there was nothing there. "Did you touch the cabinet?"

He nodded. "Sure. Had to move it."

"Can I see your hands?"

He lifted them, palms out. They weren't clean, but the spell particles were gone or neutralized. "Hmm." There might have been the faintest traces of my magic, but if I didn't know better, I'd say they had been completely absorbed— or maybe smothered. "Do you know how you do that? How you manipulate Mother Earth into bricks or how you absorb dirt and change it into what you want it to be?"

He stared at his hands. "No."

Without any sign of worry or curiosity he walked away. He was either really in touch with his karma or he was just plain touched.

I waited until the cabinet was settled in the lab before handing Lynx the note from Tara.

He drifted outside to read it in private, leaving me to inspect the lab. To my amazement, the outside walls were nearly finished. The roofers would be able to start in another day or so.

Tracy hit the showers while White Feather drove the truck back to Dad and picked up burritos.

That left me to wash up and change clothes before putting together a salad. At the rate we were plowing through food, I had better cook up some refried beans and beg tortillas from my mom.

Lynx finally joined me in the kitchen, but turned up his nose at my offer of a carrot. I chopped vegetables and snacked on the results. On my worst day I wouldn't have asked Lynx why he and Tara had broken up. Even asking him innocent, well-meaning questions was often dangerous.

Lynx glowered at the carrot on the counter with artistic disdain, ears stretched back as though he was half switched to cat. Instead of commenting on the inedibility of vegetables he said, "Tara called me *Bob*."

My hand jerked involuntarily. The celery stick I was dipping into the ranch dressing nearly sent the bowl over the side of the counter. "What?"

He picked up the carrot from the bar and chewed as though eating poison, smacking his lips rudely. "When I left her at your house and wouldn't take her with me to the job at Tent Rock."

My mouth dropped. "Tara called you Bob instead of Lynx?" The deliberate use of his shifter form of "bobcat" rather than his chosen name of "lynx" was either an insult or a threat to expose his true nature. Lynx was already sensitive. He didn't need a girlfriend touting that she knew he was a bobcat rather than a lynx. He definitely didn't need her implying that a bobcat was somehow inferior to the name he'd chosen to call himself.

Lynx did not glance my way, but one ear swiveled, and his eyes flashed bobcat yellow.

"Oh." I had no idea why Lynx had chosen the name he had. Maybe it was because a lynx was larger—although definitely not meaner—than a bobcat. Then again, the kid had been younger than twelve when he found himself on his own, living in the streets. He might not have known the difference between the two cats when he picked the name. I choked on my next bite of food rather than ask.

Lynx happily smacked me across the back while my eyes watered.

"That's exactly the way I felt." He seemed deeply satisfied with my reaction, even though my choking had little to do with Tara's words.

"Enough," I gasped out, waving him off before he killed me. I swallowed a sip of iced tea. "She has a lot of issues, you know."

He cut his eyes to me, eyes that had reverted to full human.

I held up my hand before his attitude went further downhill. "Not excusing it. But you may as well find out early how mean her mean streak can be." With Tara it went past nasty, circled back to ambush, and had no trouble escalating from there. "Bottom line is she has family and because of that, she's used to being forgiven for just about anything."

Lynx didn't have family. He'd never had family. Tara was the baby of the family. They had tried to train her, coax her to do the right thing, coerce her—and even when it all failed, they still loved her. This was not a concept that Lynx could understand, but I tried to explain anyway.

He finished his soda and half a package of crackers long before I was done stuttering on about family nuances. He scratched his chin. "Are you saying I was supposed to," he cocked his head, "just forget about it?"

"Oooh, no," I shook my head. "If Kas had pulled something that dirty, there would be hell to pay. She's my sister and I love her, but no. No, you don't take that sort of thing sitting down."

His lips curled in either a smile or a snarl. This was language he understood. "Exactly."

"But," I finished setting out plates and utensils. "That's where it gets tricky. See, I could stop talking to Kas, but she'd still be my sister. Because she's my sister, I can't throw a harmful spell at her." I looked down, guilty. "Well, nothing lethal, you understand."

Lynx never made noise when he laughed. From the way he leaned over and the delight on his face, he was probably almost hysterical with mirth.

"Are you sure Tara is worth bothering with? It's not like you're related, and there might well be someone...less...a lot nicer out there."

He turned his back on me, putting distance between us. "That's the thing. I don't *know*."

Obviously, the kid missed her. Tara had probably attempted to make amends, and the note proved she wasn't done trying. "Well, I can't answer that either. That's something only you can figure out. I can tell you that her insult doesn't mean anything other than stupidity. She's spoiled and not used to paying for stupid remarks or even idiotic actions that put other people at risk."

Tara had put me in danger, herself in danger, and if Lynx hadn't been bobcat, he'd have been in danger too. "Yeah, that part I learned. She doesn't think very hard before she decides she has a great idea."

Lynx had followed her "thoughtless" ideas a time or two before he wised up. I hesitated, but it needed to be said. "I also don't know her well enough to know if she likes you for you or if it's because you're a shifter."

His back stiffened.

"Don't go all feral cat on me! You want to hear it from me or do you want to find out the hard way?"

When he whirled to face me, his hand was raised in a warning cat-swipe.

I folded my arms over my chest. "I mean it, Lynx. I've been down this road playing the helpful friend and then gotten blamed because the message was ugly."

For almost a full minute we stared at each other.

"Women!" he said with some heat.

"Yeah." His eyes stayed brown with no hint of cat so I told him, "Back when all those women were getting killed by shifters, Tara claimed she wanted to date a werewolf. She spent a lot of time telling White Feather it was perfectly safe."

"It is."

"Not then it wasn't, and you know it. But the thing is, I don't know if she was yanking his chain or if she wanted to flirt with danger. I don't know if she really cares about you or if she has some other game she's playing."

He was quiet for a bit, but then he asked, "What's White Feather's beef with shifters?"

I grinned. "Nothing. So long as they aren't dating his sister." Before the fur on his neck could ruffle, I added, "He's got a thing about *any* guy dating his sister. My dad is like that. Some sort of an overprotective, all guys are trying to get in a girl's pants thing."

His face relaxed into a smirk.

"It's also one of those family things I've been explaining. If you have a daughter, you'll be the same way."

He blinked once, fast. Then his eyes widened as if it was the first time he connected "relationships" to kids. Or in his case, maybe it was the first time he connected kids to family.

It took him a moment to get his feet back on the ground, but he finally asked, "How does a guy figure out if a girl is for real?"

I sighed. "The same way us women have to figure out if a guy is worth the trouble. Roll the dice."

"Doesn't seem like good business."

"It's not. But you shouldn't do it for business reasons anyway." I bet he had tallied every business and logical reason for dumping or dating Tara. The kid had perfectly normal hormones, but he had survival instincts second to none. "Survival and love don't always mesh well. When the combination is right, it makes you stronger. When you get it wrong—" I hesitated. "It might not kill you. Presuming you don't date anyone who is even more lethal than you are."

Speaking of lethal, I provided Lynx with the rundown on Zandy breaking into Mat's. "He was feeding a vamp a few days ago. What's he up to?"

Lynx shrugged and did his human-cat hiss, which was close enough to the real thing that it included a guttural growl. "He sticks to the hills mostly. Lately he's been in town telling everyone he's a chupacabra on account of that witch, but it ain't true."

"Given that rumor has it a chupacabra is a crossed coyote and a wild pig, I'd almost believe it, except I saw him changed. He's still just a mangy coyote."

Lynx nodded. "Plus I've seen chupacabras, and he ain't one. They're mean as a wild pig, so that's the only reason he's been bragging about something that stupid. But he was short more'n a few circuits before Sheila the witch started injecting him with her experiments. She didn't improve him any."

"So what's he into?"

"Same as always. Mostly stealing, because a coyote can weasel around things that a human can't." He tilted his head, listening to something only he could hear. Maybe cats did that to hear their own thoughts. "Thing is, he never minded staying coyote, especially in tough times. Oh, he liked the action with the ladies, but it was the easy money that attracted him to that deal. Mostly he's too lazy to work." Lynx nodded sharply. "I'll do some looking. See what easy cash is keeping him around town instead of eating some dead carcass something else already killed."

"Lynx, he's dangerous. If Patrick is right about his blood making it possible for a vamp to enter my place, you better watch yourself. It's likely that last concoction Sheila injected in him had your blood too."

I heard the growl without the hiss. "I know. I don't mess around with him and his crap. That's why I don't know what he's into. But I'll find out."

Chapter 18

My new lab had walls, and it now contained my equipment, but it wasn't finished. I scowled over how the equipment had appeared without my permission. Maybe White Feather felt this same sense of crowding when my Dad showed up and tried to take over building his house.

My foot tapped. That last visit from Patrick had not helped things. White Feather was determined to protect me, whether I wanted to be protected or not. I stared at the diamond on my finger. If it indicated he was in trouble, I'd go to the ends of the earth, right through her if I had to. Hmm. I still didn't like being moved over here without him asking.

Because Tracy had agreed to help repair Mat's place for the next day or two, progress in the new lab was stalled. I pondered my choices. I could still use my old lab for testing purposes, even though it was now empty, but if there was ever a spell that needed improving, it was the flying spell. Testing it meant an outdoor excursion. For a lot of reasons, it fit the mood of the day.

I dug through boxes until I found the heliotrope I had purchased from Mat. It was one of Martin's stones. Since Martin was dead, getting more magic from him wasn't possible. That made this particular heliotrope very valuable.

White Feather was in the bedroom sorting through a box of items we had recovered after the storm blew his lab and half his house across the landscape. Haunting notes drifted across the room even though his lips were nowhere near the mouthpiece of the flute-like instrument he held in one hand.

"I didn't know you played an instrument."

The music stopped. He'd been concentrating so hard, he hadn't sensed me coming. "Learning. It's good exercise to direct air precisely rather than let it flow through all the tiny holes at the same time." He held up the wooden flute and demonstrated. Without his fingers ever covering a single opening, he played the melody to "Blowin' in the Wind."

"Wow. I couldn't do that using all ten of my fingers!"

White Feather shrugged. "I had five of these in the lab, but could only play two of them at the same time. This is the only one I found intact."

Only another witch would understand the need to practice controlling five spells at the same time. I smiled. "Can I borrow some helium for my measly rock that doesn't make any music at all?" He already knew the heliotrope could hold helium because he'd used the stone before. "I want to practice the flying spell."

White Feather lifted one eyebrow. "Something tells me I'm not invited to this practice session."

I frowned. "Not yet. Not until I'm closer to success."

He eyed me thoughtfully, but didn't argue. He hit the heliotrope with a blast. The stone sucked up the energy. When the breeze came around the edges, he stopped.

"Be careful with that thing," he warned.

"Of course." I wasn't even considering blowing my way to the top of Tent Rock like he had done.

White Feather wasn't impressed with my easy agreement. He chased me down the hall with the piercing sound of Kenny Loggins' "Danger Zone."

Thinking about the last time we'd used heliotrope is probably why my car found itself in the parking lot at Tent Rock. The air was crisp with cold, the sun mostly behind low, snow-threatening clouds. The burned area at the top of the climb didn't beckon me. In fact, coming here didn't provide any fond memories. I let the cold wind soothe me, freezing out any dread. Even though the earth was mostly sleeping as winter drew closer, there was still comfort to be found if you knew where to look.

I hit the trail to avoid any people from the two other cars in the lot.

There was more than one source of strong magic in Tent Rock, and that wasn't counting the individual columns of stone that rose and guarded the place. I easily reached the bowl shaped depression where Mother Earth was particularly strong. It probably wasn't a bad place to practice, but if there was too much magic it wouldn't be a very good one either.

I held the heliotrope and felt for the wind, but the power contained in the stone was as alien to me as the errant breezes against my skin. I thought to push it or pull it, but it was not like silver or any of my other spells.

I frowned. My other flying spell worked with magnets and compression. There was compressed wind in the rock, but how to direct it?

The magnets in my shoes would only lift me so high.

"Squeeze it."

The grinding voice startled me into dropping the heliotrope. I raised my silver and spun around so fast, I nearly fell when my feet lost their purchase in the shifting sand.

It took two searching passes before I saw—"*Martin*?!?" The color of smooth sandstone, he nearly blended into the rock behind him and in fact, had he not spoken, I'd never have seen him. Then again, maybe he resembled the stone because he had no clothes on and the stone behind him was more visible than he was. His body was nearly transparent.

I blinked. This was the second time in my life I'd seen a ghost. I was even less pleased than the first time it happened.

"Push the rock, not the wind."

"What are you doing here?" I blurted out.

His chuckle was more crumbling concrete than mirth. In fact, he was more stone than wrinkled human ghost. His arms were not as rounded as human limbs. Harsh planes carved out his face. Oh, his beady little eyes were the same though. They traveled up and down my person suggestively. The only difference was that now his eyes weren't watering from having imbibed too much alcohol. "Wasn't quite ready to cross all the way over." His sing-song voice now had the benefit of gravelly drums. "No rush."

"You just hang around here?"

Even though breathing couldn't possibly be required in his current state, he sucked in a snort of air and spit.

"Martin!" I jumped two steps to the right. Who cared if it was ghost phlegm? Stuff was probably poisonous. It was definitely creepy, as was the grinding chuckle that followed.

"I rested a bit," he said. "The songs didn't bother me anymore, not like before. I could sleep."

Right before Martin died—or in his case, blended in with Mother Earth such that the difference was moot—I'd started to suspect that his close tie to the earth was the reason he drank. But there was no way to shut out Mother Earth, not really. She sang through the plants, she reflected back the warmth of Father Sun, she rumbled through the stones and gems of which she was made. She was the mountains and the heartbeat within.

That beat echoed through my own heart. Martin had roamed far and wide hunting her treasures and selling the magic, but he hadn't been able to stand her constant thunder.

"Now that you're awake, don't you think you should be moving along?" Was it rude to rush a ghost through to the other side? Wherever that other side was?

"There are things here, interesting things, in-between. I closed the gate. But there are these little holes. Tiny ones that pop open when black magic calls dark energy over to your side." He waved a hand full of knobby fingers. "Then I heard my stone. Nice of you to keep it. To remember me." He reached out as though to touch me.

I flinched and stepped back. I hadn't wanted him groping me while he was alive. We all owed Martin, but gratitude didn't cover pawing—dead or alive. "What little holes? Here in Tent Rock?"

He smiled and swayed side to side as if he were still a drunk. "Magic. Not my kind. Not your kind either. Little bits of demon spit that leak out, hunting blood. Black magic attracts demons and ghouls. If the magic is strong enough, it will call them through. You don't want to mess with those things even if you're resting here in-between." His voice was soft and getting softer. "Nice of you to remember me."

"Martin, wait! You haven't explained—"

His mouth was moving, so I shut mine, but being Martin, he just had to get in the last disgusting word. "Squeeze the stone like a fart. You don't grab farts, you squeez'm out."

"Oh, for Moonlight Madness on a pin full of Aztec sacrifices!" I whirled around to make sure he wasn't sneaking up from a different angle. For the first time, I realized my silver hadn't heated up, not in the least. Of course, Martin hadn't been a magical threat in real life, and he was an earth witch. A very strong earth witch who had felt me using one of his harvested stones even after he died.

I glared at the heliotrope and bent to retrieve it. Martin hadn't changed. He was still annoying, and made very little sense. Or no sense at all.

Crouched down, I fingered the green stone with its streak of blood red. Bloodstone and wind stone. I wrapped my hand around it and concentrated on the stone rather than the wind. I squeezed tight with my fingers, trying hard not to imagine anything farting, including the stone. Using my grounding as an anchor, I pressed the stone.

The heliotrope remained hard, but wind leaked out in all directions. "It works!"

I squeezed harder.

The wind spurted out, matching my excitement. A gust pushed my hair back. Sand scattered around my feet as if White Feather's stored magic were bursting to escape. I not only rose three feet in the air, sand and rocks swirled alongside me, gifting me with a mouthful of dust. "GakPtttPttt!"

I stopped squeezing, but the wind didn't die down. My head went one way and my feet the other. I had no idea how to compensate. I gasped for a breath of air, hoping it wasn't all helium.

The wind spun me with a last vengeful gust and then cut off suddenly. I dropped straight to the ground.

"Moon—ptth." I coughed and choked. Spattered fistfuls of sand plopped onto my denim jacket.

Somewhere in the rock cliffs, there was the echo of a laugh. It was either Mother Earth or Martin. In this spot, from what I'd seen, that was one and the same.

Chapter 19

My hair was tangled half in and half out of its braid. Oh, who was I kidding? The only remnant of my braid was the tie dangling from knotted strands. I looked as though I had been dragged through the dust, only in this case, the dust had been dragged through me by a self-inflicted windstorm.

I let myself in the front door and headed to the bathroom.

White Feather was turning from the fridge, orange juice in hand.

One glimpse of me was enough for him to nearly choke on his juice. After a sputter, he asked, "Are you all right?"

My lips pressed together, biting back the annoyance that had only grown on my trip home. I was actually less injured than on some excursions, but I was not accustomed to returning home to a witness. Lynx had seen me a time or two, but he didn't count because I didn't care what he thought.

"Yes," I mumbled. I relaxed my fists in order to catch my sliding backpack. A drop on the tile would probably break everything inside.

"Uh, spell didn't go well? Or did something else happen? You look," he tilted his head, "furious."

"I saw a ghost," I snapped out.

His eyes widened briefly.

Before he could pester me with a million questions, I said, "It was Martin."

He set his glass on the counter, smacking the bottom dangerously hard. "Oh?"

"Do you know he had the nerve to appear in front of me *naked?*" I flapped my hands, freeing more sand to fall on the tile. "I have to be haunted in the desert by a naked ghost? What did I do to deserve this?"

White Feather closed his eyes and for a few seconds there was complete silence. Then, to my disgust, he started laughing. Hard.

"White Feather! It isn't funny! The guy was obnoxious enough while he was alive. The last thing I need is to have some sculpted ghost appearing naked in the desert when I'm trying to work!"

He stopped laughing long enough to gasp out, "Sculpted?"

I glared at him and jabbed my finger in the air. "He looked like stone. Naked stone. I thought ghosts were supposed to be wispy."

It was a while before he sucked in enough air around his chuckles to say, "He did save our lives. And it appeared that his rescue turned him to stone. Interesting." Thankfully, the intellectual side of things penetrated his brain enough that he was able to hold his hysterical laughter down to a couple of guffaws as he thought about the situation.

"Don't you think you should be concerned that a naked man is appearing in front of me and flirting outrageously?" I demanded. "I wouldn't be very happy if a naked woman showed up in front of you!"

He coughed away another laugh. "Martin? You expect me to be jealous of Martin?" An attempt to sip orange juice to clear his throat almost choked him. "He is still dead, right? And what do you mean by flirted?"

My breath puffed out in a sputter. "I didn't want to see Martin running around the desert naked when he was alive. I don't know why I have to see him now."

"His ghost actually flirted with you?"

"White Feather!" My face flamed.

"You made up that part."

"I did not. He always did—does, this look over where he checks me up and down. He still did it even though he is *dead*. And let me tell you, it wasn't pleasant when he was alive and smelling like rotted beer farts. Now that he's dead..." I shuddered. "I don't even want to contemplate what that ghost might think is sexy."

White Feather snorted, trying hard to stifle another laugh and failing. A stray tear of merriment leaked out the corner of one eye. "Did he have a reason for appearing, or was it to scare the daylights out of you and flirt?"

"Who knows?!? He is still Martin. He delivered some cockeyed message from the grave about demons and tiny holes in the gate, whatever that means. He said he hasn't gone through to the other side." My eyes narrowed. "And he was younger than I remember." Now that I had time to ponder it, there were other differences. "He wasn't drunk either. But he didn't seem particularly sad about dying. He was just Martin, only he looked a lot healthier than he ever did when he was alive. His whole body was perfectly carved, like granite or marble, but he wasn't stone because he moved around. Maybe he bathed recently or something."

"Hmm." White Feather raised a single eyebrow and set his glass down again. He stalked me, his eyes locking on mine. "Maybe you're right. Maybe I need to do something to erase this picture you now have in your head of a sculpted man."

I backed up automatically and barely managed to mutter, "It was *Martin*."

White Feather snagged my waist, but I squealed and made a mad dash for the hallway. "I'm covered in dust! And I'm traumatized!"

He was close on my heels when he said, "I've decided you're right. You shouldn't be imagining someone else naked."

There was no point in mentioning that I hadn't had to use my imagination. I found myself busy with more important things. The first time White Feather and I had ever been together was in the shower. It didn't seem possible to improve on such an experience, but White Feather proved me wrong.

By the time we were done, the only images in my mind were of the living.

Chapter 20

We were finishing up dinner when Lynx called. "Something going down at the nail place up from Mat's—Tam's salon," he said. "Zandy and a pal went in there, Zandy came out."

My first fear was for Mat. She'd already been attacked once, and knowing Zandy, he wasn't smart enough to give up. "Did you see Mat?"

White Feather met my eyes and pushed a button to switch on the speaker phone.

"No sign of Mat, but you better hurry. I smell blood and that tat stink from before."

"Who was with Zandy? Any idea?" White Feather asked as I raced down the hall to grab my backpack.

I paused when I heard Lynx say, "Some homeless guy. I seen him around."

If I hadn't been so frantic rushing behind White Feather to the car, I'd have thought to call my dad or Mat before leaving, but we were both buckled in before "homeless guy" and "Tracy" merged in my brain. If Tracy had gone to help my friend only to meet his demise...the address was the nail shop. Tracy had no business there, of course. But he had been repairing the wall at Mat's place. Mat had been attacked by Zandy.

"Did Lynx say anything about Tracy?" I demanded as White Feather squealed the tires taking a corner too fast.

"No, but he'd have mentioned if the homeless guy was Tracy. He worked with Tracy the other day."

Relief warred with worry. "True. Probably. But with Tracy working at Mat's, what if Tracy walked up to the bakery when he was done and then went into Tam's shop with Zandy? The man eats an entire loaf of bread in one sitting."

"Tracy isn't the type to frequent high-end bakeries. Besides, didn't your dad or cousin pick him up like they always do?"

"I don't know."

"Lynx would have recognized Tracy whether he was with Zandy or in a limo. That kid doesn't miss a thing."

White Feather was right. "Yeah." I didn't want to cause any panic, so I didn't call Mom or Dad. Whether Tracy was fine or not, they'd demand to know what caused my alarm.

We parked in one of my usual out-of-the-way spots and skulked the rest of the way on foot. The streets weren't well lit, and the alleyway behind Tam's Salon was awash with shadows. Luckily, White Feather checked ahead with a casual breeze. It was tempting to search for some silver to test whether I could glean information the way he did, but now was not the time for experimenting.

Before we were anywhere near the back door to the shop, Lynx hissed at us from atop a garbage dumpster. He hopped down and said in a low voice, "It's been quiet in there, but it ain't good. Zandy picked up the homeless dude from the park. They walked here. Before they went in Zandy told him it was a nice warm place to sleep."

Whenever Lynx was nervous, his speech slipped into the cadence and street talk of his youth, an old habit of blending in when lurking in back alleys. His nerves were not a welcome sign, but given that Zandy was involved, his reaction was understandable.

"Zandy isn't the type to offer charity to homeless people," I said.

Lynx agreed. "He ain't one to buy'm beer either, but he kept this guy limping along with more than one before they got here."

"Then Zandy left?"

"He was in there about a half hour before he came out. I didn't see anyone else, but Zandy was talking to someone. When the door opened I smelled the ink and blood. Didn't hear anyone else until after I called you; then there was a yell. After that someone left through the front door. I wasn't expecting that." He sounded almost apologetic, but he couldn't watch both the front and back at the same time.

"Nothing since then?"

"I checked the front. Whoever left must have been dipping in the blood and ink. Maybe the homeless guy put up a fight 'cause the stinks were all mixed in there, including the magic, but not like yours. Yours smells like earth when the sun hits it; a bunch of herbs or something. That guy smelled like old blood and new blood and I dunno. Something like earth, but not."

"Black magic?" I hadn't smelled a lot of black magic and even if I had, every witch's magic was different. White Feather's breeze had its own signature just as my earth magic did.

Lynx shrugged. "From the smell of drying blood, I thought for sure the homeless guy was dead, but after Zandy left out the back and the other guy left out the front, there's been some noises. The homeless guy must still be in there so maybe it's no big deal."

"Zandy doesn't do no big deal," I muttered. "He wasn't breaking into Mat's place for a cup of tea."

It didn't take White Feather long to pick the locks on Tam's back door. He cracked it open and listened with his ears and wind.

Lynx and I inhaled deep breaths. My silver flared protectively. I couldn't smell the blood, although there was a tang of paint or ink...then again, it was a nail salon. Maybe that was all Lynx had smelled?

Yeah, sure. Zandy had no doubt been delivering a new customer to have his nails painted after hours. I let out the breath I'd been holding and breathed in another. There was another tingle, but it wasn't my nose that alerted me. A current bumped my silver and reflected off. *Magic.* Not Mother Earth. Not something that silver conducted.

I nudged White Feather's arm, but he shook his head. "No idea. The breeze indicates someone in there who hasn't bathed in a lifetime or two."

"Homeless guy," Lynx whispered.

"No one else that I can detect. "

"It's not earth magic," I said. If it was a shifter Lynx would know. It wasn't a magic I recognized, but that meant nothing either. Lots of magic reacted to silver, some good, some not. "There was no magic there when I was here to have my hair styled."

White Feather snapped his head in my direction. "This is where you had it cut?"

"The owner was skilled for sure, but if she's a witch, no magical currents registered at the time." I thought hard about the work stations and the people. My silver hadn't reacted, and I'd been wary because her son had tried to give me a card. "Nothing. If she has any latent ability, I'd have guessed it leaned towards the healing arts because of her skill with hair, but that's a stretch." The wonderful smell of lemon grass conditioner came to mind. "Maybe some basic aromatherapy."

"Looks more likely a setup for another robbery than a witch's lair," White Feather said. "Getting in the other places didn't leave much of a mark. Zandy didn't bust in here either."

"Door was open," Lynx said. "Whoever used the front entrance didn't break any glass entering or leaving. Definitely some of the same smells as at the other places."

Had Zandy been trying to rob Mat and found easier pickings up this way? And why bring in a homeless guy if the door was already unlocked?

White Feather jerked his head at Lynx. "Watch the front for us."

"Back might matter more," Lynx decided.

"I can cover that." I went to the alley entrance, leaned over and left a silver bead. I placed two more in strategic locations and then scooted in place behind White Feather.

Lynx waited and watched as he always did, curious.

"You have anything on you that can hold silver?" I asked him, curling my fingers over my gold and diamond ring. He could carry gold, but I wasn't about to hand over my ring.

He frowned, but extracted a sachet from under his shirt. I'd given him the packet a long time ago. The potion inside might not even work anymore unless he kept it current. Knowing him, it was current. He didn't miss much, and if he had any inborn talent, his nose could sort the various herbs enough to keep a spell active.

I carefully inserted a silver ball into the packet.

He peered inside, still frowning. "I don't want that in there all the time. It will bug me."

"Even through the leather?"

"Yeah." Without another word, he disappeared around the corner of the garbage dumpster, nothing but a shadow in the night. He'd stall anyone who came around the front way or at least make enough noise to provide a warning.

White Feather ducked in first, flashlight low. I focused half on the silver outside and half on where I was placing my feet. This monitoring silver from afar was going to require some practice.

"The back room is separated from the front," I whispered. "Light probably won't show except through the doorway." The one small window into the alley wasn't visible in the salon part of the store.

A short hallway with two doors led us into the hair styling room I remembered. The sink yawned black in one corner. The massage table was center stage twice, once for real and once reflected in the mirror at the hair station. Inky blackness full of a nasty aura oozed across my skin and jewelry.

The homeless guy may have started out on the massage table, but he had rolled off and onto the floor. Someone had been thinking ahead because the floor was covered with a blue plastic tarp, something we hadn't seen at the other robberies. Maybe it explained the lack of clues at the previous places, because there was dried blood as well as new smeared across the tarp.

The latest blobs of red dotted the plastic and most of the guy's arm. There was no coat in sight, but no way had the guy been walking around without one. Homeless people tended to overdress even in the summer.

His ratty pants were the drabbest of olive green and well-camouflaged with dirt. One hiking boot wasn't tied; the other had a mixed selection of wire and string holding it on. His face was ashen, dirty and bearded. Wisps of greasy hair clung around the bottom of his head.

Tattoos bled and this one was worse than most, but whoever had done it hadn't worried that leakage would ruin the design. There was no plastic or bandages covering it.

I shivered, remembered my silver watchdogs in the alleyway and mentally checked outside.

The homeless guy could remain here undiscovered until when? Why were these victims at the robberies in the first place? Why roll him in here, and if they were using the victims to transport a familiar of some kind, where was it?

The clues were jumbled together worse than a drunken witch's brew.

There was no sign of any tattoo equipment, but the wound was very fresh. Lynx hadn't mentioned any stops for tattoos and hadn't smelled the ink until after Zandy brought the guy here.

Mr. Homeless wasn't looking very healthy, but he dragged in a ragged breath, leading me to mistakenly believe we weren't too late. Blood puddled around his shoulder, a slow dribble.

White Feather stepped closer, his hand reaching to check for vitals.

I didn't see the dragon until it swooped down from the cabinet. Wait. *Dragon?*

It was the size of a beagle with long wings. Its entire body was ink blue with black around the edges of the scales, flashing iridescent reds. Blue, jagged teeth aimed at my face.

"Eeeeeeeeaiakk," I screamed and ducked just as White Feather smashed it with a blast of wind.

The gust caught it hard enough to suspend it mid-attack. It screeched in defiance, but my own hysterical shout did a bang-up job of drowning out the dragon.

Neither of us saw the second nightmare until it was too late. White Feather's arm was stretched my way, exposing his ribs. The purple cousin to the first dragon darted out from under the sink, launched like a crazed poodle, and crashed into White Feather.

Fear spun me sideways, an instinctive distancing from the attack.

The wet crunch of teeth ripping flesh had me jumping straight back into the fray. The gold ring on my finger pulsed once. "White Feather!"

The steady breeze holding the blue creature in midair abruptly ceased blowing, and the dragon tumbled nearly straight down. I ignored it in favor of grabbing the feathers and scales of the purple beast trying to make a meal out of White Feather.

Grunting, I dragged at the frenzied creature. "Mayan...spawn of hell!"

White Feather yelled, "Get away!" His voice cracked with pain at the end.

My silver flared to life again, hot, then cold. As if I hadn't figured out we were in danger. Hoping the creature was more dog than snake, I clamped my fingers on the sides of its jaw, pushing flesh under its teeth. The silver in my turquoise ring sizzled when it came in contact with the scales. The gold and diamond ring sparked, a lick of flame that was very real and very hot.

I pulled Mother Earth into the diamond, hoping that doing so wouldn't somehow provide the half-dog creature more power. My ring sucked in power like a vortex.

What had been a flickering flame from the ring flared into a white-hot stream. I gasped from the heat, only partially shielded from the diamond by the gold. The laser light hit the blue creature and smoked. Black blood spurted, a steaming mix of melting blue goop that puddled on the floor.

The dog-dragon howled a decree from hell, but released its bite on White Feather.

The weight of it toppled me backwards. The side of its mouth was still on fire, but it wasn't done fighting. My grip slipped. I shouted a desperate warning, "White Feather look out!"

The tail whipped around, but White Feather fell between it and me, catching the creature with a blast of air that spun it backwards. The creature smacked into the wall hard enough to crack bones.

White Feather wasn't done, either.

I rolled to my knees, watching gusts of air tear the construct into pieces, one scale at a time. Silver up and ready to burn, I searched the darkness for more danger, but the original dragon was gone. By the time my eyes circled back to the first mess, there was nothing left, not even a growl.

"What...White Feather? What happened to the other one?" I spun forward and then reversed. There was no puff of smoke, no lingering scream, nothing. I stumbled to my feet, my back to White Feather, searching the corners of the room.

The two creatures had disappeared as if they had never existed. Whatever nether hell spawned them had reclaimed them. I squinted in the light of the dropped flashlight. It was hard to be certain, but the homeless guy no longer appeared to be breathing.

White Feather eased to the ground, emitting a strange wheezing bubbling noise. He clutched his side. "Need...a bubble."

How would his protective bubble help? I felt for the silver beads in the alleyway. The silver conveyed a sense of garbage on its way to decomposing and within the earth's burrows, rats or mice scuttled.

I reached for the silver bead Lynx carried, but couldn't find it. "Lynx?" I called out. I concentrated harder on the silver bead I had given him, but it wasn't in the front or the back.

Time ticked by at an alarming rate. I knelt and examined the mess that was White Feather's side. From the noises he made, his lung had been punctured, but the bubbling had stopped.

Something he was doing blocked air from leaving his lung.

When I would have put my hands over the wound, White Feather shook his head.

"Can you hold it? How long?" I asked.

He nodded at me, but stayed still on the floor.

Frantic and needing better light, I used the fallen flashlight to hunt for the light switch. Secrecy was moot. We needed help and fast. Racing back to White Feather, I focused again on the silver Lynx carried. I located silver inside a nearby shop, but it wasn't the bead Lynx carried. "Lynx, where in moonlight madness have you gone now?"

There wasn't time to find him. White Feather required medical attention immediately. "Lynx?" I yelled loud enough to bring the dragon and twelve of his friends back from the dead. I dug through my backpack for my phone, still probing the front and back for the missing silver bead.

Nothing. The kid was nowhere. What had gotten to him? He wouldn't abandon us even if he had witnessed what was happening inside. *Right?*

I dialed my mom, rattled off my plea and the address, and then dialed 911.

"Lynx is gone," I told White Feather. I could feel the silver in the alley and even move it, but that would be pointless. We were on our own.

Chapter 21

The homeless guy was dead. There had been no indication that he had controlled the creatures, but after examining the blood remnants on his arms, albeit from afar, it was suddenly obvious the designs resembled the dragon and the dog-dragon thing that had attacked.

I recognized the shape of the dog-creature mainly because of the long tail that went all the way to the man's wrist and ended in a dripping, barbed point.

Blood still seeped from both of the tats, but there was no color of ink remaining on his skin.

My eyes flicked from White Feather's wound to the tats, to the wall where the dragon had been torn apart before disappearing. Blood constructs, they had to be.

But who controlled them? More importantly, who created them and why? The dead guy had no reason to pay for a tat and release the constructs to rampage. There had been no sign of movement from him even when the things attacked.

Thinking through the problem kept me distracted from White Feather's pain, but it didn't stop me from hunting for vials of holy water inside my backpack. I emptied both of them into my water bottle. "Constructs are black magic." I peeled back White Feather's shirt. The bite was bad, jagged and bleeding profusely. The dog-dragon had been substantial enough to snap at least one rib and rip into White Feather's lung. I sprinkled the holy water on the wound.

Like peroxide, it bubbled and frothed. "Moonlight Madness! I guess simulacra don't like holy cleansing."

Before all the water completely dribbled out, I refilled the bottle from the sink. Holy water was still holy water, diluted or not.

White Feather never protested; he concentrated on breathing.

Lynx had smelled magic, ink and a lizard-like scent at the other sites. The lizard smell must have been a remnant of the basic nature called to be the construct. But what purpose did the construct serve? And if it killed the originators, you'd run out of volunteers in a hurry. Of course the homeless guy hadn't been a volunteer. He'd been lured here.

"Kidnap a victim. Punch a tat all over his arms. Power the tats. Rob the place. Shoot. Whoever was here had a key!" But they hadn't necessarily had keys to the other places. And the lizard and tattoo smell had been on a broken window and under a door, indicating the tat constructs had entered without disrupting any alarms. The small chink in the window was barely noticeable. A lizard-creature sliding in under the jewelry store door might raise suspicions if caught on camera, but the lizard's entry didn't breach any alarms. Once in, the controlled creature or the humans who followed could erase the files that recorded the construct.

"Power a construct. Send it in ahead of time. Turn off the alarm?" Plausible.

The salon probably had a bottle of real peroxide, something I didn't happen to carry in my backpack. A quick survey of the cabinet above the sink supplied both rubbing alcohol and peroxide. Too much of the alcohol would be bad. It would also burn like a cattle brand, which could be disastrous for a guy focused on controlling his breathing.

I did the best I could, muttering cleansing spells, but not about to pack the wound with herbs, not until he had a real healer examine him.

There was nothing more to be gained by waiting longer, so I called Gordon to report the body. He didn't pick up, but I left the address and a cryptic message. My focus remained on White Feather. The front door was locked, but a quick check out the front windows showed nothing moving in the dark.

I returned to White Feather, lending him spiritual strength and a whole lot of worry. His brow beaded with sweat, but his concentration held. He squeezed my hand.

I examined the wound again, muttering another protection spell. Healer I was not, but he had lent me the power of wind magic at least once. Mother Earth was an energy source for me, and he wore my ring. Maybe a little silver from the ring into his system would kill any ill spells.

My help may have been negligible, but the moment I drew in energy, the silver at my wrist tingled a warning, a lingering connection to the silver balls in the alley. The current was a vibration, footsteps across Mother Earth. One of the beads was in motion.

"Lynx!" I jumped for the back door even though it was propped open.

Seconds later, he arrived with unexpected reinforcements. "Tara?" She might not be as experienced a healer as Mom, but then again, she was better than nothing. "He's in here."

I probably should have warned Tara that "he" was White Feather because she stopped dead in her tracks when she spotted him.

I shoved her forward. "Hurry! His lung is punctured. The other guy is past helping."

White Feather gasped for air. Blood and bubbles oozed from his side. "You...shouldn't be—"

"Don't argue," I yelled.

"Ground for me," Tara cried, clutching my hand. "I have to save him." She faced away from me then, covering the wound with her hand. "I need my hands to work. Touch my shoulder or my head and ground!"

She hiccuped in complete panic, but placed both hands over the wound. Her breathing was as harsh as his was bubbly. Grounding I could do, not that it had done any good before. I put my hand on her shoulder, only to have fire race up my skin, scalding like steam. I tried to jerk away, but Tara grabbed my hand, sending even more pain slicing across my wrist.

"Please!" she begged. "You have to help me!"

The skin under my bracelet went red and then blistered, but even as my arm shook with the effort to escape, the electricity followed me. A hundred knives stabbed and then seared upwards.

I did what I always did when in danger. I linked to earth as if my life depended on it.

Tara didn't waste any more time. She pressed her hand on White Feather's ribs. Whatever she was doing hurt like hell, but if it helped White Feather, so be it.

My teeth clenched and nearly cracked from the pressure, but I stopped fighting the electrical charge that was Tara. If I hadn't spent my entire life grounding I'd never have been able to hold the link. Mother Earth didn't want the current surging through my arm. Her acceptance was a begrudging groan, a protest that accepted the flow and returned heat.

Steam rose through a tiny crack in the concrete, floating directly to my silver.

White Feather gasped a clear breath, but his eyes stared straight up, unseeing. My shoulders hunched from the strain of the odd fire traveling into my silver. My feet and legs gained the intimate experience of a lobster boil.

White Feather gasped again.

"I only know how to knit it closed," Tara mumbled. "I can't heal like some others can."

Perfection when it came to stopping blood loss and closing a gap was hardly required at the moment. As long as she could seal the lung puncture, he'd make it. He hadn't lost enough blood for it to be dangerous, but the lung injury could be fatal.

Tara rotated the pressure of her hands as if washing a plate. His blood didn't suck back in, and the wound remained a mess of torn skin and muscles, but his chest started to rise and fall more naturally.

"I can't—I don't know how to fix it better." She hiccuped, wiping one bloody hand down her jeans.

"Can I let go of you?" I hissed between my teeth.

Tara collapsed off her knees onto her butt, exhausted. "I don't think I can do more. The rib might hurt it again too." She glared at me with accusation. "You aren't a decent ground for me. My God, your Mom said I'd have to work to find a good one, and that some people wouldn't be able to do it at all, but that was horrible."

"It wasn't that great from my end either." I settled next to her and checked White Feather's side. The tear made by sharp teeth wasn't bleeding anymore, but it still looked as if White Feather had been dragged across concrete. "That was the most awful grounding I've ever had to hold."

"Healers can't ground," Tara said. "That's why I was never able to do any side magic. I thought I was just stupid, but turns out the healing comes from within so we have to have an outside ground or there is nowhere for all the pain and suffering to disperse. We couldn't live with all the buildup so we have to conduct it elsewhere."

My mouth gaped, but no protest came out. My mother was at least part healer. Why didn't I know she couldn't ground?

Maybe because she'd never used me as one?

The answer was not hard to figure out. Dad was her ground. "Why can't I ground for a healer?" I inspected the blister under my bracelet. As gently as possible, I moved the piece of jewelry to my other wrist.

Tara shrugged. "Earth magic and healing don't mix. Your mom said fire burns off the pain so it accomplishes a grounding very well. I think I could use White Feather because he could divert it through wind. But the earth thing. Man. That hurt."

"Yeah, I'll say."

"Well, I'm not that good yet at pushing it away from me. I've never had to do anything like this either. Your Mom taught me all the enhancements for first aid. Stopping blood flow was the first. But she said I'd need a different teacher to learn to knit skin, bone or muscles properly. OhmyGod this is such a mess. Your mom would totally freak out at the mess I made."

The dragon had made the mess, not Tara, but when White Feather groaned, the thought fled. We both reached for him at the same time. I grabbed his hand and Tara soothed hers over the wound.

"I mashed things back together, but we'd better take him to the doctor."

Doctors weren't my favorite, but she was the healer. If she said he needed one, he'd get one. There was no need to check the dead man's pulse, but once White Feather was sitting up, I did it anyway.

Gordon arrived just in time to escort Mom in ahead of the ambulance.

Chapter 22

White Feather was not an ideal patient. He was tense, moody and downright threatening as we prepared to transport him to a safe place. Since Mom would likely be more help than most doctors, we hustled out and left Gordon to deal with the ambulance and the dead guy. Besides, it would be impossible to explain to medical personnel that White Feather needed antibiotics for a dog bite. Tara had closed the punctures. And how would we explain the deep claw marks? Yes, sir, he's been attacked by a giant chicken?

Tara went from saving the day to a ball of weep. My mother drove her to the house, while I drove White Feather and myself.

As we shuffled in the door, Mom said, "Healing is very emotional. Earth is excellent to draw from, but it doesn't take emotion or human pain."

Watching Tara sniffle and tremble, I wasn't sure who was in worse shape, her or White Feather. White Feather was still in agony, and even though Tara wasn't standing next to him, she was not only reacting to his pain, but the residual effects from the healing and the emotional baggage because he was her brother. "She's a mess."

"The healing, it tears you up inside. The pain is gone, but the after effects drain." She turned to Tara. "Remember what I taught you. Take the emotions and transfer them to strength and happiness. Convert them." She gave her a pat on her hand and bustled over to examine White Feather's wound.

It didn't take Mom long to deliver the bad news. "There is a spell here."

"Aztec curses." None of the spells we'd seen at the salon had been benevolent ones.

Tara let loose an agonized moan as if she were caught in the bad spell herself.

I lost patience. "Tara, get your act together. Transfer all that emotion into something useful."

My mother shot her best witch's glare at me for my attitude. We rarely clashed, but this was White Feather! We didn't have time to stop and train Tara.

"Tara," she said gently, "remember your exercises."

Tara blubbered, "Ceeenter. Feeel. Bloock."

It was painful to watch her hiccup and sob around the mantra. She was trying, I'd give her that, but the girl had enough emotional energy for an elephant, and she wasn't the only one in the room panicking.

"Oh, for pity's sake." Since I couldn't heal, my only usefulness was teaching Tara to ground. "Go somewhere else, like you did when we practiced the witching fork."

"I can't ground on my own!" she wailed.

"That doesn't mean you can't find a partial way to disperse the emotion. And just think, if it doesn't work, I'll ground for you. Then we can both hop to the hospital in case there's anything left of us that can be saved."

She sucked in a huge gulp of air, and it came out a half laugh. "You're so stupid."

"Only sometimes."

"Hang onto it," Mom said softly. "Keep the laugh. Channel the rest there."

As soon as she concentrated, Tara lost it again.

White Feather opened one eye balefully. His stress was as deep as my own; I didn't even need the ring to feel it.

That jolted me. "The angst." He was in pain physically and still angry about the attack. "Mom, can you soak up some of his emotion? Tara's super-sensitive to him." I positioned myself so that Tara's view of him was blocked and asked her, "Where can you go that is calm? Take a deep breath and go there."

"I can't! My room is too boring! That barely worked for the witching sticks!"

People not tied to the earth and its huge pool of peace confounded me. Mother Earth was such a natural link for me, I couldn't imagine being without her. If not earth, what?

Something to tame emotions...water. Mountains. Whoops. I was back to earth. "You've got to redirect. Think of your favorite book. Or a movie that makes you laugh."

She hiccuped two quick breaths, filtering my suggestions. "Okay. But I hated Harry Potter. Everyone knows magic doesn't work like that."

"She always blames other people for stressing her out," White Feather grumbled. He glanced her way and then sighed deeply, winced and grounded.

The vibes from him hadn't particularly bothered me, but as soon as he settled himself, the difference was a breath of fresh air. My bracelet cooled. My ring had been tingling, but I hadn't even noticed, maybe because I knew the source or was stressed myself.

I scooped up his hand. He squeezed my fingers. Emotional grounding wasn't just for healers. The calm between us was a loop of comfort. Maybe we could help Tara if we understood it better, but the mere thought of dealing with her made my nerves ratchet up a notch.

Mom smiled. "Better." She completed her examination, but was less than pleased. "He needs surgery to have the tainted skin removed. It's not right. There are pieces from a nasty spell. The magic glows black."

"Can we unspell it? Use some herbs?"

She traced a finger across his rib. "Did you rinse it with holy water?"

I nodded.

"Good, good. But there's an odd blue tint embedded in the skin. His body, the white blood cells, are attacking the bits and pieces in his blood and muscles. Those are surrounded and being beaten. But those left in the skin cells sit there in fragments. I don't know what it is."

"Tattoo ink!"

She blinked. "He had a tattoo?"

"No." I explained about the dragons. "It bit him. The construct was formed from a tattoo."

She groaned softly. "Tattoo ink is impossible to remove. Most things in the skin are." She chewed her lip. "Your father could burn it."

"Why not cut it out?" White Feather asked through clenched teeth.

"What about lasers? Wouldn't that be safer?" Last time Dad used fire around one of my boyfriends, the result hadn't been pretty. Sure, no one was hurt. But that didn't mean the idea was a good one.

Mom tapped her forefinger against her thumb as though itching for the right balm. "Lasers work by opposite light, but it would only make the pieces smaller. You don't want this stuff absorbed by the body. It needs to be expelled."

"Is he stable?" I demanded.

"For now. But that ink has to come out. The tattoo ink won't spread, but it's still a spell that the owner can activate depending on the witch and what the spell does."

"Someone already used that ink to suck a victim dry," I mumbled, rummaging in my pack.

White Feather said, "I'll block anything that tries for me."

We really needed a sample of the ink in a spell that blocked and protected against it. Then again, the ink might be drawn right to the ink in his side. "I'll be back. I need to research something."

"Lynx can do it," Tara said suddenly.

"Do what?" I asked.

"Expel things. He does it when he changes. It's a shifter thing."

If Lynx could teach us to do it, that might work. Otherwise what good was it to White Feather?

Before I could continue to the lab, Mom caught my attention with a question of her own. "Can you see what Lynx does?"

Tara nodded. "Sure. Like when you tell me to focus beneath the skin and see the blood and muscles. It's like that."

"Can you channel it through you?"

Now, doubt and emotion contorted her face again. "I don't think so."

"Can you do it, Mom?"

She shook her head. "No. It's why most healers are no good against cancers. We can help, but not find every bad cell or correct the things that caused the bad cells in the first place. We can knit. We can stop blood flow. If we learn to control our emotions, we can heal the spirit and that helps heal much that is physical. But expelling every single cell that has become embedded in the layers of skin would be impossible." She shook her head. "It is easier to build a strong barrier than it is to cut something out, especially something this fragmented."

I turned on my heel, lest anyone read the fear in me. "Research. Be back." I headed to the bedroom to use White Feather's computer.

Mom followed me. She extracted a jar from her purse. "You need some salve on that burn. This has aloe in it." She talked as she spread the salve, which told me she was worried. I googled "removing tattoos" while she inspected the blister that had formed under my bracelet. She may not be able to remove tattoos, but she did a darn good job on burns.

"Certain lasers break up tattoo particles. The color of the light has to be right and hot enough to break apart the particles. The pulse has to be fast enough that it doesn't burn everything else. That tattoo was mostly the standard blue with some black and maybe purple." I scanned more text. "Moonlight madness, why would anyone want a tattoo? The ink is full of toxic minerals, paint and even blood to create specific colors!"

"It is possible that Tara can help if she is able to team up with Lynx," my mother said softly.

My fingers froze on the keyboard. "Really?" The idea was preposterous. Lynx wasn't all that cooperative with people he liked. And Tara was a mess. Setting the logistical problems aside, there were other barriers. "Can she possibly heal that way? Technically, I mean?"

Mom shrugged. "She is more talented than I am in many ways. She hasn't trained so she doesn't have the set notions I have either. I would never have dared examine a shifter with my sight."

"Mom, you don't know any shifters to examine!"

"This is what I mean. In my day, we wouldn't admit to knowing any if we did know them. She doesn't have this notion."

"How can she shift tattoo ink?"

"That is something I would like to witness. And if she and Lynx can't do that part between the two of them, maybe I can figure it out by studying the shifting. Although I'll need to use either White Feather or Lynx to ground unless we invite your father."

It was a new experience for me to work deeply with the witch side of my mother. She was my mother. First and always. And sure, she did healing now and then, but she wasn't a witch, not to me. She didn't have a craft that she studied and excelled at...only she did. And more openly since Tara had entered the picture. Maybe Mom realized she didn't have to stay quite so hidden, quite so old school.

"I guess we better call Lynx then. Only he's a cat. He'll be thrilled to hear that you and Tara want to run an experiment. And that we're all planning on watching. Oh yeah. He'll be one happy cat."

My mom sighed. "You let me know when he agrees, mija. In the meantime, we can look into this laser thing. There is probably a doctor who will do it."

"Or a witch who manipulates light. Do you know any?"

Her head tilted. "Not right this instant. But that doesn't mean we can't locate one."

And if her network didn't know of one, one didn't exist. At least we had the right people on the job.

Mom smiled and kissed my cheek. "I will teach Tara a few more tricks. She needs to practice transferring and channeling. Meanwhile, we will have to watch White Feather's wound carefully."

Mom emptied her purse, leaving me with enough salves to cure several people of various ailments. Sadly, none would fix the tattoo.

I added a few ingredients to the burn salve to block black magic and smeared more on my arm. Even though it wouldn't help, I dabbed some on White Feather's side.

There wasn't any food prepared, but we settled for the next best thing: scrambled eggs and bacon. Having a mother-in-law who raised chickens was coming in handy. White Feather never ran out of eggs. Of course, if he had cooked, he'd have made a nice, neat omelet. Since it was up to me, I diced crispy bacon, tossed it in with eggs and cheese and stirred the mess until it was cooked through.

Fed and showered, you'd think we could sleep, but White Feather was restless, unable to find a comfortable position. "You should never have been at the scene of the crime."

I raised up on one elbow. "You're right. I should be living at home, probably with a vampire feeding on me." I nodded sagely. "I never get into any trouble on my own."

He glared at me. "I'm not taking any painkillers."

"I know. You can't fight if you're drugged up."

He struggled to sit up. "If this thing in my side turns into a dragon and attacks you, how the hell will we stop it?"

I laid back down so that maybe he would. "Hmm. You attract dragons, and I attract insane vampires. We'd better stick together. How else will we survive?"

He fell back against the pillows. "Quiet, you. I need to concentrate. I was trying to make a point."

"Maybe you need to sleep instead. Tonight, I play bodyguard." I rested my head against his arm.

He didn't say anything for a while. Then, after I thought he'd fallen asleep he asked, "When do I get to be your bodyguard?"

"Seems like you've been doing that all the other nights. Moving me in here. Moving my furniture without even letting me remove the protection spells. I'd say you were doing your level best to protect me. It's my turn now."

He grunted. "Moving the furniture without asking may not have been my best idea."

"It could have used some finessing."

"I didn't like you stopping over there with Patrick showing up all the time."

"Him showing up all the time is definitely a bad idea. You overprotecting me and trying to run things won't work either."

"I might have been worried you'd decide to move back in there if I didn't get you moved in here."

"I might have been feeling a little pushed to live here."

"You're not Tara. You don't need babysitting. But you find more trouble than anyone I've ever known."

"You should have stopped with me not needing babysitting."

"I'm new at this," he protested.

I nodded against his arm. "I didn't even have a business partner before. Now I have this thing where I don't know if I'm supposed to be checking in with you all the time or what. I'm pretty sure I don't want to, and yet when you wander off to investigate dead bodies, damn right I intend to be there because what if something happens?"

He grunted. "I'll probably ask before moving furniture the next time."

"I'll definitely go with you to the next dead body."

He groaned, but it was theatrics. I slid sideways away from his arm so he could rest. "It's not any easier for me," I told him. "But tonight I'm bodyguard. Tomorrow, we'll worry about who is in charge." I held his hand and listened while his breathing evened out.

The dream catcher spun in the window, reflecting moonbeams. I hoped it was strong enough to keep a dragon out.

Chapter 23

Morning dawned cold and not so clear. I phoned Lynx first thing and left him a message that was upfront about what we needed, but didn't divulge all the nitty-gritty. His phone was never turned on when he was working. He'd show up when he got around to it if he didn't leave town entirely and refuse to ever do business with me again.

Tracy had returned to build more walls, and the roofers arrived to start the lab roof.

While I scrambled eggs for breakfast, I asked Tracy if he knew the homeless guy we had discovered at the nail salon. Describing the guy was difficult and came out as a rambling list of his clothing. I had never seen the color of his eyes and his hair had been so dirty it was impossible to know if it was gray covered with dirt or a brown combination.

Tracy listened until I stuttered to a stop. "There's a lot of us. Some hobos, lots of winos, some families. There's this one guy. He rides trains all the time. Tried it with the bus system, but he ended up locked in the luggage compartment for three days. Almost died."

"The guy I'm talking about liked beer and was hoping for a warm place to sleep," I remembered.

Tracy nodded. "Maybe Nick. He's a wino. He'd go anywhere for a beer. Warm place for the night, maybe not, but a beer or wine, yeah."

"Did he have any tattoos?"

Tracy nodded again, never once looking up as he shoveled in a final bite of food. Before he finished chewing, his plate was in the sink.

Since Tracy didn't offer anything more, I pressed. "What did they look like?"

He stepped outside and hummed an almost inaudible tune, a greeting to Mother Earth. My bracelet vibrated once as if hit by a silver tuning fork. This house would be an artistic monument when he was done.

I followed him to where the house met the outside. "Do you remember what the tats looked like?"

He paused, but then resumed removing the plastic sheeting that protected the kitchen. "I don't remember." He scratched his nearly bald crown and then added, "I need to light the brick oven."

"Any idea at all?" I grabbed a jacket and trailed in his wake.

He wasted no motions, but every now and then, he'd hum his little greeting. Finally he said to me, "He wore his coat mostly. But he had some on his arms. Blue, faded. A lot of lines."

"Dragons?"

He shook his head.

"Did he have one in the shape of a dog?" I could name shapes all day and get nowhere. "Any idea what the shape was?"

"Was more like a cross, but not exactly because there was a sun in the center or something like that. He said he had them done in the army."

Ah. Maybe we could trace him through there. "Do you know his last name?"

Another head shake. Something told me that homeless guys didn't offer up too much personal information. "Are you a wino?" Martin had been.

His eyebrows lifted, but he still avoided eye contact. "Me? No. Used to smoke, but it's hard to find enough butts lying around and isn't worth the trouble."

Yeah. Finding butts. "Thanks."

He hummed again as I retreated.

I scrambled more eggs in time to greet White Feather easing into the kitchen. Moving around was taking him a lot longer than normal. "With all the noise here, we should go to my house," I suggested. "You can relax there while I pack the rest of my things."

"I'm not able to lift much."

"Nope."

He'd get no rest here, and he needed it. Dark circles topped with pain shaded his eyes. He accepted the eggs and balanced on the edge of a bar stool. "Gordon called a minute ago. He brought Tam and her husband, Richard, in for questioning. Said she was all fired up because she's certain someone has gone in the salon at night before. But nothing was stolen so she didn't report it."

"How many times, did she say?"

White Feather nodded. "Two or three. Could have been more, but she didn't notice right off. She said she started leaving little piles of hair on the floor and small ribbons trapped between the cabinet doors. Twice for certain, someone opened the cabinet doors and the ribbons dropped to the floor."

"What did the hair tell her?"

"She said she usually uses a steam mop at the end of the day. One morning after she put off mopping something wasn't right, but she wasn't sure what. So she started leaving a small pile of hair here and there. One of the same nights the ribbons fell, the pile of hair was scattered all over."

I thought about the tarp. It would scatter hair, especially if someone shook it out. It had been heavy cloth. Hair would stick to it. "Twice. That she noticed. And that doesn't count last night when we were there. White Feather —"

"Yeah. Someone has been using her studio as a location to secretly create the tats."

"What about the bakery?"

"Never been broken into that they know of. Her husband started leaving things he could track as well, but nothing ever indicated an overnight visitor. On the way to your place, we should stop back at the jewelry store. With the new information we have, maybe now we can figure out what they were doing and how."

"You up for that?" I asked worriedly.

"Might as well keep moving."

As soon as he finished eating, I washed up and we headed out.

"I almost forgot. Before we stop at Piercing Hoops, swing by Mat's place. Gordon said he'd meet us there. He had one of the police sketch artists draw the tattoos from the wound. Since we saw the constructs, he figures we can tell him how closely the tats match."

"Mat's speaking to Gordon, then?"

"Sounds like it. He didn't say much other than he planned to run the surveillance on Tam's from Mat's place. The bakery up the street makes it easy for daytime checks; her place will suffice for nighttime."

Since the nail salon wasn't within eyesight I guessed, "Cameras?"

He nodded. "And he'll be right there if something goes down."

"That's good because if Lynx happens to follow Zandy back there, it's better if Gordon is already nearby to watch his back."

Mat's shop wasn't yet open, but she answered the alley door as soon as I knocked. She held a very large cup of black coffee in one hand. She was much less grumpy than she normally was at nine o'clock. "We haven't been to the bakery yet," she said in greeting.

"That's okay. I'd better avoid eating there or I'll get fat." I gave her a hug.

Gordon sat at the kitchen table sipping from another of Mat's giant mugs. Her mugs only came in two sizes, large and larger. Gordon had either just arrived himself or was classy enough to be fully dressed, including his sidearm, so it wasn't completely obvious whether he had spent the night.

I slid my eyes to Mat. From her cool stare and quick nod, I guessed that while things weren't perfect, she had decided to give him a second chance. She wasn't cutting him a lot of slack, however. Instead of hovering close to him, she remained detached, leaving a business edge on things.

Gordon was nothing if not professional. He had the folder ready for us and spread the pictures across the table as soon as our greetings were out of the way.

"Once the police artist knew the wounds were tats, it was easy for her to add in detail."

"Wow. These are impressive." The artist had taken the time to draw a colored snake from the first robbery, a lizard from the jewelry store, the dragon and the dog-like creature we'd fought, and what appeared to be a lizard with wings from the house owned by Tam and her husband. The colors were all done in common tattoo inks, but she had added scales, claws, and nasty snouts with teeth.

The winged lizard reminded me of an Asian dragon, more snake than the typical fatter European ones. The fact that Tam and her husband were Asian may have been why the thought occurred to me, but between that and the drawings, I realized I'd been missing something important. "Tam's son draws."

"He's an artist? As in a tattoo artist?" Gordon sat up straighter.

"Not saying he does tats or has anything to do with these. But he does the artwork for the front of the shops, and he's offered Mat designs for her new purses."

Mat's eyes widened slightly. "He's good. But why would he rob his own parents?"

"He must have a key to the place," Gordon said.

"Both the home and the shops. And he'd also know the money was at the house the day it was robbed."

"They didn't leave any money at the salon," Gordon said. "I assume White Feather told you the break-in there probably wasn't the first time someone used the nail salon as a place to do the body art. We're checking all the employees out. I'll add the son to the list. What is his name?"

"Lynx can check him out too. His name is Kevin, young guy, still in high school or maybe just out. Definitely has talent."

Mat sighed. "That he does."

"You've seen his work?" Gordon turned to her. "Anything resembling any of these?"

Mat swallowed, sounding like she was forcing down more than coffee. "There were dragons in his notebook, I remember that. I didn't pay close attention to them because I was after much cuter designs, ones that would match the nail designs or the spells I sell."

"An employee or the son in on it would explain how someone happened to walk in and out of the salon through both the front and back doors. Whoever it was had a key," Gordon said.

Mat's place wasn't large enough for White Feather to pace, but he made two attempts back and forth between the kitchenette and living area. "They didn't have a key to either of the jewelry stores. Tam's house matched those two robberies pretty closely—break in, leave body, get out."

I frowned. There were other inconsistencies. Zandy had come after Mat in broad daylight. He'd approached a homeless guy and lured him to the nail salon at nightfall. Had Zandy intended to keep Mat quiet in her own shop and do a tat on her? They could rob her place and then use her later to feed a construct. "Moonlight madness. It's almost as if they are testing techniques, trying to figure out the best way to create and control the constructs."

"It has to require practice," White Feather muttered.

"So do break-ins," Gordon added. "The first jewelry store netted them almost nothing, but they took almost everything of value from the second one. The burglary at Tam's house was obviously premeditated. They knew exactly when the money would be there." Gordon made a note. "And if they perfect their methods, they could break in just about anywhere. Since the constructs disappear when the body fueling them dies, half our evidence is gone."

Gordon handed White Feather copies of the recreated body art to take with us. I didn't hold high hopes for finding any additional clues at the jewelry store, but it wouldn't hurt to check.

Piercing Hoops was already open for the day. From outside the door, I studied the drawing Gordon had provided. "Those dragons that attacked us had more bulk than I would have guessed from the tats on the guy's arm, but they weren't huge." I spaced my thumb and forefinger across the body of the lizard. "A small lizard could fit under this door, probably even before the weatherstripping was removed."

"Easily," White Feather agreed.

We went in. The proprietor had the golden tones of a Hispanic or Native American, and he wore his dark hair braided with a beaded headband. That would convince most tourists that this was an authentic place to shop for American Indian art.

The jewelry in the counters had been replaced. Small works of pottery and at least two copper sculptures were arranged across the top of the glass display cases. The paintings of the Rio Grande remained on the left wall, opposite the camera system. A red light on the camera indicated it was running.

The door to the closet office was partially open.

"What can I show you today?" The man behind the counter stroked his bushy thinking-about-graying beard.

"Just browsing," I murmured, making sure to do so. There was nowhere in here that wasn't accessible to a construct. I hadn't paid attention to the bottom of the office door when we were here before because it hadn't seemed important. But a lizard could have easily slid through the one-inch gap even if the door had been locked.

Once in the office, the lizard could shimmy up the desk and tap keys on a keyboard. It could probably climb the sheetrock walls, especially if it had claws that were anything like those of the dragons we'd seen. Whoever controlled it would have to be able to see through the lizard's eyes. That kind of trick required a lot of power, the type that might easily drain a victim of every ounce of life.

White Feather asked the guy about the origin of the new inventory while I checked out the actual items. The guy had quality, but modern, jewelry. The sculptures were all abstract. If they were supposed to be recognizable, it was completely lost on me.

One of the pieces of jewelry, however, did catch my eye. White Feather must have heard my breath catch because he turned quick enough to elicit a gasp when he twisted his injury.

"Sorry," I said to him. I asked the owner, "Who made this piece?"

"The obsidian wrapped in silver? It is lovely, isn't it. New artist. I've not carried her stuff before, but was recently robbed. It allowed me to procure some new things." While he talked, he slid a green velvet pallet onto the top of the counter, unlocked the jewelry case, and carefully displayed the sunbeam shaped rock.

Obsidian flaked easily and formed a sharp edge; it was prized in making arrowheads because the first cut from a new edge was sharper than a steel knife. These edges were protected by silver drizzled around the sides. The obsidian was rounded, and either in the making of it by Mother Earth or by the hand of the artist, a hole had formed in the center. The artist had filled it with molten silver. The obsidian and silver design resembled a sun symbol, a throwing star with sharper edges.

"It's nice." I downplayed my interest. "Do you know the artist's name?" I was buying the thing anyway, if for no other reason than to see if it could be duplicated. I created my own pieces, but that didn't mean I ignored special talent when I saw it.

"Goes by the name Amber. Would you like to try it on?" He moved a mirror to the counter.

I picked up the chain, an exquisite collection of five strands of liquid silver that came together at the center of the pendant.

White Feather rolled his eyes. "We better discuss price before she falls any more in love with it."

"Ah, now, can you really put a price on keeping your wife happy?"

"Yes," I said before White Feather could. "He's not buying it for me."

We haggled. White Feather haggled. We paid too much, but not more than it was worth. I'd find Amber and buy direct next time, but this was a one of a kind piece. I was fairly certain that the odd shaped hole in the obsidian was a gift from Mother Earth rather than a carefully carved addition. Obsidian chipped easily. The artist had recognized the gift and enhanced it.

I left wearing the chain. "If I can duplicate this design, it would be an incredible weapon. With the silver embedded like it is, I bet I can shoot this thing several yards and hit a target."

White Feather reached to tuck me to him, but the second he raised his arm, he winced and grunted with pain. His wind magic brushed against me as though in defense.

I squeezed his arm. "Don't hug me. You already bought me this gorgeous necklace."

He kissed the top of my head, but his face remained tight. "Try not to send it into battle first thing."

"That's why I want to duplicate it. I need material I can drill and fill with silver. It will be great. Next time something big and ugly comes our way, I'll be ready."

He sighed. "You're such a delicate wife."

"I know."

Once in the car, White Feather asked, "Did we learn anything? Besides how to make an arrowhead that you can push and pull at will?"

I nodded, dreading the truth. "Whoever is driving these constructs is not only siphoning energy from the victim to power them, he's attached to the constructs in some way."

"What makes you say that?"

"Because no lizard is intelligent enough to scoot under a door, find the alarm box, climb the wall and *read* the code on the wall. The pilot had to be watching through the eyes of the lizard."

White Feather stared out the window. "Given that you noticed all that, I suppose you are also assuming that whoever is powering them saw us last night?"

My hand cramped from clutching the steering wheel, but I forced my voice to stay even. "Fighting instincts in a construct wouldn't require being controlled by higher intelligence, but the nature of the break-ins does. And if he was seeing through the eyes of the constructs for the break-in, why wouldn't he do it when he left the constructs on guard at the nail salon?"

"That's a lot of power to maintain."

"And whoever is doing it is getting stronger because at Tam's salon there were two constructs rather than one."

"These break-ins feel like an effort to obtain something more than money or jewelry," White Feather complained.

I agreed. "Even if it didn't start out that way, whoever is creating the tats is learning. It won't stop with the theft of a few pieces of jewelry here and there. There's a lot of bad blood in that spell." And right now, some of it was embedded in White Feather.

White Feather kept his face turned to the window when he said, "Some of the blue ink has shifted."

My silver flared hot, then cold as I struggled to control my reaction. I pulled over rather than crash into the car in front of me. "You're sure?"

White Feather nodded. "After we left the house. The ink may not have physically moved, but there was a pull, a...it doesn't matter. I'm able to block it."

I didn't mention that he had to sleep. I didn't grab his shirt and rip it off to check the wound. I dialed Lynx and left him another message. I dialed my mother next. White Feather swallowed his protests when I glared at him. He muttered, "I'm blocking it."

I didn't mention that whoever was creating the tats was a black magic user on the hunt for new techniques and was gaining strength. Talking to Mom without screeching was only possible because she understood the urgency.

"I'll find someone today." She hung up without wasting time on platitudes.

I pulled back into traffic and said, "If Lynx doesn't show up soon, and Mom hasn't found a witch who can use light to force the tat ink out in a few hours, we'll find a doctor to cut it out."

"I'd almost rather your dad burn it."

"There is always that option." It was only a matter of time before whoever controlled the constructs found a way to piece the remnants together and call it, control it, or destroy White Feather trying.

Chapter 24

White Feather didn't take long to fall asleep after we arrived at my place. From the color of his drawn face, it was obvious the wound and the tat was taking its toll. I packed the wound with blocking herbs and warded the room with every dream catcher left in the place. My house had even more wards against hostile magic than his did, but only because parts of his house hadn't been rebuilt.

I spent the day packing, checking on him and searching through an old phone book for possible doctors. White Feather was right though. Dad burning it would not only be faster, it wouldn't require long explanations or finding a doctor who could do it *now*.

I paced and muttered protection spells, willing the phone to ring with a call from Mom or Lynx.

By five-thirty, I was greatly relieved when White Feather woke himself up. Sleep would help him heal, but awake, he and his magic were on full guard.

We headed back to his place with the final load of my belongings. Dusk brushed its fingers along the hillside. It echoed the claws of worry and exhaustion dragging at my heart. "Dad must have come for Tracy," I said, leading the way in. The house was blissfully quiet. The kitchen wall was also nearly finished.

"The roofers will be able to finish your lab and start the kitchen roof," White Feather said.

"I've never seen anyone with Tracy's skills. And he's fast." I rested my hand on the new wall. There was the faintest echo of the tune Tracy hummed. Or maybe I imagined it because surely the wall couldn't sing the magic for long.

White Feather was no better rested than when we had started out in the morning, but he pulled items from the fridge anyway. Protesting wouldn't do any good, so I scooted out to retrieve the last of the things from the car and make the phone calls that needed to be made.

As soon as I opened the door, the gold in my ring tingled a warning. It wasn't completely dark yet, but I snapped the porch light on. Ordinarily, nothing came this close to White Feather's domain without him figuring it out, but he wasn't in top form. The second I knew, he knew. He was behind me almost before I sensed him moving.

I had always been afraid of Patrick, but since the rogue vamp had attacked, my fear was worse.

Patrick waited politely off the porch, exhibiting his usual control.

"Did you dispose of the rogue vamp?" I blurted out. "For good?" How did you ask a vamp if he had killed another vamp when they were dead to start with?

Patrick stepped closer to the porch, but kept his distance. "The only good vampire is a dead vampire," he said without a trace of humor on his face.

I rewarded him with a glare for his bad pun. "I already knew he was dead. I meant is he gone completely?" There was no polite way to say it. "He's destroyed, won't come back, buried, incinerated, gone?"

Now, he was full of humor. A hint of fangs and even a chuckle. It had that sexy vamp undercurrent, almost a caress. I'd never been fooled by vamp glamour, but around the time I started wearing White Feather's ring, there was an additional doorstop against the illusion. One ear heard a sexy laugh, but the other heard a quiet inhuman whine. Instead of shaking off a flirtatious laugh, my insides froze in fear. My body screamed *hunted* and demanded I conceal myself.

Patrick switched off the chuckle in an instant. He either smelled my fear or heard my heartbeat tick up as it prepared to run. He was never all warmth and friendship, but my reaction switched him instantly to wary. Couldn't say as I blamed him. Someone not fooled by the glamour of vamps was a danger to him.

I held my ground, but avoided his direct gaze. He was a beast who hunted human blood. It didn't matter if he obtained his blood from the hospital blood bank; it barely mattered that he had ethics.

"I've never met anyone who can push back glamour," he said quietly. "And your skill is improving."

I made a fist over the ring. "Sorry." But we both knew I wasn't.

He smiled, no fangs. "What do you see when you look at me?"

"Exactly what you show the rest of the world."

Fangs. "And that is all?"

I nodded. "That is all."

He didn't believe me, and it wasn't because of his vamp powers that he saw through the lie. "Is it because you believe so strongly in what I am that you overcome what your eyes tell you?"

I hated his questions. Even if the answers didn't matter to me, once the question was asked, there was no stopping my brain. Answering was a bad idea, but avoiding doing so was a type of sparring that was nearly as risky. "Spells aren't visual. I don't rely on sight to know if they are active. Magic for me functions on a different level. You are a different level. It doesn't matter what I see."

"Thus, anyone who has grown accustomed to using enough of their senses can see through the guise." He gave a sharp nod. "It's possible. And you're gaining in your ability, but it doesn't matter. You were never fooled in the first place."

We stared at each other, stalemate. Patrick finally acknowledged White Feather positioned protectively less than a step away. Of course, that only meant he spared him a polite nod, as if White Feather wasn't prepared to blast him with a tornado at the slightest threat.

"You'd have been perfectly safe from me had you decided to remain in your own house." Patrick's tone was flat, not angry or charming. From this, I deduced he was furious about me moving out.

"Until you changed your mind? You're faster and stronger than I am. I sleep during your waking hours, you're stealthier than night and my spells can only succeed to a degree in protecting me."

"I would not change my mind. And you could have rescinded the invitation."

I hadn't known that for certain, but it wouldn't have changed things. "I would have had to do so in person, yes?"

Now, there was a tiny flash of humor before it evaporated behind the cool beast. "You did know about it."

"One does wonder about such rules after having two vampires in her living room—one of whom was uninvited. I figured if the uninvited vamp won, you might get bitten and go rogue. If you came back with that same—" I almost didn't say it, but what was the point in pretending? A hunter was a hunter. Pretending otherwise would be no different than him ignoring my ability with spells. "You might come back with that same uncontrolled hunger."

His eyes were already flat pits of darkness. My words caused them not to darken, but to suck at my soul. "I take it the invitation is rescinded."

He had already offered the olive branch of admitting it could be done. That had been generous in its own right, but to actually go through the ritual? My eyes narrowed. Patrick wasn't doing this out of the kindness of his heart. There was either some unknown danger to me from the rogue or some other reason for the gesture.

"It is rescinded." The slightest bit of regret tinged my tone, regret that he was no longer living, regret that it felt like a slap in the face. I feared Patrick, but hurting anything without a purpose was not my way. "I do not owe you for taking care of that trash, but I take back any welcome over my threshold."

Patrick smiled. No teeth. "Thank you for treating me as your equal even though we are not."

I frowned. As a predator, he was far superior to me. Then again, with White Feather at my side, the two of us could definitely escape, if not outright stake him. Or did he mean I had magic he could destroy, but not keep for his own? Life was always superior to death. Hmm.

Patrick's eyes shifted to White Feather and then back to me. "The human, Zandy. After he sold blood to the vampire, we offered to pay an even more generous stipend to entice him into the open. Unfortunately, Zandy suspected the original vampire had come to a disastrous end. He tested his theory by putting word out that he would only deal with the original vampire. Without that vampire, we were unable to meet with him and contain the threat."

What a polite way to say "murder Zandy without a trace." I pondered the problem, but saw no way to help. "He's greedy. Maybe if you lowered the price, he'd think the window of opportunity was closing."

Patrick shook his head. "It is too late for that. He found another buyer who is willing to pay more and is apparently less of a threat to him."

"He's still selling? Who in moonlight madness wants his blood now?"

"Not a vampire. Zandy's blood is an extreme danger to us. I'd be very interested in finding whoever he is selling to now. It must be a day creature because he is suddenly avoiding those of the night."

I added up the equation. If Zandy had figured out that the original vamp went insane, he might be selling that information—along with his blood to some very high bidders. Leverage over vampires would command a very high price. "Does Zandy know the vamp went insane?"

"He offered to accept money to keep quiet, but it is not clear if he thinks the vampire went insane or was destroyed by his blood. Either way, he knows there are those who believe they must master us or destroy us with no middle ground."

One thing was for certain. Whatever Zandy was up to, it wasn't good. He would barter with the devil to make a profit. And even if he successfully blackmailed vampires, we all knew he'd still sell the information to the highest bidder if the opportunity presented itself. "Pestilence," I muttered. "A total pestilence."

"My enemy is your enemy," Patrick said softly.

I understood he was offering assistance—or money for information. I opened my mouth to tell him again that I didn't do business with vampires, but he inclined his head once and then stepped away.

As he always did, he disappeared from one step into the next. He was a shadow, then complete darkness.

Chapter 25

Lynx was, predictably, less than eager to lend his expertise to the project of healing White Feather. He appeared in time for dinner, but because of Patrick's visit, we hadn't even started cooking.

I explained how the constructs had been partially embedded and required removal while White Feather was changing his bandages.

"I don't see why I gotta be involved," he groused from his spot at the kitchen bar.

"Do you know any other shifters who will do it?"

He snorted. "Okay, I get that part, but why do I gotta work with Tara?"

"Business. It's business, not the other."

"See, that's the thing that makes no sense. In business, I deal with who I want. This family crap, it's all messed up. I get that you and White Feather are tight." He grinned. "But you never liked Tara."

"So she says."

He grinned his silent laugh. "Nah, I can tell myself. Whenever she's around, you're tense and you smell different. Not like fear, but a lot like when you're about to throw a spell around in a fight."

Ask a cat for too much information and you get told you smell. "You mean sort of like now because you're annoying me?"

His eyes glinted. "You're holding too much worry underneath the annoyance so I know you won't waste energy throwing anything at me."

"Will you help or not?"

That shot his humor down. "Can't your mom do it?"

"What's the big deal anyway? Didn't you bring Tara in the other night? Or has she been following you around again?"

His eyes shifted to the kitchen counter. "I called Tara right after you went in the salon. That place smelled bad. That homeless guy, he was fine when he walked in that place, no blood, no worries. When Zandy left, I could smell blood as if they left him to bleed out. I thought maybe Tara could save the guy."

"You're positive the guy didn't have the bloody tats before you followed him? Maybe you couldn't smell it under the coat?"

"No way. He didn't have fresh tats when Zandy was feeding him booze. I had to stay downwind so Zandy didn't catch my scent."

"Gordon said Tam complained of other times she thought someone used her shop overnight. Why her shop? Could she be guilty? I sensed no magic on her at all."

Lynx didn't have an answer for that question. "If Zandy shows up there again, I'll know."

"So will Gordon. He's monitoring the place and checking the employees." I paced away, trying to keep my nerves from exploding.

"You want me to keep watching Zandy?"

"Probably, but you had better be careful." I broke the news that Zandy was selling his blood to someone who could use it against vamps. "You have any idea who it could be?"

He came up empty. "No. He'd sell his own blood without caring. Thing is, he doesn't like risk. He thinks he's better than humans because he can shift and that makes him faster and sneakier, but I don't think he cares whether he is better than vamps. Just maybe wants to be richer, but who doesn't?"

"You haven't heard anyone else bragging about gaining leverage over vamps?"

He shook his head. "There's always people who claim they can't wait to turn, and there's always haters. I'll keep my ears open."

"You need a masking spell that will hide your scent too. If you end up tailing Zandy again, I don't want him getting his hands on you."

"Ain't gonna happen."

"No sense in taking chances. We have enough people in danger already." I didn't let my voice slip, but my hands twitched nervously. No doubt I still smelled near panic because I was.

Lynx followed me to the lab and waited until I invited him in. The lab was usable for such a simple spell if I could locate all the ingredients. Mostly things were still in alphabetical order, but finding the right box might take some time.

Since shelves weren't up yet, I pulled items from the boxes and arranged them neatly along one wall. "This spell will be similar to the one that allows you to blend in with your surroundings. Which reminds me, I better recharge that one too and combine them."

"I'm good."

I didn't even pause in my search. It had taken me a while to realize that he practiced witchery. He had been watching me for a long time now, and at some point he had decided he could duplicate my spells. There was no sense of earth magic around him, but Lynx was a cat. He was vastly different from me, but enough alike that apparently he could work some earth magic.

"So this family thing. Do they all work like that?" he asked.

"Like what?"

"The family members." He waved to encompass an invisible mass of people. "They do stupid things and be forgiven no matter what. So you have to keep working with them?"

I nodded. Then I shook my head. I started to nod again, but decided it made more sense to think it through before answering. "Some families. Some things. I'm pretty sure murder isn't tolerated in all families. But a lot of other stuff is. It depends."

"On what?"

Now there was a question. "This has to do with Tara again, right?"

His eyes slanted. "Maybe, but I was wondering about your friend, the water witch. And the cop, and whether she'd take him back."

"Who told you—" Tara must have spilled the beans, maybe to point out that she wasn't the only one who made mistakes in relationships. Jim certainly wasn't hopping up and down telling people about it, not if he wanted to live longer than, say, yesterday.

"Here's the thing," I said. "Every family starts out with a whole bunch of hope. Everyone is perfect. Only they aren't. So when you start your own family, you have to pick someone you think you can live with. Someone you trust, who will forgive you for being stupid. And I don't mean stupid like cheating stupid, I mean mistake stupid."

"But how do you know when it's too stupid and you give up and walk away?"

"You don't know, not really. You draw your own lines. You learn from day to day if this person is paying attention and cares. And if they are stupid all the time or if they just mess up occasionally." I thought of another problem. "Until you have kids. Then, usually, the kids are so busy being the stupid ones, from what I can see, you want to pick someone who will keep you from killing the kids when they're stupid. Because that is what families are for."

"You're not very good at this stuff, are you?"

"It's complicated."

"Your family always forgives you?"

"Who says I was stupid?"

Lynx smiled, the ghost of a cat-grin. "Your mom didn't want you to be a witch. She said your sister hated you for it, too."

"Huh. Kas doesn't hate me exactly. She just harbors a few issues because I'm not like her. But she's still my sister and mostly, she'd defend me if I needed it."

"And you'd spell anyone who caused her trouble?"

"Absolutely."

"But what if she asked you not to?"

My mouth twisted. "It depends on whether she really meant no spells or she meant don't get caught."

Lynx nodded sagely. "See, that part of family, I get."

I had no idea whether this conversation was convincing him to help with White Feather or making him more certain he should run away. "With family, you do the best you can. You make it up as you go along and try to turn it into that dream family. But it's never perfect."

"It would be better if Tara wasn't White Feather's sister. Then maybe you wouldn't still work with her."

"Mom thinks Tara can help. For White Feather, I'll do it. But...yeah." I closed my eyes. "She's family now."

"I'll do it, but I ain't gonna like it. And it don't mean nothin' about me and her."

"Tell her that, not me."

When I finished his spell, I added it to the sachet he carried. If he activated it, he would be very hard to see or smell. I didn't test either one, but did notice the silver ball I had given him had been replaced with a single gold stud earring.

Lynx put the leather sachet back around his neck. "You can find me with gold or silver, right?"

Since I often used silver to ground, that association came easier for me, but nestled in the packet of herbs I had just spelled, it wasn't hard for me to sense the gold. "Seems that way."

"If I don't want you to find me, I won't wear it," he said. "How far away does it work?"

"I don't know."

He gave me his slant eyes.

"Seriously. When you left the nail shop the other day, I knew you were gone, but not where you went. When you came back, I knew, but not until I searched." I frowned. "I can't remember if I searched because I heard a noise or I was looking anyway."

He repeated, "Then if I don't want you to find me, I won't wear it. You can find any gold or silver?"

I shook my head. Then I nodded. He rolled his eyes. "Well, I think so. But now I associate that gold with you and the packet. So I can search for it specifically. It's sort of like...well, as if I know what it smells like. Randomly locating bits of silver or gold isn't all that useful. We need to do this thing for White Feather now. I'll call Tara and Mom."

He fingered the packet, contemplating. "Double rates. This is worse than all those daylight jobs you give me."

"I know."

"Let's get it over with," he finally said. "But we better eat first. I'm weak from hunger and shifting takes a lot of energy."

I hurried to the kitchen and the phone. "I'll tell Mom to bring food."

That improved his attitude. Mom's cooking was a better enticement than double pay.

Chapter 26

In the end, Lynx offered to chauffeur my mother. "If she doesn't have enough food, I can pick up extra."

I wasn't sure if he didn't want to be here in case Tara arrived before Mom or if he was hoping for extra food out of the deal. Since it was Lynx, it was probably both, along with ferreting out any new magic tricks Mom might be planning to use on White Feather's injury. He was not one to waste opportunity.

Tara raced over as soon as I called, arriving before White Feather had even finished showering. He was easily the most reluctant of the bunch, deciding to shower, shave, and change clothes. It wasn't the plan itself that was the problem; it was the fact that if this plan failed, the alternatives were worse, and we both knew it.

Tara flounced through the front door with a large denim bag that matched her quilted denim jacket. Her hair was almost all natural black now, instead of being dyed super-black. One lock was a shade of silver, but it was a lot more attractive than her previous Goth getup.

She hopped on a bar stool and pulled a tiny yellow flower out of the denim bag. Small leaves were arranged one opposite the other on the stem. "Goathead," she said triumphantly.

My eyebrows rose. Not too long ago, she had been ready to dump me as a teacher because there were no goats in my yard. I had neglected to clarify that the goatheads mentioned in the typical aphrodisiac were the plant, not an actual goat's head. Now that she had figured it out on her own, I wasn't sure whether to be happy she was studying or worried about what she was learning. "Tried it yet?"

She frowned. "You knew all along, didn't you?"

"You mean when you asked about the spell to attract men?"

"You knew."

I met her stare. "There are better ways to attract men. At your age, trust me, you have enough natural magic. You don't need herbs. Or potions. Or spells."

She smiled. "Your mom told me that too. Gave me the longest lecture on sex I've ever had, but she skipped all the basics and went right to the important part about chemical reactions and hormones. It was kinda cool actually."

My memories of Mom's lecture were not so enthusiastic. "Yeah, well, it boils down to you don't need the goathead spell. And if you plan to experiment with spells like that, try it on yourself. Don't inflict it on some poor unsuspecting male who probably needs extra encouragement like another hole in the head."

Her eyes flicked around the kitchen as she toyed with the stem. "I wasn't planning on using it on Lynx. Don't worry. Your mom dumped an earful on me about the responsibilities of using magic, especially healing or poisons. I'm not that dumb."

"Plus the spell wouldn't work because it isn't an attraction problem." It was rude of me to point that out, but moonlight madness, if she attempted to manipulate Lynx with a potion, if he didn't kill her, I would.

"There's not a spell to fix what I did, is there?"

"Sorry might work."

The goathead weed twirled in her fingers. "I'm not sure he does sorry. I owe him now, and until I make it up to him, we aren't even."

I had to agree. "At least you understand the problem."

"But how do you give someone something when they've got everything? And they can shapeshift on top of it?"

She had it bad for him. Lynx was a mystery to me for the most part; I didn't have any real advice to offer. "I don't have the answer, but I guarantee you, it has nothing to do with goatheads."

White Feather chose that moment to wince his way out of the bedroom. His black button down was left unbuttoned and untucked around drawstring khakis. At any other time, I'd have swooned, but he hadn't rewound the support for his ribs, leaving the wound on his side glaring an angry red. The red was normal for healing. The nearly invisible specks of blue embedded in his skin were the problem. Carrying around embedded remnants of a construct made of tattoo ink was on the high end of spooky and the gambling end of extreme risk.

"You know, if the tat stuff was only in his blood, your mom and I could separate it out. It's not that hard to separate out the poisons from the bloodstream because the body helps. But when it's locked in the skin like that, it's all mixed up. Nothing flows. Blood is easier. It's liquid and the body already has natural fighters there."

"What is it you expect Lynx to do to solve the problem?" White Feather asked as he took up residence on the couch.

"We better put a towel or a sheet around you," Tara said.

I went to fetch an old cotton sheet.

When I returned, Tara was explaining that if Lynx could shift skin cells, and she could see how it was done, maybe she could shift the skin cells. If not, she might be able to drag the magic from Lynx to White Feather.

My guts clenched. What if it didn't work? What if it did? Would White Feather end up part shifter? And what would that mean anyway? His magical counterpart was wind. Shifting to that wasn't helpful.

White Feather said, "They're here."

I stopped arranging the sheet and opened the door before anyone could knock. Good thing, because Lynx and Mom had their hands full. Lynx carried food and Mom carried her supplies. I rescued one of the bags, leaned over for her kiss and asked Lynx, "You ate already?"

Mom answered for him. "Enough so that we can try this experiment first. If it fails, Granny Ruth is contacting a witch who works with light. Maybe she can break apart the remaining ink, but it would be a new technique. There isn't a witch alive who knows how to shift skin cells."

"Except for Lynx," I said.

"He's not a witch," Tara said.

Lynx almost slid his eyes away from mine in time, but I caught the flicker of acknowledgment there. Good at it or not, he was practicing. Whether it would make a difference with healing was another mystery entirely.

I propped a wooden tv tray near White Feather for Mom's supplies.

Mom examined the wound again. "It's mended a bit. The spell is still in multiple pieces. Flecks here and there." She frowned. "Tattoo ink lives in the second layer. Blood reaches that layer. That must be how the construct is fed."

I updated her on the fact that the homeless guy, Nick, had probably received the tattoos the same night the ink infected White Feather.

"Doesn't matter when the tat was done. The danger is that someone knows how to call the tattoos. It's black magic, blood magic. There is blood mixed in, maybe copper because the tattoo was blue. I don't know about this idea, but you show me what you do." She beckoned Lynx over.

Lynx froze, his legs locked. He finally blinked, but still didn't join her.

Mom tapped one finger against her jeans. "I don't see how it will help, either."

Tara crouched near White Feather. She rested her hands on the skin. "We need to make the skin flow."

By the time she looked away from White Feather, Lynx had managed to force his legs closer. He was silent. Barely breathing.

Tara reached for his hand, but he flinched.

Mom tsked. "Tara, you must always ask first. Remember the patient and the healer must be willing or it does no good."

Lynx stared at them out of crystal yellow eyes. Mom smiled. "That is good. Now back."

He blinked, surprised. "That's all you want? Just the eyes?"

"But—" Tara started to protest. She stopped, not needing anyone to chastise her further. The hurt that so often surrounded her shuttered over her like a veil.

Mom tapped her finger, ignoring her for the moment to focus on the problem. "It might be easier with your hand. Can you do that? We do not require your entire cat, and in any case, it is up to you."

Lynx offered his hand to my mom. The snick of a claw snapping into place was not entirely new to me. I hadn't actually watched it happen, but I'd heard it.

Mom said, "Back again."

She held his hand, protecting it from the rest of us. I kept my distance, providing a scant illusion of privacy even though I badly wanted to help.

"Hmm. I see this flow." She shook her head. "Tara, you are right. It is like liquid. Lynx, if you are ever badly injured and cannot make it happen, I am almost certain I can help, but I am not certain you would ever need help from me. Magnificent." She continued to hold his hand and tap her fingers against her leg with her other hand.

She finally turned to White Feather. "The cells simply are not the same. Lynx has two together that shift back and forth with one or the other on the top. White Feather has only the human type of skin cell. When Lynx moves the cells, he can expel anything between them. White Feather would need a second layer of cells to do this."

Tara's hands balled into fists. "Why can't we shift the cells, one kind or not? Lynx shifts them and doesn't always move one completely in place of the other!"

Mom shrugged. "That is the magic of Lynx. I do not think he can give this magic away, even if he wanted to." She released his hand and examined White Feather's ribs again. "I can see the bits of cells that don't belong. I could cut them with a knife and remove them. But I cannot shift them."

"But we knit them together! I knit them together when they were not!" Tara cried.

Mom frowned. She hovered over White Feather, concentrating. White Feather grunted. I couldn't see anything happening so I scooted a few steps closer.

Mom gasped. "Ground for her," I warned White Feather. "She's not that good at it without Dad around."

White Feather responded with a wild-eyed stare and yelped. "Ow! That spot hurts like hell!"

My wedding ring may have warmed a tad, so I grounded for him, cycling it through my ring to his. It wasn't as strong as if he held the link himself. "Mom, I am not grounding for you! Lynx, do you know how to ground?"

Now Lynx shot me a panicked look, one that had a lot of "run and ask questions later," but despite twitching, he stayed rooted to the spot. He didn't reach for my mom. He didn't move at all.

Tara said to him, "You've grounded for me. You did it on the mountain."

His gaze switched to her, but it was over. A pinprick of bloody blue bubbled to the top of White Feather's skin.

With a gasp, Mom slid off the couch to the floor next to Tara. Sweat dripped down one side of her face. "Mi Dios. And that one was nearly on the surface."

"You moved two skin cells!" Tara crowed.

"I didn't. I squeezed them to push that one drop out, but it was close enough to the surface it was more of a splinter than a tattoo." She shook her head. "It would be impossible to do them all. I can knit them, but this unknitting, squeezing thing, that is counter to the magic."

White Feather's lips showed white around the edges. "Burning it out would make more sense."

"With lasers or light manipulation, there is the danger of some pieces being absorbed," Mom said. "I had really hoped this would work."

"Let me try," Tara urged. She didn't dare look at anyone directly.

Mom glanced at her in surprise. "You saw how I did it?"

She nodded.

Mom said apologetically, "It is not so much healing. But she is stronger than I am. She can force more of it to the surface."

Mom's face had lost all of its color. "Mom, do you want hot tea or coffee?"

She sighed a big breath. "Tea."

I made tea while Tara studied the problem. She looked sideways at Lynx twice. His eyes changed from human to glowing cat. I couldn't tell if that was a threat or if he thought he was helping.

Tara finally sat back and said, "I need a splinter. Something I can jab Lynx with. Then he can change. I want to see if he breaks it up or expels it."

Lynx's eyes snapped to mine, all human. It was asking a lot, too much. And it was not my call to make. He had done what he had promised, and it had provided Mom with some insight. My insides roiled. His fear was different than mine, but visible all the same. He was trapped out in the open and forced to deal publicly with his ability to shift.

Mom's eyebrows raised. "It might not matter how Lynx does it. White Feather is different."

"Maybe not. But it might."

Mom glanced at me with a smile. "She is stubborn, like you."

I bit down hard on my reply. Lynx's ears swiveled between the players. He stared down at White Feather's wound. Then he looked at me, but his eyes drifted to my hands, and I realized they were clenched. His nose twitched, and I knew he was telling me that I smelled worried or afraid or insulted.

"Very funny," I said.

He did a half of a silent laugh, but it cut off as suddenly as it started. I might smell different, but he probably smelled funny too because he didn't like Tara or the situation any better than I did.

"Not silver," Lynx said. "Wood's okay."

I stalked into the lab, hurrying, but my hands weren't all that steady. I feared for White Feather. A part of me feared for Lynx. None of us knew what we were doing.

I shaved off a few small pieces of a pecan stick and returned to the living room. Lynx reached for them, but my mom intervened. "I can place it just so," she said. "I do not see how it will help, but it will be less painful if I do it."

She split one of the slivers with her fingernail. Lynx offered his hand, and this time when Tara reached out, he let both of them hold it. Mom slid the splinter in carefully. His head tilted, but if it hurt, he didn't jerk away.

"Change," Tara said, her voice a low chant. She was focused now, centered. Somehow she had grounded, probably through Lynx. He didn't seem to notice, or if he did, he allowed it. His hand changed, first the snick of claws, then fur rippled across the back of his hand.

I held my breath. Mom was right. It was magnificent. I could feel the magic, even if I didn't understand it.

The front of his hand toughened and changed colors. He changed back, almost before the paw completely formed.

Tara kept her concentration. She didn't ask him to do it again, nor did she pick up the sliver that now rested on his fingertip.

When she turned to White Feather, his intake of breath was as loud as mine. Her hands hovered for a moment, but then she swallowed hard and began. I felt a swoosh of wind and warned, "Ground or it will burn like the devil."

The wind trickled to a breeze and we locked eyes. I linked to earth again, willing it to hold against his pain. He latched onto my link and added his own. The breeze came through the diamond now, but I trapped it and fed it to Mother Earth.

Lynx clasped Tara's shoulder hard. She struggled to keep her breathing even. Instead of a small pinprick of blue, it was like water bubbling from an underground spring. Tainted blue ink pooled across White Feather's ribs, forming a small puddle before dripping down onto the sheet. Mom wiped it away, watching everything closely. There was no blood on his skin. There was no open wound.

White Feather let out the breath he was holding. So did Tara. She closed her eyes and started to shake.

"Stay centered," Mom and I ordered at the same time. We recognized the draining that left you feeling as if you'd run a mile full out and all of sudden your muscles dropped out of the race.

"Release it slowly," Mom said to my, "Ground through Lynx."

Tara laughed shakily. "That was...hard."

Mom rubbed her back, but her gaze was on the blue ink staining the sheet. "I didn't examine the cells of the ink carefully enough. I concentrated on the human ones. I didn't realize...the ink cells, they are similar to Lynx. There are sets of two, rubbing against each other."

Tara nodded, finally sitting back, but still trembling. "They're like the shifter cells. So I shifted them back and forth, back and forth. Reverse of what Lynx did. I expelled White Feather from the ink."

It took a minute to understand what she said, but then I shouted, "Shifter cells?!? As in—"

Together White Feather and I swore, "Zandy!"

"Patrick said Zandy was selling his blood to someone else! And Zandy was there. Tats use blood for color...or in this case, to create a construct."

White Feather groaned. "He's selling his blood to a tattoo artist who creates tattoos that turn into constructs."

"Or he learned to do it himself, the fiend. But, no. Patrick said Zandy found another customer. Apparently the new customer isn't interested in vampires at all—he's using Zandy's blood to create constructs. The blackmail thing must have been just another attempt by Zandy to make money from nothing. That coyote has more than one death wish."

White Feather flexed his shoulders and stretched his side. "I feel a whole lot better." He tugged a strand of Tara's hair. "Thanks, kid."

She blushed.

I nodded and added my own gratitude. "Took guts to try that after my mom failed and all of us standing here expecting no better."

Mom smiled. "She's stubborn like you. She'll make a good witch. She just needs patience."

"Hmm."

Tara lifted her head, her face drawn, but it was a good kind of tired. A half-cocked grin lit her face before her eyes dared find Lynx. "Thanks for grounding. I can't do that part."

There might have been the slightest sheen of respect on his face, but then he blinked. "Let's eat," he said. "I'm hungry."

Chapter 27

When you obtain the blood of your enemy, if he is dead, you burn it. If he's not, you make sure that Lynx has smelled it, and then you bury it in the backyard where it can do you no harm. But you have it if you need it.

White Feather tended to blow bad spells away, so he didn't have an area for evil spells until we dug one, lined it, added a holy water barrier and encased it in protection spells.

It was after midnight of a very long day when we finished, but we both slept better knowing the spell was outside and not inside White Feather.

White Feather beat me into the kitchen the next morning. He whistled while preparing breakfast. When I came in dressed in jeans and hiking boots, he raised an eyebrow along with his spatula.

I sniffed. "Is that hash browns I smell? Mmmm."

"We can't live on bacon entirely, even if Tracy and Lynx vote that way. You look set for spell practice."

I hesitated, still not really used to running my less-than-logical ideas by anyone. "Martin mentioned something about demon spit, ghouls and black magic. I was wondering whether it has anything to do with constructs."

"Demon spit. To form tats?"

I shrugged. "What Martin calls things and what black magic really is could be one and the same. The energy comes from somewhere."

"From the dead bodies, it looks like the victims are providing the energy. Throw some Zandy blood in there, maybe some blood from the conjurer and how much more bad energy do you need?"

"True. But I started wondering how much Martin can see. If he sees black magic or demon spit coming through to our side, maybe he can see who is casting the construct spell." I dumped Mom's leftover salsa on my eggs and hash browns.

"And he might be able to tell us where the person is?"

I nodded. "Or describe the person. Or something."

"Would Martin pay attention to details like that?"

"Who knows? Not when he was living, not unless he was sober, and that wasn't very often. At least now he's sober." I thought about it. "Well, I think he's sober. He's so weird it's hard to tell for sure."

I finished breakfast and decided that if we kept eating big meals, I would have to do more outdoor spell casting—like about ten miles up a canyon. My jeans were definitely squeezing me. "Martin always noticed magic. That's what enabled him to excel at finding stones. He's like Tracy. He hears magic."

"I'll go with you," White Feather said, joining me at the sink to wash his own plate. "No need for you to meet up with a ghost by yourself. We don't know his intentions."

"What?"

"He flirts with you."

I blinked up at him, not sure if he was teasing. "He's dead. I don't think he has any serious intentions, good, bad or otherwise."

White Feather swallowed the last of his mocha. He set the cup down and wrapped his hand around the back of my neck, bringing me closer to him. "May as well let him know that when you cross over, you're still mine."

He kissed me good morning and made me wish we'd never gotten out of bed.

* * *

There were a few necessary chores to take care of before leaving. I couldn't put off adding my magic to White Feather's lab any longer. At the rate Tracy erected walls, if I didn't do it today the lab would be completed before I had a chance. Plus, helping Tracy might teach me how he talked to Mother Earth.

I was up to my elbows in mud and dirt when White Feather came outside to tell me that Gordon had called. "He has some mug shots of tat artists who are known or suspected of dabbling with some dangerous inks."

I snorted. "From what I read, all the inks are potentially lethal."

White Feather nodded. "They're made from noxious chemicals even before magic is involved. Gordon collected samples of inks from about four shops. It's a long shot, but we might be able to pick up an aura that matches the stuff that came out of me. A match would point to the artist responsible. Since you're knee deep, I'll go while you finish up here. Gordon's at Mat's place, minding the store."

My head whipped around. "Minding the store? No one minds the store except Mat."

"He said she had an important errand."

"Hmm. Well, we can hike Tent Rock this afternoon. I won't be much longer at this."

He left to take care of his business, while I continued to stack my rows of bricks. If Tracy thought it was odd for me to build parts of each wall, he never said anything. Of course, he rarely said anything anyway, so what was the difference?

While I slathered mortar around, I listened. Tracy didn't so much hum as vibrate, but whatever it was, my bracelet sang back. I hummed a version of the tuneless little notes, but the vibration wasn't really his voice, it was his magic. He drew Mother Earth into his work as surely as I did.

As I headed inside to clean up, Mat drove up.

It was a few minutes before ten o'clock, which was usually when she opened shop. Her red hair was braided and looped up. She wore jeans, albeit Ralph Lauren ones, but worst news of all, she had on running shoes. Even though she was dressed in her version of battle gear, she oozed delicate beauty.

The good news was she probably hadn't stopped by to ask me to kill Gordon because her eyes were no longer red-rimmed or puffy. Plus, he was minding the shop, whatever that meant.

"You look dressed for special projects this morning," I said after waving off her hug. "I'm filthy. Let me wash up."

"Your kind of job, not mine. Patrick stopped by last night. His vamp friend is dying. He asked if I had any potions or ideas."

"Guy named Joe?" I rinsed off the worst of the dirt at the kitchen sink.

Mat sat at the bar and rested her chin in her hands. "I didn't meet him. He's at the hospital. Patrick said you'd know where. He said they would both be there even during daylight if I thought of anything. The only thing I thought of was you, but he said he'd already asked you."

I dried my hands and arms. "And so you stopped by because?"

"Wits end. I know you don't deal with the vamps, and I don't deal with them much either, not anymore. He's desperate."

"What if he thinks witch's blood is the cure?"

Mat shrugged. "He would have asked me to sell him some if that were the case."

I gasped, but she just grinned at me. "I didn't say it would be *my* blood. But there are always those willing to sell for a price. I don't actually carry the stuff, but could put him in touch with someone."

"Unbelievable," I muttered.

"There's ways to provide it that are anonymous, and apparently it carries a lot less consequence if not done directly, but it's not something I normally negotiate. There's actually a number of clients who would purchase witch's blood, but I don't want that kind of responsibility."

"Unbelievable."

"You said that already. What do you think? Will you come?"

I fidgeted. "I can't fix what ails that vamp."

"Me either. But I'm not sure that is what his request is about. He considers us friends." She nodded hard at my stricken look. "Especially you. He wants to do everything he can even if it's futile, and that happens to include us."

"It doesn't sound safe."

"He's a vamp. It can never be completely safe. Half my clients aren't safe. What does that have to do with anything?"

She had succinctly stated all the reasons I did business through intermediaries. The less I dealt with the actual client, the better. But I had been dealing with Patrick for a while now whether I wanted to or not. "You're asking me to go chat with Patrick as a show of support?"

"Unless you actually have a spell that would cure Joe?"

"That has got to be one of the most messed up pieces of logic I've ever heard." I headed around the bar to the living room. "Let me sort through the lab. Maybe I'll think of something. Patrick did let me rescind the invite into my house. Maybe he did it knowing he needed a favor. Maybe not. Why are we allowed to do this in broad daylight?"

"Gordon's watching my shop for me," Mat said. "He owes me, and I didn't want to show up early, wake you and drag you to the hospital at all hours. Vamps are also weaker during daylight so if we must take chances, we may as well have the timing on our side."

I invited her into my messy lab. About the only spell that came to mind was holy water. What good would any healing stones do? He was *dead*. He didn't need to be healed, he needed the opposite.

I shook my head and was pretty sure something rattled. Obviously there was more than one screw loose up there. "If he's dead and doesn't want to cross over, does that mean he isn't dead enough? Or is he too dead? If you don't heal someone, you injure them."

I ransacked my boxes again and selected a string of coral. "I don't know if this stuff works against the evil eye after you're dead. It will block witchcraft, and I would think that would work after death, but who knows? I have some arrowheads too."

Arrowheads were a ward against evil and evil-minded witches. Because of the possibility of them being effective against witches, I didn't normally house them in my lab, but because of the move, they were currently locked inside a metal jewelry box and secured behind another lock inside my cabinet.

"What about bloodstone? It's a healing stone," Mat suggested.

I shook my head, while I tried to decide which arrowhead was best. "Bloodstone isn't likely to help because healing stones are gifts for the living, not for the dead and not gone. Mother Earth is very happy to take back what is hers, ashes to ashes, but don't ask me how she feels about vamps. Plus if a normal healer would be of any use, he'd have hired Tara or someone like my mom."

"Probably so. I thought the bloodstone might cure him if whatever he had was some sort of vamp blood disease." She reached into her purse and extracted a dark green piece of bloodstone, aka heliotrope. "I ordered a bunch more heliotrope since I'm in short supply."

"Thinking of enticing me to trade for Martin's last stone?" I grinned. "No way. It's a done deal." I told her about the Martin sighting in the desert. Only Mat could be disappointed to have missed something like that.

"Next time you see him, ask where he parked his trailer and who inherits all the stuff he collected."

My eyes widened. "I hadn't even thought about it."

"I asked Gordon to be on the lookout now that I know he's a cop. I could use Martin's stash, even if I have to purify it."

"Hmm. You're right, it would be nice to find." And I could possibly, remotely possibly, find it using the heliotrope he had gifted Mat. It was twice removed from him now, but he had felt the stone and come back to talk to me. "I'm pretty sure we won't be able to explain to a court that a ghost left us a bunch of stones."

She raised coy eyebrows and smiled. "Who else will want them? He didn't have any relatives."

"Maybe." Tracy didn't act as though he had any relatives. But being a loner and hoboing around the states didn't necessarily mean you didn't have relatives.

"Just a few more things and I'll be ready." I collected several extra loops of silver, a turquoise and silver ring, and four silver bangle bracelets with crosses dangling from each one. I handed her a crucifix, but she shoved her shirt sideways, revealing the one she was already wearing.

"Looks like we're set."

We jingled worse than wind chimes all the way to the car.

On the way to the hospital I said, "I take it that you didn't tell Gordon about this mission of mercy?"

"Need to know basis," she replied tightly.

I sighed and dialed.

She nearly jumped a curb, protesting. "You hate telling people what you're up to."

"I'm finding it's easier to do before rather than after. And if something goes wrong, he'd know and then...it's just easier." I wasn't about to confess that if Patrick came after either one of us, White Feather would know almost as soon as it happened. It wouldn't be a pleasant way for him to find out about this endeavor. Slightly better was the phone call ahead of time.

After a single string of curse words, and several questions, I heard Gordon say in the background, "They're going *where?*"

White Feather was almost more mature about it. "I'll head over and meet you since it's on the way home."

"On the way" wasn't even a stretch because it was so far out of the way. "You can't go everywhere with me," I said. "Not all the time. You married a witch. It's my job." I wondered just how much he was regretting marrying me.

"You aren't the problem," he bit out. "Neither is your job."

He hung up, leaving me unsure exactly what he meant by that.

Chapter 28

The hospital where Patrick was employed as a nighttime nurse was on the opposite side of the road from the Santa Fe Indian Hospital. Its location made it natural to associate it with Indian Hospital, but lately I'd begun to suspect it was not funded by the same sources.

The only sign on the building read, "Specialty Center." There was a trauma entrance and a regular entrance in addition to the back one, which was the only entrance I'd ever used. My latest impression was that the hospital was privately run by an organization that didn't answer to a typical hospital board. Maybe a check with Mom and her buddies was in order. If her network didn't know for certain who funded and ran it, they'd have some scintillating rumors.

Of all things, Patrick had given Mat a key to the back door. The key might not unlock his direct haven, but the outside door swung open to reveal the concrete steps that led down to a long, dark corridor and his special room in the hospital basement. There were no visible windows in the underground cavern. The doors along the corridor were ancient metal ones with sturdy locks. It screamed "dungeon" rather than "hospital."

Quiet as a tomb, it was a perfect daytime lair for a vamp.

"I can't believe you talked me into this," I muttered.

Vamps had acute hearing. Patrick whispered into existence outside one of the cinder block walls. I distinctly remembered there being a visible door when I last left the lair, but it wasn't evident now. I studied the bricks behind him. I'd never have found the door if he hadn't been standing right in front of the outline.

His guidance might be a necessary evil, but chills still traveled down my spine.

"Welcome."

My nod was cursory. There was no point in chit-chat. Patrick looked as he always did to me, mostly handsome and debonair, but with a blurriness that upon close inspection, revealed hints of something else. "How's Joe?"

"Another day or two in this state, and it will be merciful to put an end to it."

Maybe we should have brought a stake. Maybe that's what Patrick had meant when he asked Mat for a spell. If she was thinking the same thing, she gave no indication of it, staring around with avid curiosity mixed with a healthy dose of wariness.

Searching for silver to sneak a peek in the room before entering was a waste of time. There would be no silver in the vamp cave. Besides, I wore so much silver on my person, the weight of it might very well block out anything less than a silver mine with the mother lode of finds.

I sighed and followed the two of them into the room. The door made no sound as the false lines in the bricks sealed behind us.

Joe rested limply in a hospital bed. He was still paunchy and had the high sheen of someone who tended to sweat too much. His eyes were nothing but hollowed shells, with lids that fluttered half open and then shut again. A light sheet covered all but his arms and face.

Before, his face had been a cross between that of a teen with acne and a boozer. Now it was shrunken with vague red spots. One arm was hooked to an IV dripping blood, of course. His shoulder was completely covered with a harsh red rash that extended partway down his chest. The rash reminded me of drops of blood oozing...

A roaring in my ears shut out everything else. Mat shook me twice before I stopped holding my breath.

"For crying out loud," Patrick burst out. "He's not a threat to you in this state. He has had plenty of blood and yet he withers!"

"How did he die?" I squeaked out.

"What?"

I waved at the vamp. "Die. How did he die?"

"Here in the hospital. Sepsis. Infection in the blood."

"Aha. Wouldn't blood infections be detrimental to a vamp?" Mat asked.

"Not much is detrimental after death. Only this. Whatever it is." Patrick watched me watch Joe. "You shouldn't have come if you weren't prepared to deal with death."

"Death doesn't bother me," I muttered. "Unless we're talking about my own." I set my backpack down and peered closer at the rash. Backing off, I let my focus slide away from it, seeing it peripherally. "What was it?"

"What was what?"

I pointed. "His tat. And where did he get it?"

Mat sucked in a breath.

Patrick frowned. "He did have a tattoo, but when you change, they don't last. No impurities like that make it across, generally. Why?"

"Can you wake him up?"

"He is awake. He hardly sleeps. That is part of the problem. His cycles are mixed up. That's one of the reasons I'm here during daylight instead of in my own home. He'd walk out into sunlight without me watching him. He has no sense of night and day. It's as though he's only half changed."

"Joe?" I said.

His eyes blinked frantically. After a moment or two, they remained opened, but he squinted.

"He's better when the lights are off."

There were no windows. No lights with two vamps was too scary to contemplate.

Mat conveyed my thoughts on the matter. "Only if you leave the door to the hallway open. Wide open."

Patrick not only complied, he raised the light level in the hallway with a dial that was outside the room. The switch was higher up than a person would normally expect.

"Where did you get the tat? And how soon was it done before you died?"

With a question to focus on, Joe revived a bit. Done setting the lights, Patrick adjusted the bed up so that Joe was half sitting. He was little more than a puddle of death.

"It's a secret," Joe said, the ghost of a smile lighting his decaying features. "I always wanted a tattoo of a vampire. I planned to become one after I died. I researched it. I knew I had to find one, and I did. Think about it. You can live forever!"

The actual shape of the tat was hard for me to identify, especially since it was only a rash. His chest did sport a longish humanoid shape, but it was more bat-like with long wings, one of which stretched across his shoulder. "Is that where the infection started?"

Joe frowned. "I don't know. Who cares? I didn't die and that is all that matters."

My heart beat double-time. Patrick stepped away, staring at my chest, and it wasn't because he was interested in my boobs. I couldn't control my heartbeat. "Sorry," I said. "Who did the tat? When and where?"

"I got it at church." He chuckled weakly.

"You're a *priest*?" Matilda screeched too close to my ear.

"Nah. Records and historical collections." He straightened his shoulders. "Worked at the Library of Congress for two years, and that got me a job at the church to run their archives. Sorting old documents may sound like a measly job, but not just anyone can piece together and organize important stuff. Some of those old papers explained all about vampires, so when the time came, my decision was made."

"Who did the tat?"

"A friend. I couldn't visit any of the pro studios, because the bishop is always harping against all that stuff; drinking, earrings, tattoos. Bogus rules. The job didn't pay shit either, and I wanted the best." He rubbed two puffy fingers together, except he missed and ended up looking like he was flicking off something nasty. "My friend set me up. We met at the church. I didn't even have to leave my late shift."

"Who did the tattoo?" Mat repeated quietly.

"Zandy, my bud, set everything up for me. No girly shops where church members might see. Had to be secret. So Zandy and his friend met me at the church."

And I had feared Zandy would run short of volunteers. My shock was such that I might never have moved except Patrick swore a string of curse words that started with the name "Zandy" and blistered my ears. Joe actually perked up, leaning forward as if to catch the stream of violent energy.

Hoping to settle my churning stomach, I paced away from Joe. "Was the church too holy to allow black magic?" That was possible. Magic in a church could go badly wrong. I had definite proof of that because I'd tried an innocent spell in a church once. "But why would it affect a vamp? Wouldn't black magic be erased after death like most magic?" Blessings had affected the rogue vamp, but he was already changed. If a blessing worked against the rogue vamp, what would a construct of black magic do in a church?

I hovered over my backpack for a moment and then unwrapped the arrowhead from the silk. "What does an arrowhead normally do to your kind?"

Patrick shrugged. "Unless it's blessed for some reason, nothing."

"Here. Hold it."

He stared at me, but I ignored the intensity and held out the silk with the arrowhead. Finally, he reached out and picked it up.

Nothing happened, at least nothing obvious. Malachite was a light protection against the evil eye and arrowheads were a defense against evil witchcraft, also known as black magic. My eyes weren't evil and I wasn't cursing him, but I was a witch. The blur around Patrick lightened. His glamour was suddenly stronger, as though blocking my eyes. If I tried, I could probably still see around it, but who wanted to see what was underneath anyway?

My attention slid to Mat, but I wasn't certain how much she could detect beneath his glamour under ordinary circumstances. Now wasn't the time to ask.

"Okay, let Joe hold it." If it pushed away a curse, or evil eye, what would that mean? In and of itself, it was more likely to push me away as it had done with Patrick.

Joe accepted the arrowhead.

My stomach hit my toes, flipped and left town. Mat choked and almost turned it into a cough to hide her reaction.

Instead of blocking my witch sight, the arrowhead revealed a gaunt skeleton peering from underneath his odd and ugly glamour. He was hairless and nearly skinless. The view was blurry, but the guy was a walking corpse. It shouldn't have been unexpected, but even Patrick's true self wasn't a corpse. It was more like a beast. A strong beast, not a half-dead human.

I swallowed and pretended nonchalance, completely ignoring Patrick's burning stare. Had to hide the fear. Fear made me more attractive to a predator.

"Okay." My voice was steady. Good. "What about holy water. Burns, right?" I accepted the arrowhead back onto the silk and dug out my holy water.

"It burns?" Joe parroted.

Patrick rolled his eyes. Not a pretty sight since the whites of his eyes were already whiter than human eyes. "Yes."

"Oh well, that was before I died anyway," Joe said.

The room was already silent. I swear even the IV stopped dripping at that point.

"You used holy water?" Mat finally managed in a near whisper.

I had read up on tattoos way more than she had. "The ink!"

Joe nodded. "It was too thick. Had to be thinned and the holy water was sitting right there."

I squeaked. "He mixed holy water with black magic in a tattoo. On church grounds."

Patrick lost patience. "Do you plan to explain what you are talking about sometime today or should I order in dinner?" His tone lacked the sense of humor I would have preferred to hear when a vamp mentions dinner, but at least his fangs weren't out.

"Not funny," I complained. But I told him about the robberies and the victims. "Zandy's new customer appears to be a black magic user harvesting Zandy's blood to create constructs. The victim ends up at the robbery site and by the time all is said and done, the victim and constructs are completely used up or dead."

"And Joe was meant to be such a victim," Patrick growled.

"Looks that way. He ended up with Zandy's blood, holy water and a tattoo that wouldn't turn into a construct. The holy water wouldn't have been sterile so it probably caused the sepsis, which killed him. You tried to turn him and it didn't take, not completely."

"He didn't turn because of the holy water or Zandy's blood?"

Mat chewed her lip for an answer so I gave it my best shot. "I'd guess the holy water. Could be the church too. He's not insane, but he never drank Zandy's blood. I don't imagine it was healthy for him though."

"What if we removed the tattoo?"

I shivered. No way in any play book was I offering Tara's services. Her gift of healing on a vamp would be black magic. It was too close to necromancy to even consider. "No idea."

"If it contains holy water, I am not sure it can be removed," he mused.

I agreed. "That would be a blessing, not a curse. And I don't know how you can remove a blessing if you are one of the damned."

"He is not cursed then. He is blessed." Patrick laughed softly. He showed none of his usual restraint; his fangs gleamed.

Mat crowded closer to me.

He didn't cease his awful chuckling.

"Pretty sure our tasks are done here." My feet barely paused long enough for me to grab my pack on the way to full speed.

Patrick was still cackling, his voice floating after us as we tore down the hallway. "We need a curse that is worse than vampire blood. Now I wonder what that could be?"

Mat and I nearly knocked each other over shoving our way out the back door.

Chapter 29

White Feather was waiting at the back of the hospital, which saved Mat from having to drive me home. Gordon wasn't with him. I was surprised Gordon had stayed away until White Feather explained, "He gave his word that he'd watch the store until she came back or he had to leave on a police emergency. It was a matter of living up to her trust, and he's running a bit of a deficit in that area. "

"He's going to kill her," I said.

"If this is her idea of payback, I'm guessing they're even."

I shook my head. "She didn't expect him to find out." When he lifted an eyebrow, I explained, "I'm private about my work. She knows that. She had no clue I'd call you to tell you where I was headed. And I had no idea Gordon would be right there listening."

He thought for a long while before he said, "Thank you."

I stared out the window. "It's what I'd want you to do. I'm not used to answering to anyone. And I wasn't asking permission."

"I got that impression."

I unclenched my fists. "I didn't want you to find out the hard way if something went wrong."

"No, that wouldn't be good."

I wasn't sure I'd ever be entirely comfortable with this relationship responsibility, but I'd made my promises. I'd keep them.

It was easier to focus on the case than personal issues, so I ran through what had happened at Patrick's lair. "All of the crimes are happening in close proximity to the nail salon. And whoever robbed Tam and Richard's home obviously knew the nail salon's routine. Mat's place is down the block."

"An employee at the bakery or salon? Their own kid, Kevin? Or are you thinking of an employee at one of the places that was robbed?"

I shrugged. "Mat doesn't have any employees unless you count Gordon, and I suppose we can safely eliminate him. Right?"

His bland expression told me not to press my luck.

Instead of hiking Tent Rock after lunch, we postponed the trip in favor of carefully testing the auras on the samples White Feather had obtained from Gordon.

Despite enhanced witch forks, not even the barest of twitches indicated any kind of match.

The results weren't unexpected, but it was disappointing. After everything was tested, we added some additional safety measures to the new holding area in White Feather's backyard and stored all the samples.

As the sun went down, we finished securing the sand-packed enclosure. Since the sand was exactly the same as all the other dirt in the yard, a spell to blend wasn't necessary, but I buried an arrowhead under the dirt to prevent the magic from attracting the eye of a witch.

Darkness and arrowheads reminded me of Patrick and his sick friend. Would they be roaming the night in a last ditch effort to locate a cure? What might they try? Joe wouldn't hold on much longer.

I was glad to hurry inside where vampires couldn't enter. Well, not unless Zandy fed one again.

My shivers weren't only from the cold.

* * *

My priorities shifted overnight. Meeting with ugly vampires, one of whom wasn't even a proper vampire because Zandy was dumb enough to offer black magic tattoos on church grounds, made me determined to limit my vulnerability to the coyote.

"I need better weapons," I told White Feather over breakfast.

"And we need a hell of a lot more information about this case. It's time I hunt down some wind spirits and see if I can convince them to talk."

"Wind spirits?" I blinked. "The last time we dealt with wind that had a mind of its own, it ripped half your house apart!"

"Don't worry. Normal wind spirits are nothing like that monster." He reached over and tugged on my hair. "They're playful breezes, little sprites collecting dust here, leaves there, and along the way, bits of information."

"Playful? Just how playful?"

He shrugged. "They're basic elementals. It's the same thing as when you talk to the earth, right? Earth spirits, wind sprites or spirits, same thing. The wind sprites are like little kids with the attention span of a gnat and about as reliable, but sometimes they are worth questioning. I'll take a couple of quick hikes and see what the breezes know."

"Why can't you do it here? Maybe use your grandfather's sacred place?"

He moved to the sink. "The magic that grandfather guarded isn't tied to the here and now. I need to reach specific breezes that have danced through town, swirled up into the mountains and collected tastes of the recent past. Then I need to tease those bits together."

White Feather had always been able to glean more direct information from the wind than I had been able to from Mother Earth. It wasn't until I concentrated on a single element of Mother Earth that I'd been able to get any concrete messages from her. My brow furrowed. "You're saying there are separate whirlwinds you talk to?"

"Your breakfast is getting cold."

I put my spoon down. Oatmeal was not my favorite and this was far more important. "Are they dangerous?" Mother Earth was alive. I had not thought of the wind quite the same way. Mother Earth had moods and...yes, various parts of her were more or less dangerous, more or less informative. She had different smells and different voices.

"No more so than when you hike Tent Rock and run into ghosts like Martin."

"I didn't...that's not hiking...?!?" I sputtered.

He laughed, a quick snap of air tugging my hair as his hand had just done. "There's no risk to me. But I need to be away from distractions. Find the right breeze. Tease out any clues the wind sprites might know. It's like listening to a hundred songs at the same time and quite possibly as useless.

"When I'm able to convince them to cooperate it's a lot like when we hunted for Lynx with the witching fork, only less precise. You knew an area to search so we were able to narrow in. I'm looking to narrow our search area by asking the wind spirits to focus on the tat smell and tat magic."

I shook my head. "Finding Lynx wasn't much more than luck until we found that overhang."

"True, but the air doesn't forget. The right breeze might have seen something and convey an important clue. Right now we've got nothing."

"I'd better go with you to watch your back. If you're focused on chatting up wind sprites anything could happen."

"You'll just distract them and me." He leaned over to kiss the top of my head. "You hike and work all the time. Same thing, only I bet I don't even see any ghosts."

I frowned. Ghosts were hardly the biggest worry. "Do not find any dead bodies. With or without tats."

While he prepared to leave, I washed my dishes. Unlike me, he didn't collect a backpack of supplies. He simply put on hiking boots and a coat because it was cold outside.

He kissed me good-bye, leaving me feeling distinctly unsettled. He was a powerful warlock. He could take care of himself. When I was at home, and he was here working, I was never concerned.

I glared at the closed door. I wasn't used to this whole marriage thing and having a partner. Of course, the wind spirits didn't sound particularly dangerous. Unless one of them went rogue and spun him down the mountainside. Then again, he could control the air and defend himself against it.

"Hmph." At the moment, he was the only half of the partnership focusing on an accomplishment. I was standing here like a ninny.

Okay then. Defense. Even with half a lab, I could pound silver. Arrowheads didn't have to be pretty. They needed to be sharp and fast.

Since Mat could use a silver weapon or two, I created enough for both of us. She'd probably refuse to use them because they were so misshapen. Too bad. If she had them and was near me, I could use them. I notched holes in the arrowheads to loop on my bracelet alongside the round silver beads.

Feeling clever, I attached a few of the arrowheads to small pieces of ash. Mini-stakes in the form of darts. The wood might not be ash because I had never gotten around to labeling the wood pile, but we weren't after vampires anyway. It was more for the sake of art. I could combine warfare and art; I just needed the right incentive.

Once I had a pattern, it was a matter of pounding, shaping and sharpening.

White Feather hadn't returned by one o'clock, even though it was lunch time. When I toiled over spells in the desert, I was gone for hours.

I made a quick foray into the kitchen for a snack, made four burritos for Tracy and took a quick peek out the front door.

Nope, he wasn't home yet. The tiniest hunt for his silver wedding ring resulted in a warm tingle across my gold band. Could he feel me checking on him? The touch wasn't strong enough to glean a sense of place, but it did make me feel better.

Feeling like an idiot, I closeted myself back in the lab and arranged a flat board on one end. It was time for target practice.

It didn't take long for me to discover that aiming at silver was easier than pushing silver randomly and hoping to hit a target. Once a silver arrowhead was lodged in the plywood, I could accurately shoot the rest of my weapons to within a quarter of an inch.

"Excellent." Anyone or anything wearing jewelry would be an easy target for me. Of course, most of my enemies, by their nature, didn't sport silver accessories. Shame, that.

Within the hour, White Feather returned. Hyper-sensitive, I knew the minute he drove up. I dithered over whether I should greet him or continue working.

"Moonlight madness." What was the point in standing here when I wanted to be out there?

I didn't quite yank the front door open.

White Feather was already on the porch. "Good, I won't have to set these down." He peered at me over two huge bundles of willow branches, one dried and one green.

I grinned like a happy idiot and accepted one of the bundles. "This is...you're entirely too awesome!"

He rolled his eyes. "Most women expect roses. You, you think dead sticks are the stuff of romance."

I laughed. "Willow is worth more." If it hadn't been for the willow in the way, the kiss I gave him would have lingered on even longer.

When I stepped back, he followed me to the lab with his half of the branches, only to stop in the doorway with one raised eyebrow. He stared at the board full of silver arrowheads. "Practicing your aim?"

"I've improved it greatly."

He grinned down at me, set the branches against the wall and pulled me in for another kiss. "I'm glad you're not most women."

I was very glad he wasn't most men, too, because most men probably couldn't handle living with a witch at all, let alone know the right gift to make my day.

Still locked inside the circle of his arms, I asked, "Did you learn anything from the wind spirits?"

My question broke the pleasant mood. His brow furrowed and his eyes flashed dark brown. "It wasn't good." He loosened his hold on me as though he didn't want to taint me with the news. "They conveyed the smell of death and old magic."

"We already know people are dying."

He shook his head. "This was decay. Like a body left somewhere that we haven't found, but the breezes shied away from talking about it. The magic and blood they hinted at was even older. You may have been right when you said I should use grandfather's room to hunt information. There's some ancient magic at work here, something someone dug up and delved into."

"That doesn't sound like a promising lead."

"I just wish there had been a sense of direction, but the deaths and tats have been in several places. That makes it much harder." He sighed and stretched his back. "I need to take a shower and get something to eat."

He left me standing with my new piles of willow sticks. I fingered one, wishing I knew a spell to ferret out the root of the evil. They weren't any good for that, but if I spelled the green branches now it could improve the finding ability once the sticks aged.

I ran through my list of clients mentally. Lynx's new client, the one with the matched packet finding spell, might hire me to locate one of the packets someday. It wouldn't hurt to spell some willow with dust from amethyst and red garnet. Repeat clients were my beans and tortillas, and it never hurt to be prepared.

I whittled away at the sticks while I considered more weapons for my arsenal.

Chapter 30

Next morning, I headed to Mat's with my silver presents. The bakery was definitely on the way from my parking spot.

Fortunately, great minds think alike. Mat was already installed inside the cafe, sipping coffee. She spotted me coming through the door and waved with a happy smile.

"Split an eclair?" I offered in greeting.

"I'm being good. Only having coffee." The coffee was topped with whipped cream, cocoa and some cute colored sprinkles. No doubt the almond biscotti was strictly a stirring implement, not meant to be dipped and eaten.

"Yeah, that looks low calorie all right. Okay, I'll eat the entire eclair, but it's your fault if I get fat."

I ordered the eclair and picked up two forks. The Asian man at the counter, Richard, I assumed, was kind enough to cut the eclair in half, saving me the trouble. He grinned wide, stuffed my dollar tip in the tip jar and beckoned the next customer forward. It sure would be bad news if his own son were somehow involved in the robberies.

I set the tray down at Mat's table. She helped me arrange the plates and accepted her half of the eclair without blinking an eye.

"Brought you something." I pulled a set of five darts from my backpack. "These aren't much, but I also brought you my spare dagger. I'll give you that at the shop."

"I don't need the dagger. I bought one, but thanks." She pulled the box her way and opened it. "Interesting...What in spell's bells are they? Something from an African war chant?"

I laughed. "They're darts."

"If these were from anyone but you I'd refuse them. I now have a dagger and colloidal silver located strategically all over the shop."

"Excellent! I can manipulate that too."

She sipped her coffee. "The colloidal liquid is fluid enough for me to call it like I do water." She fingered the little darts. "These look like mini stakes."

I nodded. "Kind of. I considered enhancing them to be attracted to Zandy specifically."

"You have something of his?"

"From a long while back, and now something more recent. Thing is, he's dangerous. I don't want him tracking *me*."

"Can he do witchcraft?"

"Not back then. But someone is using black magic now. What if Patrick is wrong and Zandy isn't selling his blood, but he's using it to create the constructs? I don't want anything of his anywhere near me. So the darts are clean, no magic. Throw them or use them in a bracelet that conceals a wrist knife."

"Why haven't you designed a wrist wrap for one of your knives?"

I jingled my new charm bracelet. "Don't need one. I can pop these off and send them flying. I'm improving too, although from a distance, I have trouble keeping the point aimed correctly."

She reached over and examined the various arrowhead "charms" on my bracelet.

"Armed and dangerous," Mat said with satisfaction.

I wanted to ask her a few questions about Kevin, but since his father was manning the bakery it would be stupid to discuss his possible involvement here. I swallowed another bite and casually asked how her designs were turning out.

"Awesome. I've picked out the material for the purses and have a couple of prototypes embroidered. I'll show you when we get back. They are absolutely gorgeous."

"You're using Kevin's drawings?"

She nodded and twirled her fork, her eyes darting to the counter where Richard was wiping down the espresso machine. "I came here this morning to pick up his notebook. Need to flip through it again to see if there is any other artwork I might want to use."

"Oh." I was betting Gordon wanted to see the notebook, and Mat was his excuse to get his hands on it. My stomach fluttered nervously. "You found what you were looking for then?"

To my dismay, she nodded. "You name it, the kid has done it. Dragons. Snakes. Flowers." Her eyes flicked to the counter again.

"Any matches to anything else you've, uhm, considered?"

"Close enough."

We really should have waited until we were elsewhere to discuss this. Kevin's father was busy, but that didn't mean he couldn't hear between lulls in the noisy conversations around us.

Mat filled the void with more innocent conversation. "If he hasn't drawn it, he can. But I had to talk him out of Kokopelli. Why does everyone insist that little beast is cute?"

I nearly choked. Mat definitely wasn't talking in code about the notebook anymore. She'd always disliked Kokopelli. "I don't think the magic of the fertility symbol counts if it's in your store for sale."

"I'm not taking any chances. Yeah, yeah, he's also the rain guy and the music guy, but I'm in a relationship." She dropped her voice to a whisper. "I do not need 'fertility' complications!"

I laughed. Mat had potions out the ying-yang, sold most anything and negotiated with vamps. One little fertility spirit, and she refused to do business.

As we packed up to leave, Richard bustled over, wiping his hands on his white apron. He cleared the table efficiently while asking, "Was good, yes?"

"Delicious!" we declared unanimously.

"Ah good. You come back then. I look for you."

Mat rolled her eyes. "Don't pretend you don't recognize me. I've been here almost every day since you opened!"

He smiled. "You are my best customer. I hear you talk of Kevin. He is a big help, yes?"

There went my smile, but Mat was a better saleswoman than I'd ever be. Her composure never slipped while she babbled praises.

He refused another tip, and we couldn't leave fast enough. I really hoped Kevin wasn't involved.

We skipped down the street to the alleyway behind her place. Mat chattered on about the spell packet designs. "No matter what happens, the new packets will be totally awesome. I bet even you will want to sell a spell or three in my store."

"Hmm." She knew I wouldn't sell them openly. "If you get a special client, we can talk about you being the intermediary. Lynx is busier than ever these days, but I still only work on request, and only for clients you've checked out." That was closer than I'd ever come to selling in her store.

Mat stopped and clapped a hand over her mouth to trap a squeal of delight. Around her fingers she asked, "Really?"

My eyes narrowed. "Why? Do you have a client in mind?"

She shook her head. "Nooo. I've sent a few people to you, but always through Lynx. I'd love to go more direct."

"You can be direct. Just leave my name out of it. And I'd prefer clients you already know and trust."

"I'll sort through my client list today! This is like winning the lottery."

Since she was focused on me, she didn't notice the discarded jeans and t-shirt tucked near the dumpster, but I did. My feet halted. I checked the rest of the alley before Mat noticed my wariness.

I pointed to the jeans. "Last time there was a pile of clothes in your alleyway, Zandy was inside about to make mincemeat of you and Gordon."

She went unnaturally still and the side of her neck turned the brilliant flush that only a redhead can maintain.

"He might not be in your place. You said you have silver in there?" Liquid silver might not provide me with as much information as regular silver, because it was stored in a jar. "And a dagger, right?"

Her eyes went distant. "Lend me your water bottle."

Since I almost always carried one, it wasn't a stretch for her to know it was attached to my backpack. I extracted it from the side pocket.

"Thanks." She unscrewed the top. As a water witch, if she had a few drops of water or even a mirror, she could pull reflections, especially standing this close to her own environment. Not knowing how well her magic would perform under these circumstances, I concentrated on finding the silver she had told me about.

She was way ahead of me. "That is absolutely it!" she screamed.

The ground under my feet rumbled.

"Uh, Mat..." Any water within reach roiled and churned as viciously as her temper. There was a roar, a crash and yelling up the street. From the sound of things, the hydrant's new moorings went the way of the water in my bottle, tossed aside like so much garbage.

"Mat, we'll stop him! We'll get backup. Trap him in there and this time make sure he doesn't have another chance to return."

Like a whirlwind, she flew at her backdoor, twisting the knob. The lock was intact, but she already had her key ready. As she threw the bolts she yelled, "*You dare, bastard coyote!*"

"Or I guess we can just kick his ass ourselves," I said. As I scooted behind my friend, the ring on my finger tingled. For the first time, my head was clear enough to detect the magic flowing through it. My fingers squeezed the gold, which squeezed the diamond. Half of that was raw emotion, but it was enough to suck wind in, and the guy on the other end was very attuned to wind.

I had just put White Feather on notice that I was running straight into danger like a fool.

Chapter 31

Maybe if I hadn't been so focused on the ring, I'd have heard the footsteps behind me. Then again, maybe not. The guy was good and obviously had some martial arts training. He had my arm yanked back and would have pinned it solidly except my backpack was in the way. He was strong too, swinging my body sideways into the door frame.

Luckily I twisted, an instinctive reaction. The brunt of the blow bruised my shoulder and cheekbone rather than breaking my nose.

My assailant smashed the backpack out of the way using my own arm against me. That kept most of my firepower trapped between the two of us. Setting off any of the lethal spells in the pack would burn me as much as him, maybe more.

I spun my bracelet with my fingers and flicked the catch. I pushed the beads and arrowheads all at once.

The guy mangling my arm jammed my face in the door frame again. I directed the silver and heard the delightful sound of popping and smacking, even as a stray silver ball grazed the side of my own head. The only failure was the lack of sizzling flesh as the silver hit. The guy wasn't a shifter.

I called them back almost before they could ricochet off the adobe walls.

"What the hell?" the voice near my head muttered.

Since he wasn't a shifter, I concentrated harder on the arrowheads. It was impossible to say how accurately they hit, but he yelled, "Ah!" and his hold loosened enough for me to twist partially free.

I lifted on my toes and smashed my head back, but I missed. "Moonlight mad—!"

He crashed against me, flattening us both against the wall. My cheek throbbed, but it didn't stop my fingers from searching along the side of the backpack still caught between us. If I could reach...the fireball packets on the side...

From inside, Mat screamed, "Die, bastard coyote, die!" The smell of burning fur billowed out the door, followed by the yelp of a coyote.

Hadn't Zandy learned anything?

My groping foot found an instep. I slammed down, still flinging silver beads at the enemy. He gasped, either from the foot or another lucky strike. Mentally, I reached for the silver knife I had intended to give Mat, but it was inside a leather sheath and my backpack was zipped.

I twisted my hand, locking my fingernails into his skin. He yanked me in hard, cursing in my ear, a muttered threat as he struggled to secure his grasp. My new necklace danced sideways, and I teetered against the doorway.

The necklace was silver and sharp. I wasn't that controlled in my aim and couldn't see my target, but I flung the strands of silver anyway. The obsidian nearly choked me as it flew backwards.

My diamond ring flashed heat.

I twisted again. Gravity tumbled me sideways, but in a half crouch, I found myself facing the enemy.

"Lee," I gasped his name out in accusation. The nail tech from Tam's salon batted ineffectively at the silver raining down on his head. Blood dripped from a cut across his nose and neck, but he launched a karate kick anyway.

The wall trapped me, and the kick sent a shooting pain through my thigh, buckling my leg.

I rolled and divested myself of my backpack. With my hands freed, the fireball packets in the side pocket were better than a chocolate bar. I crushed the first packet, whispered the word of power, and threw it. His fancy high kick left him vulnerable.

I aimed an arrowhead squarely at the blood already leaking from the wound on his neck. I smashed another fireball, mixing the elements. Even if the fireballs failed to start him on fire, they usually convinced anyone with any sense to run.

Even though my second lob was dead center, Lee was apparently too stunned to do more than land on his ass and roll away from the flames.

He was stronger than me and faster. The silver would have worked great against a shifter, but he wasn't one. My spell needed an enhancement or two when it came to the mundane.

I'd have lobbed another fireball, but Mat screamed.

"Aztec—" I bit off the rest of the curse, called my silver and ran for the door. Before I reached it, Lynx rounded the corner of the alley at a dead run. I paused to yell, "Keep this guy here! And don't come inside unless you have to. Silver will be flying."

Lynx was nothing if not cat. Once he focused on his prey, his eyes glowed that unblinking, predator yellow. His stare alone might keep the guy from running.

I tossed my remaining fireball to Lynx. He knew many of my spells required crushing. He didn't know the word to set it off, but Lee didn't know that.

Lynx caught the spell with the speed and dexterity of swishing claws. Those lethal points ought to be more than enough of a deterrent, even without the fireball.

I paused long enough to extract my silver dagger from its sheath and dashed inside, feeling silver everywhere. That message from Mother Earth was confusing until I sorted it with my own eyes.

Mat was not in as much trouble as her scream implied, but she was definitely enraged.

Zandy was nearly bald from splashes of colloidal silver. He was half changed so that he could rub the silver off or expel it, but whatever she had concocted, it was sticky.

From the way she was holding her own silver dagger, it was possible she needed a lesson or two on proper slashing techniques, but she had enough colloidal silver smeared on her person that it didn't matter. Zandy couldn't touch her.

"You're dead!" Zandy screamed. "He won't wait around for you to trap him! He'll use your carcass until you bleed dry like the rest of'em."

Zandy had always been big on talking and whining. "Yeah, yeah," I interrupted his tirade. "If you move, I'll beat you to a pulp and clean the floor with whatever is left." I wasn't covered in silver like my friend, but the silver beads were right behind me, ready to roll.

He was not impressed. He attacked, changing fully to coyote on his way to me.

I was much better with my aim this time around. He swallowed two pellets. The arrowhead hit him in the eye and stayed there. I slashed with the knife and spun sideways. Very helpfully, Mat hit me in the chest with a water balloon full of silver.

I did lie though. I left the floor bloody instead of using Zandy to mop up the damage.

Chapter 32

Gordon was stuck with the pleasant job of preparing Zandy to be carted off to the hospital. Normally shifters healed fast, especially if they could change a few times, but healing was more difficult when the wounds were due to silver. In Zandy's case, changing was nearly impossible, coated as he was with the sticky stuff. On top of that, he was nearly incapacitated from having swallowed two silver pellets.

Zandy was much less threatening as a human, but only because of the lack of snapping canines. His brown hair was tangled where it wasn't outright burned. He was as wiry in his human form as he was as a coyote. His pale brown eyes were just as shifty too, with a cruel glint that flickered when one of the cops dragged a burned and bruised Lee into the shop.

Gordon snapped on special handcuffs made of sterling silver. He used the excuse of the wounds to wrap Zandy's wrists underneath, but any squirming would put the silver bracelets in direct contact.

White Feather assured me that Gordon's team knew how to handle Zandy.

"But how often do shifters end up in the hospital?" Zandy was as wily as coyotes came. "He pukes up those silver balls and changes a time or two, he'll run."

White Feather frowned, but Gordon didn't have time for nosy questions.

Mat was out of sight washing up and recovering what she could of the silver. I was in awe of her water balloon idea. She'd aimed and fired like a baseball pro. Other than the one she had gripped too tightly and exploded on her person, she had hit her target unfailingly. The one that doused her had played to her advantage. Zandy stood no chance of attacking her without injuring himself.

"Twenty of the things," I gushed. "She went all out. I'll add silver to my fireballs so that I can call them to me. Store them in an area of my backpack where they aren't tied down. If I redo my dagger sheath, I could call it too."

"I'm going to put *you* on a tether," White Feather muttered, encircling me with his arm and squishing me into his side. "I'd much rather rescue you myself, but thank God Lynx was in the area when I called him."

"Ah, that explains how he showed up in such a timely manner."

"I phoned his cell while driving here. He had been tracking Zandy, narrowing in. He might have arrived anyway."

It wasn't quick, but Gordon's team finally hauled Zandy away. I made sure that Gordon knew about the two pellets Zandy had swallowed. "If he expels those, he'll require a silver jail cell to keep him from escaping."

Gordon passed the info along to the parties who needed to know.

Since Lee's burns were painful but not critical, one of the officers supplied first aid cream, but Gordon didn't process him right away. His shirt was nothing but tattered and burned remnants. If he was cold, who cared?

Not me. My own face still throbbed from being slammed into the door frame. Lee deserved nothing more than the third degree, starting with who he worked for on the burglaries.

Lee squirmed under our combined glares, but he answered. "Guy calls himself Jedi 'cause he says he can call the force. He's an old white guy, more like Shatner than stupid Jedi, but he's into all those stories, Frankenstein and Dracula crap. Thought he was all talk when we started casing a few joints, but the guy is for real. We just had to help him with a tat. So, I let him and Zandy into Tam's place. Kevin leaves his designs there all the time. Customers sort through them for their nails."

"You had a key?" I demanded.

"Sure."

Gordon stared him down.

He didn't even drop his eyes. "I borrowed it from Tam one day and made a copy."

"Borrowed," Gordon repeated.

He shrugged. "It was on the counter."

"Okay," Gordon said. "You stole a key and some tat designs. Then what?"

"Easy. We found someone who wanted a tat, no problem. No reason not to use Tam's place. There was already a table and supplies."

"Yeah, other than it was breaking and entering," I muttered.

He shrugged. "We didn't take nothing. Jedi did the tat. I knew where things were in the shop, alcohol swabs, whatever. Then he said he was gonna call the force. Zandy and me, we about busted a gut laughing, but Jedi, he made the tat come alive. It was like he said, some kind of Frankenstein. The lady, she was a zombie, lay'n there drooling, but the tat, it did whatever Jedi told it to. He said he used his blood in the tat so it had to obey him."

"Then you dragged the lady to the jewelry store?"

"Couldn't. Zandy was sure the whole thing was bunk so we didn't have a target ready. Zandy and Jedi made me stay with the lady while they found an empty place to hit. I about shit myself. That tat lizard sat there in the corner, zoning on me. It breathed when she breathed. I never touched it, I swear."

"Not that time, I bet," I said.

"Not never. Jedi told me he'd know if I messed around, and he'd feed me to the tat if I so much as touched it or the lady."

Gordon cleared his throat. "So Zandy and Jedi cased the first jewelry store. Then what?"

"Jedi left Zandy on watch at the jewelry store. He came back for the tat. We loaded the lady and the tarp in the car, and we hit the joint. The tat crawled under the door and turned off the alarm. But the lizard thing, it was like, weak. We barely got inside and it just disappeared. The lady, she strangled. You could hear her dying. We hightailed it outta there. Didn't get a thing for our trouble.

Man, it was terrible."

"Terrible. Yet you went ahead with the next robbery two weeks later."

"It wasn't easy like that! Jedi had this new plan. He said he'd use his own tats so he could control the energy, and he wouldn't die because he'd call back the tats if he got too weak. It was gonna be perfect!"

"Except another lady died." Gordon tapped his pad of paper as though it contained a full accounting of wrongs.

"That wasn't our fault," Lee grumbled. "Jedi tried his own tats, but it damn near bled him out. I thought he had bit the dust just trying it, but he showed up again with another plan. We were able to hit the second jewelry store. But that lady died too."

"And somehow you thought it was a great idea to keep right on killing women?" Gordon stabbed the page again. "You robbed your own boss's home."

"Jedi swore the next chick wouldn't die! All we needed was an athlete, someone strong enough to withstand the job pressure. He grabbed this buff runner. I told him we didn't even need a tat for robbing Tam's place, so it wasn't my fault. I could have tricked Kevin into telling me the safe combo. But Jedi was positive the lady would live. Only problem was, she was some kind of body builder. She kept fighting him and bled even faster where the tat had been."

"You could have stopped the killing. Walked away."

He nodded frantically. "Damn straight. Those tats creeped me out and Jedi was one sick dude. One or two more jobs, and I figured he was gonna croak on us anyway. But Zandy, he just kept on. Said we needed someone with more power, like a witch. He said it would work because witches, they have some kind of force too, like Jedi."

My fists clenched. "Only Mat wasn't an easy target." I'd like to show him how lethal a witch could be. Lee may have burns from the fireballs, but he deserved worse.

"I didn't have a thing to do with it after Tam's place."

It didn't take a genius to see the lie. "You kidnapped a homeless guy and did a tat on him *after* Zandy attacked Mat," I spat out.

He shook his head. "No way. I told them I'd keep selling them tat designs and rent the place out. Why not? If Zandy happened to bring clients to the salon for body art and left them hosed while he checked his next target, that's none of my business."

"You were with him today!" I shouted.

He rubbed at the burns on his chest, but with a wince, left them alone. "Different biz. I was only the lookout. Zandy said if I helped him take down the place, I could have all the potions. He didn't want any of them!" His eyes glimmered with greed. "You know how much cash I could make selling that stuff on the side at the salon? And it wouldn't even be illegal."

Mat's lips tightened with barely repressed rage.

"Stealing them in the first place is illegal. On top of that, you don't know what any of the spells are for," I pointed out. Mat labeled the potions with broad strokes, leaving many a jar completely unlabeled. Instructions for any spell came only with the purchase.

"Doesn't matter. They'd buy the stuff. Those ladies, they have nothing but time and money. I'd tell them all that shit would make their husbands go wild. Or the eighty year old ones that they could get a boyfriend instead of shopping for a cure for loneliness. I could work that."

Despite another twenty-five thousand questions, we squeezed little else of use from him. He admitted he knew Zandy was still using the shop, and he admitted he considered getting back in on the deals, but he swore he hadn't met anyone other than Jedi and Zandy. His physical description of Jedi as "some old white guy" was zero help. He didn't know where he lived, but assumed he'd been staying with Zandy somewhere.

Before White Feather and I departed, I pulled Lynx to the side. "Thanks."

He shrugged. "Looked like you had it under control."

"Did you use the fire packet I tossed to you?"

"I lost it?"

"Liar. Do you want to know the word to set it off or are you just planning on copying the spell? I could train you, you know."

His eyes gleamed. "Lemme study it first. I can usually twist things to work. I can't start them from scratch like you do, but I can keep them going."

The kid was...no longer a kid. But he was still a marvel. "Do not blow yourself up, okay? You know where I live if you want to *ask* questions instead of doing things your own way." I hesitated before moving on, but it had to be done. "Can you get us in the hospital?"

"Tonight?" Before the word popped out of his mouth he was already shaking his head. "You are not gonna do this one in the daylight!" The end was a feral hiss.

"Patrick works there at night, Lynx!"

"That could be a bonus, you know that, right?"

"Nighttime means he'll involve himself. That is not something I want to see. And I do *not* want to owe a vamp anything! Not a favor, not an implied favor, barely a truce."

He set his mouth in a mutinous line. "I'll see what I can do."

"Lynx, we have to get Zandy to talk *before* Patrick gets to him. Zandy isn't just a threat to you and me. His blood is a huge problem for Patrick."

"Patrick doesn't want his blood. He isn't going to drink it."

"No, he's not, but he won't stand around letting us ask fifty questions while a perfect weapon against vamps recovers in his hospital."

"He might let you ask your questions before he takes care of the problem."

I crossed my arms and waited.

"Okay, Patrick gets to him tonight, it's gonna be a short fight." Lynx made fangs out of his fingers. "You gonna tell White Feather?"

"Are you kidding me? You think I'd try to force info out of Zandy on my own?"

Lynx grinned. "Just checking. Plus if White Feather is with you, maybe he can spin you two up to a window. I open it, let you in and we're done."

"In broad daylight? We can't go sailing two or three stories into the air!"

"I tol' you daytime was a bad idea."

I'd walked into that.

Lynx wore a smug smile as he disappeared out the back door to "take care of business." He was such a *cat* sometimes.

Chapter 33

Much to my surprise, we didn't need Lynx to sneak into the hospital. After we were done with Lee, Gordon suggested we meet him at the hospital at three to "talk" to Zandy. Maybe his being a cop did have its uses.

Gordon said, "Zandy should be stabilized by then. We can't torture him to obtain answers, but it wouldn't hurt if you brought a load of silver."

"Never leave home without it." Was he crazy? I'd refill at the house, and while there, strap on my sheath for my dagger. It fit under the leg of my jeans and was easier to reach than the backpack. There wasn't enough silver in the world to make me feel safe around that coyote.

Mat had a big mess to clean, but instead of mopping up, she pulled out a container of colloidal silver and began filling balloons.

"How about using thin blown glass as a container?" I suggested. "The broken glass would embed the silver into the skin. You could even sell beads like that to me!"

"Good idea," Mat agreed. "The glass would break easily enough and the added damage would be a bonus."

"We could add a spell or two into the mix."

"A curse."

"Excellent. I have a few in mind that won't stick to the good guys."

White Feather asked, "How many silver balls did you lose?"

"Just the two." I had already called the remaining balls back and loaded them on my bracelet. "The arrowheads need to be sharper. Or better yet, I should create a throwing star, shaped like the necklace you bought me."

"Since the colloidal silver was effective against Zandy, I'll add a balding spell to a couple of these," Matilda muttered.

Gordon squawked before quickly muffling the noise. He patted his own head of hair, and then shifted from one foot to the other as his gaze traveled between me and Mat.

White Feather laughed softly.

"What's so funny?" I asked as White Feather guided me out the back way.

"Nothing. I don't think Gordon quite understood what he was getting into when he started dating Mat. He thought he knew all about witches and warlocks because he knew me. But I don't invent weapons as though I'm in hot competition with Los Alamos, and I never fall into the kind of situations that you find yourself in."

"What?!? I'm not the one who was half eaten by a tattoo!"

"That never happened before I met you."

"It never happened to me before I met you either!"

White Feather chuckled. "True. But I have a feeling that Gordon saw a beautiful witch and set about seducing her without realizing she could blow him into tiny pieces or spell him into knots. He had no idea that the witch he was dating was truly *dangerous*. Sure, he's arrested a witch or two, but at least one of those was a fake. He knows two other shifters who play ears in the underground now and then, and I'm pretty sure one of the guys on the force is a shifter, but Gordon has never dealt with them changing, and none of them attacked his girlfriend."

"And none of his other girlfriends blew up a fire hydrant twice in one week either, I bet."

"Nope."

"Well, it was an aberration. She doesn't do that sort of thing all the time."

"Uh-huh." He opened the door to my car. I sat but didn't swing my legs inside because he crouched down inside the door. "I'll be right behind you on the way home. Adriel—" He grabbed both my knees. "Could you maybe stay safe until we get there?"

I leaned my forehead against his. "I promise. Zandy is in custody. Lee is too."

"I love you."

"Me too." He squinted at me so I corrected with a grin, "I love you, too."

He didn't tailgate me, but it was close.

I showered, changed clothes and loaded my backpack. White Feather strapped on no less than four silver knives. Good. If mine wasn't enough, I could call his.

Just before the doorbell rang, White Feather said, "Lynx is getting faster and sneakier. He didn't drive all the way up."

When I answered the door, Lynx said, "Problem. I can't find Patrick."

"Not a problem." I explained that we had been officially invited to the interrogation.

Lynx paced inside, his head tilted. "He's not answering his phone, even the number for an emergency."

"Is that unusual?" I had never tried to call Patrick despite him offering the number.

"His back room is always available. That's the point. If it's not, he's still the contact for a vamp finding a safe house."

"It's broad daylight. Vamps won't be hunting for a safe house right now."

His head tilted the other way. "Mostly true. Any vamp outside right now would be too fried for treatment. But the thing is, he treats more than vamps. And the rooms in the basement have always been available if you know the code. But he didn't answer. Or call back."

"How do people usually gain access to the treatment rooms if he's not there? And what good does it do them if he's not there?"

Lynx gave me a blank stare.

"Okay, okay, too many questions." Lynx guarded client information better than Fort Knox guarded gold. I had been treated in Patrick's special room during daylight hours. During that emergency, it was possible that Lynx had reached Patrick before Patrick left his night shift at the hospital. But Patrick had also given Mat a key so there was more than one way to deal with Patrick.

"Do you have a key?" I asked.

"Not the way it works. There's a system, but he doesn't hand out keys."

"Hmm." Lynx didn't need to know Mat had one. He wasn't the only one who could keep a secret.

"You don't need me for the Zandy thing, then?" he asked.

"No, that's set." I knew what he was thinking. "Lynx, be careful."

He was halfway to the door. "Always am."

"Lynx." He paused, his hand on the doorknob. "After we're done with Zandy, we'll help you find Patrick. If he's lost. You know where he lives, right?"

Cat eyes. "I'll do some checking. He's always answered before. After you're done with Zandy, maybe you can see if he showed for his shift last night."

Before I could agree, Lynx was out the door and moving. Great. Just what we needed. Another problem to solve. I didn't necessarily like Patrick, and my life would be easier without him in it. Still, I didn't wish him any ill will either. Quite the contrary. Most of the time, I wished he were one of us—alive and someone I could trust.

I headed to the lab to finish packing necessities. White Feather followed me.

"Could Zandy possibly be creating constructs on his own?" he wondered.

"He's so lazy, I can't see him figuring out black magic. And spell casters, especially the black magic ones, aren't likely to explain as they mix their tricks."

"There were two people at the shop drilling tats on the homeless guy, Nick," White Feather mused. "But Lee said he wasn't one of them."

"Lee could be lying a blue streak in the hopes of a reduced sentence."

"True, but he has to be telling the truth about that night. Lynx would have recognized his smell if he had been there."

"Whoever they are, they kept the same MO that he described. Take a victim, do a tat, check the joint is empty and rob it."

"Only we interrupted the process with Nick."

"For what good it did." I rolled a ball of silver between my thumb and forefinger. "The best curses are spelled to a specific person. But I could load a couple of these with a curse. Or a fireball spell. Be good to have some silver shrapnel flying around, right?"

White Feather kissed the top of my head and left me to my spells. In the end, I made a fireball with silver, holy water, stinging nettle, and some explosive firepower. "Hmm. A little of Granny Ruth's spider poison in here would force a neurotoxin into the blood along with silver. A shifter could have a real problem staying upright."

Borrowing from the design used in the arrowhead necklace, I melted silver to the back of a steel tip and packed the spell. I used the kitchen burners to complete some of the work. It wasn't entirely safe, but until my lab was finished, it was the best I could do.

White Feather appeared from the bedroom. "Ready?"

I jangled my silver bracelets. "Showtime."

The entire way to the hospital, I pondered what to use as leverage to convince Zandy to spill his guts. Difficult that. He was on the hook for murder. Lee stood the better chance of negotiating a plea deal with prosecutors, and he'd be more than happy to place Zandy at the scene of the crimes. Deals weren't my cup of potions anyway. Gordon would be the one to offer or fake it.

As expected, Zandy had been admitted to the building across from the main Santa Fe Indian Hospital where Patrick worked nights as a nurse. Come nightfall, if Zandy was still a patient, there was no way he'd live through the night. He was too treacherous for the vamp community to allow him to continue breathing.

"That's it!" I whispered, even though we were alone in the elevator headed to the second floor. "I bet Zandy knows Patrick works here, because all the shifters and vamps know Patrick has a safe place in the basement. Zandy knows Patrick is on the lookout for him after that vamp went rogue. We can tell Zandy that if he cooperates, we'll transport him to a nice safe jail cell before sundown."

"Good idea."

White Feather's phone rang the second we stepped out of the elevator. "It's Gordon." He read the text. "He's running late."

"Good. Then he won't hear our conversation about Patrick."

We knew the room number, but even if we hadn't, the guard was obvious.

White Feather showed his ID, and it was enough to gain us entrance. That was the good news. The bad news was that we were too late.

Zandy wouldn't be sharing any secrets ever again.

Chapter 34

White Feather dialed, even as we stared at the lifeless body that had once been Zandy. The hospital curtain had been secured more than halfway around, blocking anyone entering from immediately seeing the damage. An IV hooked up to his arm dripped slowly, but the blood could in no way replace the amount that had been taken out.

"Bled dry," White Feather said into his cell.

That was a good assessment. The ripped carotid artery at his neck wasn't leaking more than a drop or two anymore. Whoever had done it had been fast and clean. Or really hungry. My eyes flew to the window. It was still daylight. "Aztec sacrifices!" It had to be the work of a vamp. But it wasn't dark outside.

Gordon being late must have meant "Gordon is waiting in the parking lot until we ask our questions" because his voice boomed in the hallway as White Feather provided a terse description of the situation.

Gordon burst through the door, breathing hard. "Shit. Damn vamps. What shift does your vamp buddy work? Did he have to be this obvious? Some kind of freak warning, maybe?"

Fear began to build in the pit of my stomach. "Patrick didn't drink his blood. Not on his worst day."

"Now ain't the best time to stick up for him." Gordon gestured at Zandy's form in disgust.

I shook my head. "His shift is at night. He's a *vampire.*" I looked at White Feather for backup. "Insanity, remember? Patrick said Zandy's blood drove the other vamp insane. Patrick didn't like Zandy, but he isn't stupid. There is no way he'd bleed him, not even a mouthful."

An uncomfortable silence followed my declaration.

"Then who—or what—did it?" Gordon asked.

"It can't be a vamp. It's still three o'clock. No sane vamp would attack in the daytime. Only a completely dumb vamp with no survival skills whatsoever...wait a minute!" My thoughts raced ahead of my mouth. "Fat old guy who tried to use his own tattoos...Lee said Jedi was sick. Joe is sick; he's somewhere past death's door. Patrick said he had to stay here at the hospital otherwise Joe became confused and went out in the daytime!"

"What?"

Neither man was following my confused ramble. I grabbed White Feather's arm. "Patrick! He disappeared. Basement! Mat has a key!" Over Gordon's protests, I confiscated the cell phone still in White Feather's hand and dialed Mat.

"We need the key to the hospital basement," I told her. "As in yesterday. Although it's really too late."

The thing about girlfriends is that they aren't like men. They understand an emergency and don't demand logic on the spot. Sure, you'll have to provide the gory details eventually, but best friends trust you'll share when the time is right. Meanwhile, they hop in the car and drive faster than the legal speed limit allows.

I hung up. "I think the key she has opens the inner door. It had better." We'd only used it on the outside door.

White Feather said, "Patrick's new vamp? The sick vamp you just visited drained Zandy?"

"Joe. It has to be him. Lee told us that Jedi decided to use his own tats to form constructs to control. What he didn't say was that Jedi had to first create new tats on himself. I didn't think of it at the time, but new tats are the only possible way Jedi could have animated them. Old tats wouldn't contain the black magic or Zandy's blood, both of which were used in the construct formula."

"And Joe died from new tats," White Feather said.

"Exactly. He died from tats gone wrong, tats he admitted used Zandy's blood. And Patrick mentioned he was staying with Joe in the basement because Joe kept trying to leave during the day. What he didn't say, maybe because he didn't know, was that Joe *could* go out in daylight because he was never completely turned!"

"Who the hell is Joe?" Gordon demanded.

"The ugliest, unhealthiest not-a-vampire I've ever seen. And the last time I saw him, he was dying in the basement of this place."

"And you're considering waltzing in there to find him? Shoot'm full of silver bullets?" Gordon's eyes bulged.

My own panic was worse than his, but for entirely different reasons. "I don't think Patrick knew any more than Joe told us during the visit, but the timing fits. Joe died about two weeks ago, right after these robberies started happening. Patrick believed Joe's lack of respect for daylight was partly responsible for Joe's illness, but my guess is that the whole turning vamp failed, leaving Joe somewhere in between. There was black magic in the tats, mixed with holy water and church grounds. There's no way any spell could have gone as planned with those circumstances."

"If Joe can operate during daylight hours, wouldn't that make raiding the basement right now damned dangerous?" Gordon asked, single-minded as ever.

"It wouldn't be any safer at night. And I wonder what happened to Patrick. Lynx said he's missing."

White Feather handed me the phone. "Call Lynx. If he's on Patrick's trail, you better tell him about Joe."

While I placed the call and left a message because Lynx didn't answer, Gordon said, "We need a plan."

He was right. Even if Joe had cleared out...Patrick had been watching over him for the last few days. He wouldn't allow Joe to go rogue without putting up a fight. Had he taken Joe to his own home? That was doubtful, but I didn't know vamp etiquette.

Patrick had kept Joe here for a reason, so why move him? They had easy access to blood here. Blood was the universal food for a vamp, right?

Thinking of the red stuff had me reaching for the IV pole before Gordon could prevent me from tainting the evidence. If Patrick was hurt or had been without blood for a while, he would be hungry. I wasn't offering anyone I knew as the main course. Better to have a safe source if we found him in time.

I tried hard not to think about Joe filled up on Zandy's blood, roaming somewhere in the daylight and soon-to-be dark. A rogue vamp who could waltz right into my old house—and maybe even my new one because he had tainted blood from an old spell.

Gordon was only worried about storming the basement, but he hadn't seen the rogue vamp. No point in telling him that basement might be the least of our problems.

Chapter 35

Gordon voted to bring in a SWAT team, but we didn't have time. The flash of his badge did buy us the information that Patrick had missed his last two shifts.

"He's been out of circulation for at least two nights. If he's been bled dry or staked, there's no rush. But if he is still...functioning, he's somewhere that he can't escape. And getting hungrier. And it takes three days to turn a vamp. I don't think we want to wait a third day to see what Joe might be up to."

"What does three days have to do with Patrick? He's already a vamp," Gordon pointed out.

"Nothing unless... well, I'm almost positive that Joe can't do any turning because he isn't a proper vampire, but I know it takes three days to turn one. Joe has been turning tats into constructs and obviously has a thing for creating monsters. We don't dare wait through tonight to discover his plans because if he is up to something that includes a three day time limit, we're about to hit it."

White Feather sighed. "Wind can only reveal so much about what might be in a basement behind a locked door. We'll have to go in."

"Why did you call Mat? She's a civilian!" Gordon exploded.

"She has the key to the basement. I don't. You haven't seen the place. It's built like a tomb. One that isn't meant to be opened all that often."

Gordon found himself inundated with the police business of the dead body that had been Zandy, but the second Mat buzzed my phone announcing her arrival, he turned the mess over to someone else.

We spent a few minutes by the basement door reviewing details, none of us happy. Dusk was no more than a half hour away and cold had already arrived.

I tried Lynx again. I didn't like that he wasn't answering, especially since he was supposedly searching for Patrick. If Patrick wasn't in the basement, he could be at his home in Los Alamos. Maybe Lynx had gone there. I shivered inside my jacket, and it wasn't from the cold air.

We had minutes to sundown.

"Let's go." I broke into the terse argument between White Feather and his brother.

Gordon glared at me and adjusted the strap on the pair of stakes he had across his back. The tips were steel with serrated edges. They'd been dipped in silver more than once. Of more comfort to him was his gun. I didn't need to ask to know the bullets were silver. I could sense them.

"There's no silver in the hallway below. I checked. Mat?"

She held up the key. Gordon reached for it and met her closed fist and raised eyebrows. The key disappeared inside the lock before he could argue with her. She did take his advice and stand to the side while opening it.

White Feather sent in his wind. "No one breathing."

That wasn't all that reassuring in this case.

We trooped in, one at a time, as Gordon had instructed. I positioned myself behind White Feather's left side. Mat hugged the right wall and Gordon brought up the rear, closing the door behind us.

My ring was warm, either from nerves or because White Feather was floating wind everywhere at once, a constant search. The lights were dim and the only switch we knew about was near the door down the hallway.

It wasn't a long walk. Lynx had implied there were other rooms down here, but if they were as invisible as the one we'd visited, it could take a while to locate them. If not for the light switch I'd seen Patrick use, finding the outline of the door we were after might have taken longer too.

As soon as I spotted the light switch, I adjusted it to full power. White Feather and I both did reconnaissance. I sensed bare hints of silver this time, nothing more than atmospheric noise. White Feather interpreted a lot more.

"Patrick's there. Vamps have a signature that wind recognizes. There's a presence with no sound."

"It's not Joe?"

"I've met Patrick on enough occasions. There's a certain smell on the wind. It's vamp and it's Patrick."

"He's alive?" I whispered.

White Feather snorted. "He hasn't started breathing, but he hasn't stopped existing either. There's a...there are two others breathing."

"Any other vamps that might be Joe?"

He shook his head. "No. Vamps are a vortex of negative energy, like an empty space, only when the wind goes there, it dries up. I'm not getting that except from the one corner.

The hall lights were at full power, but the keyhole was still almost invisible. The door itself was no more than a line of oddly layered concrete blocks. When White Feather inserted the key, it refused to budge left or right.

"Are you sure this is the right spot?" White Feather asked.

Had I not been searching for silver, I might not have felt the tingle of magic. "Let Mat turn it," I said. "Patrick gave her the key."

"You are not entering first," Gordon growled. He was still thoroughly angry at being shoved in the backseat. But a gun with silver bullets was not as advantageous as wind. It might be on par with a thrown spell, but Mat and I not only had various weapons at our disposal, we both had the advantage of having been in the room before.

Mat and I switched places, putting her within reach of the key.

She turned it easily. It didn't even click. With a hop, she was back in position behind me on the side of the door.

Gordon kicked it, forcing it inward.

White Feather was supposed to force it open with wind magic, but Gordon apparently couldn't follow the plan. After the kick, he mashed me as he spun to the side.

Nothing moved. I felt White Feather's magic sail past into the room. "No change," he confirmed.

Patrick's voice was a strained gasp from within. "You're...better off...not entering."

White Feather ducked in behind Gordon, who went in low and fast, rolling. Mat hit the inside light switch. I lobbed a fire packet. It contained silver. I could call it back. I could set it off.

It wasn't obvious at first glance that Patrick's glamour was entirely gone because I almost always saw glimpses of the beast. Instead of a cool and handsome Spaniard, a hunched gargoyle waited in one corner, his long clawed fingers intertwined in front of his belly, holding the pieces of what was left of a shredded nurse's smock.

Even without the tattered uniform, I'd have recognized him because I'd seen most of his face before. It wasn't feral so much as rock hard. His eyes hadn't changed. The cool orbs fit the gargoyle more than the human form; gray stone, unblinking. Fangs were as natural on such a face as the long, clawed feet and the folded leathery wings at his back. His body was little more than scaled muscles that rippled as he tightened them, holding himself in check.

Mat's soft gasp was the first clue that his glamour was missing. White Feather's silver ring heated, a reaction I felt through the gold on my own finger. "It's just Patrick," I said, my voice only cracking slightly.

I tossed the bag of blood to him. His vamp glamour skills might be weak, but he snagged it midair without visible effort. His hand twitched as he unclamped the bag and took a swallow. He managed not to guzzle.

I should have admired his restraint, but it was still human blood no matter how the score was tallied. "Moonlight madness." Okay. He was not human and would never be again. Time to get over it and respect what was left.

Gordon's gun never wavered off Patrick. White Feather and I split our attention, sparing plenty for the half naked humans on the right and left. Patrick was still a threat, at least until he had enough blood to control himself, but I'd bet my last spell that it wasn't Patrick who had caused the two humans in the room to be lying senseless.

"They're both breathing," White Feather said.

The skinny teenager on our right leaked blood, little beads dripping down his ribs, almost drying before a second drop had a chance to fully form. The loss was slow; a parody of a stalactite forming.

The droplets meant that tattoos had been brought to animation. Joe had moved his studio from Tam's salon to Patrick's lair. And why not? After Mat and I visited, he knew we were putting the pieces of the puzzle together. It was only a matter of time before we figured out he was involved.

My eyes frantically searched and found the first tattoo creature perched on the hanging fluorescent light fixture. The blue-red hag had a face that sagged on one side and was a distorted blob on the other. Someone had been in a hurry when drawing this tat.

Blue wings showed behind her back. Obscenely misshapen boobs almost hid the fact that she had no lower body. She was cut off at the waist, nothing but a stump. "Where's the other one?" I croaked in a bare whisper.

Patrick spaced his answer around swallows. "Joe forced the other construct to leave with him. This one protects the bodies and makes sure I do nothing but feast." He swept his arm in the direction of a large bucket. The contents weren't clear from here. "He left me Zandy's blood. That or I fight his construct for the blood of these two."

Gordon kept the gun leveled at Patrick, but he nodded to the body on our left. "Why haven't you eaten either of them?"

Patrick finished the last of the blood. He did not lick his lips, but at least he now had lips shimmering back into existence over the harsher face. "They are more interested in my blood than I am in theirs."

"Would the hag swinging from the light attack you if you tried to drink from either of the two on the floor?" I asked.

Patrick nodded. "Without a doubt."

"The tats and constructs were made with Zandy's blood?" Blood Patrick couldn't afford to drink no matter how starved he might be.

"Joe's blood, my blood and Zandy's."

My eyes traveled from the two victims to Patrick. I processed his comment about the victims being more interested in his blood than the other way around. Patrick watched us, waiting.

Finally he said, "You must kill them both. By nightfall they will both be vamps. Joe decided that humans weren't powerful enough to keep constructs fueled. He is right, of course. He intends to continue feeding these two vampires to power his constructs."

"You turned them?" I asked.

"Technically my blood was used to turn them."

"Bloodsucker," Gordon cursed.

I shook my head, seeing the truth. The rumor that a vamp drank the blood of a victim to turn him into a new vamp was backwards. "They drink Patrick's blood to turn. Not the other way around."

Patrick's head swiveled my way. "Witch, you think too much. But even you are running out of time to arrive at an elegant solution to this problem."

"I'm right, though."

Patrick's predator eyes didn't blink. "The legend that we bite a victim three times is misleading. They feed from us before they die. We provide the second and third blood meal usually through a carotid artery. The dead at that stage aren't terribly interested in eating."

"And because of the bite marks, everyone assumes you fed off them until they died, but at that point you're donating."

"Bloodsucking mosquitoes," was Gordon's assessment. He edged one step towards the naked man closest to him. The beast on the light fixture dove and would have made good on the attack had White Feather not caught the wings with a stiff breeze.

The hag didn't need a lower body to fly. With its wings open, the double sets of claws on the wings were more obvious. There was a grasping set at the top of the wing and another at the bottom where a hand might normally be.

Gordon fired instinctively, but the bullet, silver notwithstanding, went straight through the construct. It left a hole dead center of one low-hanging breast, but that didn't even count as a maiming injury with a construct.

"Step back," White Feather said, holding steady.

Gordon did so quickly, staring at the bullet hole. The construct hissed, turned into the wind and swiped at Patrick on its way back up to the light.

"Gordon...or Mat." My voice was barely a whisper around the panic squeezing my throat. "We'd be safer if you went upstairs and procured another pint or two." If we engaged the construct, and I could see no way around it, I didn't want Patrick hungry at our backs. His glamour had returned such that both faces were visible, but he'd been down here for at least two days. Make that three. Night had to be only a few minutes away.

"Will these two vamp at nightfall?" I demanded. We already had Patrick hungry, we didn't need two other vamps coming awake.

Patrick said, "You need to kill them before nightfall. They will turn, but —"

We waited in vain for him to continue. He merely stared, his gargoyle face wavering in and out of focus. "But what?" My patience hadn't entered the room with me; there was no hope of finding it now.

"The information you seek is deadly."

I snarled, "The information I already have is deadly."

"It is forbidden."

"Fine. One problem at a time. Mat?"

She nodded. "I can get fluids. Of any type. I'll be back."

"Gordon, there's another vamp running free out there. With a construct. You'd better stick with Mat." White Feather didn't have to ask twice.

They were barely into the hallway when Patrick said, "You must kill them both. I am not...what time is it?"

"Can't you tell?" If he was having troubles of that sort, it smacked a little too much of Joe's problems. Maybe he had fed on Zandy's blood. Or Joe's. Maybe he was already rogue or about to turn into some kind of sloppy, idiot vampire like Joe.

"Normally, yes. It seems close."

"Less than a half hour. Maybe five minutes. Maybe less." I didn't have my watch.

Patrick straightened and hissed. "You must kill them now!"

When he moved, the construct recognized it as a viable threat. The hag dove. White Feather swirled it sideways, giving Patrick room to maneuver.

He didn't waste it. Like a man possessed and with the speed somewhere between human and vamp, he lunged for the body on the right. I wasn't about to stop him.

The construct wheeled around and closed her wings. She tumbled to the ground, landing safely under White Feather's blast.

"A stake! Silver, wood, anything!" Patrick growled.

Gordon had the stakes. Gordon had gone to obtain more blood.

Not that Patrick waited. He grasped the teen's head and twisted it violently. The snap nearly froze me with horror, but the construct was far from out of the picture. She rolled towards Patrick as if she'd had a lifetime of training without legs.

I detached the small silver spikes from my backpack, the mini stakes meant to skewer and burn a shifter. They were very, very small, only six inches in length, maybe eight counting the silver arrowhead, but technically, they were stakes.

I tossed one to Patrick.

The legless construct screamed, her maw full of deadly teeth intending to shred.

White Feather hit the hag with a blast that rolled the thing over like a bowling ball until her flat face got in the way and halted the momentum.

Patrick snatched the stake out of midair. "What in all of hell is this? *This is the best stake you could design?*"

His outrage would have been comical except for the fact that the other vampire sat up and let out a bloodcurdling shriek.

Patrick stabbed the puny stake into the teen, driving it well past the end of the small wooden ash. Gordon burst through the door, his gun out.

"We need your stakes!" I yelled.

Gordon ignored me. He shot the new vampire, cutting off the beastly screaming. I could have called back the silver slugs and thus shot it twice, but Gordon emptied his entire clip, pummeling the chest and head into bloody splinters. Then, he staked it.

By the time I turned back around, White Feather had beheaded what was left of the younger vampire, and the hag construct had melted into a puddle of ink and blood.

Chapter 36

I collapsed where I stood. "Did it bite you?" Vamps had superior hearing or Patrick would never have comprehended the puff of air that was my question.

His answer was bellowed loud enough for patients upstairs to hear. "In twenty years of life and two hundred after, I've never known anyone who can draft intelligent spells the way you do. And this, *this* is the best stake you could envision? What kind of fairy vampire did you intend to kill with that thing? Can there even be an explanation?"

I blinked. "It did the trick, didn't it?"

Patrick was so angry both of his fangs were in evidence. "You were planning on standing that close to a vampire to use it?" He held his hand out. "A real stake, if you please." His request was for Gordon, his disgust for me.

Gordon took his time about it, not trusting Patrick.

"Give him the stake, already," I snapped. "And then some blood if you found any."

Mat stood in the doorway holding two bags. She tossed one to Patrick. He caught it in one hand and the stake in the other. He finished off the headless vampire before guzzling the bag. Given the complete lack of civilization around us, at this point, polite sipping would be egregious pretense.

"Will Joe return here when the construct with him dissolves?" I asked.

"It's too damn late. I was too weak. I didn't know it was so close to nightfall." Patrick limped to the door, pausing and visibly restraining himself to allow Mat time to step aside. She offered the other bag of O-positive, which he accepted.

"Where are you going?" Gordon demanded.

"Out."

"What do you mean it's too late?" I called after him.

"He vamped." His response was nothing more than a low growl.

Gordon stepped in front of Mat and raised his gun. Unless he had put another clip in it, the bullets were spent.

"Dammit all to hell!" Patrick howled. He fell to his knees. He wasn't panting; he didn't need to breathe, but he clutched his head as if it hurt. His skin rippled, the gargoyle winning out. "We needed more time. Even a minute would have sufficed!"

My heart hammered in my chest. I hoped he had consumed enough blood that he wouldn't lose control because my nerves were a beacon for a predator. White Feather's wind swirled around me, hard to distinguish from the man who was just as suddenly by my side.

"Pa...trick, we're going to walk around you and leave," I stuttered.

He shook his head, leaning it back against the wall. "Too damned late." He still held the blood Mat had given him. Would it be enough?

Mat and Gordon scuttled past first. Gordon must have put another clip in because he kept his gun out and aimed. When they were safely past Patrick, Gordon nudged Mat towards the stairs. She put up zero argument.

Gordon covered us while we edged around Patrick.

The vamp sat motionless the entire time, his hand clutching the blood, but not drinking it. He was weak and ugly.

Running might make things worse, so we faced the vampire and walked backwards.

White Feather checked outside, a wise move, one that wasn't instinctive for me yet. I felt for Mat's silver and found it waiting outside the door.

We stepped through the door, and the first thing I did was ground. I needed Mother Earth and her deepest strength and direct comfort. It wasn't the same as linking in the desert where her scent drifted in the air and fed my soul. It wasn't even close to being in the mountains where the earth was fresh and in a constant state of renewal. All of that was a distant echo here; packed dirt that had a history of human footsteps from eons ago through the present.

I'd have been fine except Patrick called out from within the tomb.

"Wait."

We all backed up as one, our attention rooted on the door.

Gordon unlatched a stake and tossed it to White Feather.

For once, I heard Patrick approach. He was still limping. One booted foot rested heavier on the steps than the other. There were funny pauses between each step too.

After about a decade, he reached the top. The blood bag was gone. The gargoyle was pushed back again, but my witch sight still saw it. The gargoyle was gray. The white glow that was Patrick's normal skin color was reduced to the same dull gray as that of the gargoyle.

"I cannot fathom how you can survive without knowing. Be it forbidden or not." He leaned against the door frame. "When a vampire is used to power a construct—" One hand covered his eyes, while his other flexed its talons. "It is forbidden. We do not create constructs from our own kind. We do not even do it to living humans, but from what I gleaned in the last forty-eight hours, Joe believed he could eventually power his own little army of constructs and become the greatest vampire that...never lived. The idiot had been hunting a way to riches while he was alive and when he became—"

When Patrick floundered, I supplied, "A not-vamp."

"He was just another patient who wanted to be a vampire. I had no idea he was running black magic before he was infected with sepsis."

"We need to stop him," I said.

"You have no idea."

We waited. What choice did we have?

Finally Patrick said, "When a vampire is used to create a construct that construct becomes a ghoul. Ghouls devour vampires and use the energy to become stronger. They savor living humans as well. The ghoul obtains power from a human's soul."

Mat shifted beside me. The ground under our feet rumbled, and I hoped if she went for a water attack, it wouldn't include rupturing pipes under our feet. Gordon kept his gun level. White Feather said nothing, but his breezy power was the silent type.

"You're saying that vamp powered a construct that turned into a ghoul?"

He nodded. "The vampire fully turned at dusk. Joe created the construct days ago, and the construct has been powered by the almost-vampire's energy even as it turned. It reached full vampire stage tonight. The vampire's energy was immediately drained to the construct turning it into a ghoul. Could you not feel it, witch?"

My mouth was too dry to speak. I hadn't felt it. My molecules had been too busy screaming at me to run. "A ghoul takes on the appearance of whatever it last ate." Ghoul research was not at the top of my studies. I hadn't known how one was created, but apparently Patrick did. Vampires and their damned secrets.

Patrick's beast growled low, unsettling the hair from my arms to my neck. "I'll arrange what help I can," he said. "But we vampires are solitary creatures."

"Despite rumors of hives and clans?" White Feather asked.

Patrick's talons spasmed. "Through the ages, we have been many things. Today, here and now, we are mostly solitary. We are territorial creatures, and there is no benefit to large numbers of us cooperating. The fewer of us in an area, the better for us."

"How do we kill the ghoul?" I asked.

Now he did bring his gaze level with mine. "Destroy it and its maker. Although in all honesty, you may only need to find Joe. It's quite possible that the ghoul has already devoured him and taken his guise. One of the many reasons ghouls and their lore is forbidden knowledge is because their nature leaves room for no one but the ghoul."

"Did you tell Joe this?"

A smile with fangs. "No. If you had not come to my rescue, I'd have gone to dust knowing Joe was destroyed by the creature of his own making."

"Well, I guess this means I can quit worrying about whether Joe the vampire can enter my home without an invitation the way the rogue vamp did. Ghouls don't have the vamp limitation of waiting for an invite, do they?"

"No. No, they don't."

See. No point in worrying over the little things.

Chapter 37

Ghouls were nasty, soulless, haunted creatures at night. They fed most often then, although the grimoire didn't say they didn't feed in the light of day. The book also said nothing about ghouls being created from the essence of a vampire, but it did say they were soulless twice over. Of course. A vamp was soulless and a ghoul created from one made it soulless twice.

When ghouls fed, for some unspecified time, they could take on the appearance of whichever soul they ate. I was willing to bet that unspecified time was about three days. Another vampire hint once you knew the end answer. "Joe didn't have a soul. He was a vampire. So will it take on his appearance or not?"

"A half vampire," said White Feather, not even glancing up from the grimoire he was scanning. We stood shoulder to shoulder in Granny Ruth's grimoire library. She hadn't hesitated to let us in, even though visits to her special room were generally not allowed at night.

We had ten minutes to find what lore we could. Or given the magical nature of the room, it had ten minutes to present itself or hide from us, depending on the mood of the magic.

"I don't care what he looks like," I grumbled. "He needs to die. Go away, be obliterated, gone. But if by chance Joe wasn't eaten by the ghoul, how do you kill a vampire that isn't a vampire? Joe is already dead, but he wasn't properly undead. A vampire is a cursed being. But Joe was somehow too blessed to be cursed to full vampire, so a blessing probably won't work on him."

White Feather muttered, "Ghouls can't be undone. They are created from energy that isn't of the earth."

"That's for certain. And undoing this one would bring back an idiot and a half-vamp. Not much of an improvement."

"Can't be starved either. A lack of souls only makes them desperate." He flipped a page. I hated the sound of parchment. It reminded me of my last visit here, and that had almost been my last visit anywhere. Shivers overtook my spine. I was positive that at least one of the spiders that protected this God-forsaken place had just crawled up my leg.

The light by the door flashed in warning.

Granny Ruth opened the door. "Time is up."

I slammed the book shut. Let it put itself away. Things in this room, guarded by lethal spiders or not, tended to rearrange themselves as they saw fit. The spiders might prevent ill magic from escaping, but they didn't prevent it from wandering around the enclave.

I scurried out, running my hand down my pant leg. Oh, right. I had tucked my jeans inside my socks. There was no way a spider had crawled up my leg. Right???

White Feather peeled off his set of borrowed gloves as he stepped out. The door was short, forcing him to bend at the waist. That put him about eye level with the weaver on the plant stand that stood guard in front of the secret door leading to the grimoires.

White Feather paused to examine the colorful spider. It stared back with all eight of its spooky eyeballs.

"Ick." I didn't share his fascination with the idea that poisonous spiders were immune to magic and therefore served as the best guardians in the universe for dangerous grimoires.

I removed my gloves and breathed in the humid, warm greenhouse air. Granny Ruth had dressed in the ten minutes we had been studying ghoul lore. She led the way to her kitchen where she had prepared a midnight snack. There was hot mint tea and warmed blueberry oat muffins.

Despite their huge size, I crammed half of a muffin in my mouth.

Granny patiently pushed a platter of butter my way. Her white curls were smashed on one side from recent sleeping, but her eyes were as bright as ever. If any of us had come out unscathed from the disaster at Tent Rock, it was she. If anything, she was more vibrant. "Did the grimoires reveal important secrets?"

I nodded and then shook my head. White Feather managed to clear his throat before I did. "We know what ghouls are, but not precisely how to kill one. From what I read, a nuclear explosion might be our best bet."

"It wants souls," I reported. "Lots of them. I might be able to convince Martin to tell me where it will feed, assuming it doesn't come out in the open and head straight for live humans. There must be others like Martin with their souls still attached on this side. Martin should know where those souls are waiting." I told her about seeing Martin.

Granny chuckled. "You're tired. You don't need Martin to tell you where to find souls that haven't crossed. They'd be right where his is—wherever their bodies were last."

Her point was lost on me either because it was past midnight and I was barely functioning, or because I had not bothered to educate myself enough on the subject of death. "You know where there are wandering souls?"

"Any graveyard is full of them. Lots of people aren't ready when they die. They tend to stay partially tied to their old bodies while they wait to cross. Now why Martin hasn't gone over is another story entirely. Knowing Martin, he hasn't finished exploring whatever it is that has caught his interest."

"I can believe that." I ate the second half of my second muffin. I managed to delay long enough to slather butter on this one. The tea was almost cool enough to gulp.

Granny said, "A ghoul is not a power to be shoved back to its own realm. It has to be destroyed. The longer we wait, the more it eats, the stronger it will be."

The thought of souls, even a single one, being devoured was anathema. Maybe all the vampire souls that never went to heaven or hell were out there about to be gobbled. Maybe the lost souls who had never found their way were at risk. "Our best chance is now, tonight, isn't it?"

She nodded. "If you can find it. If you can't and that thing is smart enough to figure out how to survive among us, a lot of lives and souls will be lost."

I reached for another muffin. "I have the tat ink. Not the exact same ink that was used in the construct that became the ghoul, but applied to a witching fork, it might track the thing."

Granny stood. "What I want to know is whether Joe discovered the tattoo construct spells in the church archives or the Library of Congress. Either place might have a cache of dangerous manuscripts, especially the church. If he removed a grimoire where did he hide it? Did he share the knowledge with anyone?"

I shook my head. "Maybe Zandy, but he's dead. You can quiz Lee; he's in the slammer."

She sighed. "It's impossible to keep those manuscripts locked up. The magic can wait dormant for years, but it always seems to find a way to a greedy fool. I'll make some calls. If I can recover whatever text he used, my spiders will guard it."

In case something bad happened to White Feather and myself, I told Granny where to find the tat ink we had buried. "I'll ask Mat to hunt Martin at Tent Rock while White Feather and I search graveyards. If the ghoul stops long enough to eat in one area, I bet Martin will know."

Granny waved, but she was already halfway to her lab. With all the spiders she kept as pets, she never had to worry about locking her doors.

Chapter 38

I found Lynx where I least expected him: hiding in my new lab. Lynx was often silent, moody or feral, but I'd only seen him run mindlessly scared once. By the time he'd stopped running that time, there had been no inclination to gibber on about packets, fireballs and tattoo monsters.

This time he babbled as if he only had moments to tell us the facts. "I couldn't find Patrick, but I backtracked places Zandy had been. Figured if there was a problem with Patrick, Zandy might have had a hand in it. Started at Mat's place and first thing, there was this guy, he smelled like blood, like the guy at Tam's place—he was scouting Mat's store from the alleyway."

"Joe. You never met Joe. He's a half vamp."

"Not anymore, he ain't. He had a tat slinking along with him like some kind of dog, only it looked more like a snake."

"Thank God Mat was with us," I muttered.

"That thing wasn't fooled by your invisibility spell. It could see me, smell me and damn near ate me!"

"The construct?" I asked.

Lynx's head jerked and had he been cat, he'd have done nothing but hiss. "It *was* a tat but then dusk hit. I thought it was safe to get closer."

"Moonlight madness!"

He did hiss then. "Joe got eaten! Right there in front of me! If I hadn't thrown your fireball, I'd have never made it, but I gotta tell you, your firepower needs work. Barely slowed that thing down."

"Dusk was a bad time," I explained. "Before sundown the tat was a powerful construct controlled by Joe. It was sucking energy from a not-yet-a-vamp, but at first dark, the construct spell harvested the power of the undead. As soon as the construct linked to vamp power, it morphed into a ghoul."

Lynx gulped and his eyes flashed between cat and human.

White Feather appeared, eating a bean burrito. He handed a second one over to Lynx.

Around his first bite Lynx said, "The tat had been sitting there next to Joe watching the alley. It smelled just like the others; ink and blood and magic. But all of a sudden it started growing. And sniffing. It got wind of me, and I promise you I was downwind. Looked right at me as if your hiding spell was a beacon. I tossed the fireball, and it barely paused to snap down the flames like they were the crisp edges of a burger!"

"What about Joe?"

"The dude started squealing, 'At last! Live!' like a deranged hyena. That was all the head start I got. The mouth, shit, the mouth on that tat grew bigger than my entire head. Joe's head too, because instead of coming after me, it finished off Joe. Opened those teeth and swallowed Joe's head and shoulders like a giant snake. I never ran so fast in my life."

Lynx was right about one thing. The fire packet wasn't lethal enough. I'd made better since then. How many would it take to kill a ghoul? How many chances would I get anyway?

While I mixed new fire packets from soft silver, White Feather retrieved the remains of the tattoo ink from the backyard safe. Theoretically the ink should provide us with an early warning, but the construct ink was now removed a degree or two from the actual ghoul. Still, all the tats had been made from some of the same blood sources.

I set the first part of the witching fork and White Feather set the second. The magic would either follow the convoluted path or it wouldn't.

There were only four large cemeteries in Santa Fe, but countless smaller ones. For that matter, local ghost stories—which could easily be lost souls—were as common as restaurants, especially around the churches in Santa Fe.

"We better hope the ghoul doesn't park itself in The National Cemetery. We could hike that all night and Rosario next to it and never spot the ghoul," White Feather complained.

"Meanwhile, some other ghosts or haunt will probably kill us. We'll never get this job done," was my own sour prediction.

"You do have a tendency to attract ghosts."

I sniffed. "I do not."

White Feather turned his attention back to the Google map. "San Isidro is nice and isolated, but it's small. Wouldn't feed a ghoul for long."

"National is closer to where Joe has been operating. Near the plaza and the jewelry stores. But who knows how much information the ghoul retains from its host?"

"Fairview and Guadalupe aren't really any further from the plaza than National," White Feather estimated.

Lynx finished his burrito and pulled out his cell phone. I sincerely hoped he wasn't texting Tara as a "just in case." If the ghoul ate any of us, she wasn't going to be able to squeeze us back out.

I studied the map. "The other part of Rosario is directly across the street from St. Vincent's Health Center. Plenty of new business for the cemetery. Just roll the bodies straight over, no waiting. Did Gordon agree to ask the patrols to watch for any disturbances at the graveyards?"

"Supposedly, but he accompanied Mat to Tent Rock. Do you two really think Martin will know where the ghoul is hiding?"

Lynx snapped his phone shut. "Fairview."

"What?" We faced him.

"Got a friend at the deaf school nearby. Met him a few months back, remember when you got yourself chased there?"

Nice way to phrase "running for my life" from some overzealous bouncer guy who had followed me from a nearby club with his gun. "I remember."

"My friend was in the graveyard that night. He's not supposed to be, but it's the only place he can hear. So he hangs out there a lot. Not like you were hard to find with all the noise you were making, but he could hear the ghosts complaining about you. Some ghost dude told him trouble was brewing, and once he figured out I was looking for you, he said he'd watch my back. Didn't need it, but that isn't the point."

"Wait a minute. Didn't you just say he attends the deaf school?" Lynx nodded. "And he hears ghosts in the cemetery?"

Lynx shrugged. "Ghosts talk. They don't even have to sign to him. I texted him just now, and he said there was shrieking and then nothing but quiet. Said it ain't ever quiet in the graveyard."

White Feather asked, "He doesn't hear anything but ghosts?"

"None of my business if he does. We hang out now and then. Plus, you never know where business might come from, and he's thrown some my way. He's cool."

I did not want to know what kind of business Lynx did for a deaf kid who could hear ghosts. Not that Lynx would tell me anyway. "You better text him back and tell him to stay far away tonight."

Lynx gave me his slant eyes, which I assumed meant he had it covered.

Chapter 39

Grounding in a cemetery is barely tolerable for an earth witch. Yes, Mother Earth claims bodies, ashes to ashes and all that, but it takes time and there's a lot of stuff between reclamation and died yesterday. Not every grave is peaceful either. Some are too peaceful, guarded by a sense of holiness that means setting off a spell near one would be a big mistake.

There were metals, including silver, in cemeteries. I did not want to call any of it, not even by accident. Underneath my feet, fluid was especially suspect including ordinary mud on my shoes. This was New Mexico. No one wasted water on a lawn in a cemetery, especially in the dead of winter. Anything oozing under the ground was...I did not want to know. I did not want to think about it, and I did not want to ground to it, around it or through it.

An earth witch without her link is about as useful as feathers on a cow. The cow can't use the feathers to fly and somewhere there is a naked, very unhappy chicken missing its feathers. I was that chicken.

It was four in the morning, and cloudy and cold enough to freeze a naked chicken, even though I'd worn my ski jacket. It had lots of pockets, which was a requirement because I'd emptied my backpack into them. The lethal stuff was on my bracelet, exposed for immediate access.

We parked the jeep along the roadway closest to the center of the graveyard. The jeep was one of White Feather's projects, but at the moment, we needed it more for its clearance and space than its ability to run on alternative energies.

Lynx tagged along, much to my complete surprise. His mouth set tight, he had plopped himself in the backseat of the jeep and said not a word. I don't know what he thought he could accomplish. I wasn't sure what any of us could accomplish.

If we failed, our backup was Granny Ruth and Patrick. There was no doubt Granny was hard at work on a spell, but spells take time, and leaving a ghoul running loose for a few days to eat its way to superman strength was not a plan, it was suicide.

The cemetery road circled the perimeter and almost made a cross through it, but the right branch of the cross was angled. From the center, we could explore any of the sections.

Seen one grave, seen them all was my frozen opinion.

We trooped forward in an arrow formation, White Feather taking point and Lynx and I with the witching forks to either side and a step behind him. Using lights would only announce us as live bait, so we stumbled along in the dark. Well, White Feather and I stumbled; Lynx didn't have much of a problem.

We tried to avoid the headstones, although we only passed two that had freshly mounded dirt. With the rest of the graves it was impossible to tell which direction the body had been buried in relation to the tombstone unless the plot was surrounded by a gate or rock border. Most of the graves had been around a long time, and the dirt was hard-packed. Many of the headstones were crooked, fallen or missing entirely.

We were halfway to nowhere when Lynx grabbed White Feather's arm and yanked back, hard. My ring flared like a beacon as panic shot through me. I grounded, shutting the ring down, but it was enough to glimpse what Lynx had seen.

"Patrick didn't say anything about the ghoul digging up and eating bodies." My voice was a low croak as my brain processed the images. The grave in front of White Feather's next step was a yawning pit of darkness. The headstone had crashed over into sunken earth. Dirt was haphazardly piled, landing mostly on two sides of a blackness that was either a hole waiting for a body or a hole now missing a body.

"Watch it with the light," Lynx hissed at me.

"Sorry." I hadn't even known I could do that. Actually, I wasn't sure I *had* done it. My panic may have caused the stone to contract or White Feather's wind...no, it had been energy from Mother Earth. When I linked here, I barely skimmed, but power leaked up through the rock. I had felt the ring react before, but it hadn't been dark enough for me to fully appreciate the flare of light. With my heart trying to crawl out my throat and leave, it was not the best time to concentrate on new discoveries.

The witching fork in my hand quivered in the direction of Acequia Trail, the road that bordered the north and west side of the cemetery.

My nose twitched cold. My hands were lumps of ice. Was it because of the nighttime temperature or because we were wandering through graves and ghosts we couldn't see? Of course, if we found our quarry and didn't succeed, we wouldn't have to worry about reserving a premium spot. We'd be gobbled up; no need to dig, no need for a headstone. We'd be nothing more than an impression on the face of a ghoul until the next meal.

Before we could get our bearings, a voice broke the silence. "Some-ing 'ere." The body that went with it stepped from behind a tall grave marker on our left, the same direction as Acequia.

I almost clamped down on a shriek, but didn't quite manage it.

White Feather pulled my arm, dragging me back from the open grave and the human shape that had spoken from the other side of the pit. He smacked the human shape with wind, blowing it back and over.

"Moonlight...!" Was the human shape the corpse from the grave? Maybe the ghoul hadn't eaten the corpse. Did that mean we had to kill a zombie too? Before we even located the ghoul?

"It's Roberto," Lynx yelped. "Stop! It's my bud, the one from the school!"

The breeze cut off, leaving swirls of dust from the sudden drop of forced air.

"Roberto?" I echoed. My brain registered what Lynx said even as the witching fork conveyed its own news. Roberto scrambled to his feet and darted sideways.

The witching fork tugged in the same direction almost as fast as he moved, following Lynx's friend, the guy who was the reason we had chosen this graveyard.

Chapter 40

The open grave was between us and him. Roberto wasted no time diving behind a tall tombstone. The marker was a lumpy cherub perched on a larger platform, providing plenty of space to hide. The silver on my bracelet went hot and then cold. The turquoise shuddered its own warning.

Lynx dodged around me on his way to navigate the hole in front of us. He headed straight for the ghoul.

"Lynx, no!" I meant to yell, but it was a croaking gasp. "Lynx! The witching fork!" He wasn't as practiced as I was in listening to the subtle tugs of the magic. The fork had definitely indicated.

"Lyyn?" Roberto's voice was more ghost wail than speech. Because he was deaf, he'd probably never heard regular speech unless you counted the ghosts. And who knew how perfectly they enunciated?

Lynx loped around the open grave before coming to a sudden standstill. His hand was up; his head bowed down. The fork pull must have finally registered because he not only halted, he backed up a step, forgetting the dug-out pit yawning wide behind him. A funny sideways leap that only a cat could execute kept him from tumbling down into the open grave.

Roberto, still hidden behind the tombstone, made another noise, a gurgle or gasp.

I drew from Mother Earth through the diamond, slower this time. The contact rattled my teeth. Along with the sparks of light from the ring, the smell of decay and the displaced sound of far away wind chimes bombarded my senses. Holding this ground was worse than when helping Tara.

Metal grated on metal inside my head, but we needed the light. "Moonlight madness!" My calling light into the ring threatened to open every crypt within the cemetery. I dropped the witching fork, and snatched the silver dagger from my boot.

White Feather already held a short silver sword in one hand and a silver bayonet in the other.

Instead of Roberto pouncing on Lynx, the teen peered around the tombstone, transfixed by the light. Short black hair trapped bits of dirt and a long-lost leaf. His mouth formed a soundless cry that communicated nothing.

He scooted into the open, his hands clearly visible in a universal, 'I mean no harm' gesture.

The dark shadow that followed him was twice his height.

I opened my mouth to scream a warning, but it was far too late.

Lynx let loose a howl that must have banished any remaining ghosts straight into the next realm.

White Feather pulsed wind again, but none of us were close enough to help Roberto. The ghoul behind him was nothing but teeth and a curse.

"Get down," White Feather yelled.

Faster than a human could move, a darker winged blackness smacked into the ghoul. Roberto half turned. He never saw what floated behind him because Lynx leapt, yanked Roberto around the stone, and pushed him face down into the dirt.

I'd have happily spent some fire power, but the growling, shrieking mass of ghoul and wings rolled end over end before it came apart into two separate bodies, neither of them human.

"Patrick!" Lynx yelled. His relief was short-lived.

There was no sign of Patrick's glamour. He was all gargoyle, all beast. Seconds after he toppled the ghoul, it winked out of existence.

I blinked in disbelief, my dagger high.

The breeze swept around us, searching.

A faded outline, a shadow of deeper darkness, rippled near Patrick.

None of us had time to move. The ghoul was more ghost than substance until its amorphous arm reached for Patrick's throat, just missing and crushing the top part of his wing instead. The teeth lunged next, all deadly fangs, maybe twenty of them.

A bald troll with shark teeth would win a beauty pageant by comparison.

Nothing about the monster resembled Joe. Its form was closer to that of the constructs, a deformed hag dragon, but deadlier and uglier. It had no feet, but it floated and drifted as fast as the gargoyle fighting it, too quick for my eyes to follow.

I held up a fire packet for White Feather, and crushed the elements. His wind picked it up and tossed it, but the ghoulish nightmare either sensed it or had the luck of the devil on its side. It winked out again.

The fire ignited on nothing. Patrick ducked away from the flames while the ghoul faded again and let it burn.

The fireball provided Patrick seconds to regroup, and it allowed me time to fling silver beads with careless abandon. Some ghosts had problems with silver, although I'd never understood why. If any ghost deserved to be affected it was this one; part shifter, part vampire, black magic and one hell of a lot of ugly.

The beads and one arrowhead hit as the physical shape of the ghoul returned, freezing the silver somewhere inside the creature. It must have hurt because the ghoul roared and batted at itself.

"Go for the neck," Lynx said from my right. "Sever the head."

Patrick was fast. While the ghoul clawed at its insides after an itch it couldn't scratch, Patrick flitted forward and ripped its throat out. Blackness erupted, a fountain of rotted flesh and ooze.

Patrick stumbled back, his clawed hand and arm smoking. He shook it violently, flicking off chunks of disgusting flesh.

I lofted another fire packet. White Feather directed it, faster this time. Lynx dragged Roberto further away while the two of us crept closer. The ghoul was already healing. Its dance with Patrick should have warned us. If we didn't finish it off before it attacked again, we didn't have a chance.

I was wrong. We didn't have a chance anyway. The bottom of its jaw still dripped black blood when there was suddenly nothing but teeth in front of me.

"Damn you to the nethers of hell!" I tossed a silver ball filled with holy water, explosive powder, nettle and Granny's spider poison right into its jaws. The fire might not kill it. The curse might not follow him across whatever barriers kept him in cross-existence.

A strong wind pushed against and through the howling mass of death. I felt the silver in White Feather's sword plunge straight into what would have been Joe's heart.

The ghoul barely shivered. It reached back a clawed appendage and ripped the sword free from White Feather's hand.

I smashed another packet and hooked it on one gleaming fang as the ghoul swung the sword. The blade flashed down towards White Feather. It hit wind, but that only slowed it. My pull on Mother Earth against the silver screamed, sparking the diamond into a white hot stream of light aimed between the sword and White Feather's flesh.

I could move silver. The silver sword...would. Not...hit...*White Feather*!

The blazing fire from my ring slapped the silver back and up, smashing it into the shapeless head of teeth. The maw opened into an unearthly scream. Pain vibrated across my skin as though it had touched me. A swipe from one clawed appendage shredded my coat.

Mother Earth fed through me, enraged at the abomination. Where the light touched, the ghoul smoked, but if the creature experienced any hurt, it ignored the pain. A melting, smoking arm flashed through the center of the light, pushing soul-sucking darkness. The enraged evil was determined to extinguish my link to earth.

I lost my sense of self; there was nothing but raw earth power erupting through me across the planes of diamond. The stink of putrid smoke may have killed me off had White Feather not added his weight to the fight. The force of a tornado burst through the ring.

I sucked in air that wasn't tainted with sulfur and rot. My head cleared barely in time to spot the ghoul feeding parts of itself into a new, lengthening arm that reached around the wind and light. The other arm fought and burned without respite.

I shrieked the word of power to ignite both fireballs. The entire graveyard, dead and alive, heard me. White Feather didn't have wings, but he managed to fly backwards without slowing the power pushing against the ghoul.

For a heartbeat and another breath of fresh air, nothing happened. If anything, the explosion expanded the darkness of the shapeless monster. Then, its head burst into a mist of ghoul spray.

Like any good witch, I ducked.

The rest of the dark mass stretched as though it might contain the fireball it had swallowed. The beast flickered, an attempt to wink out of existence, but a huge chunk tore loose, releasing a soul-sucking screech that must have been the gates of hell opening.

Ghoul ichor just missed me as I rolled to the right.

The glint of a silver sword sliced through the night, cutting and slashing at pieces of a black hole.

I forgot about the empty grave behind me until my second roll met nothing but empty air.

"Aaagh." The bright glow of the diamond blinked out when I hit.

From above me, I heard a whimper and then a groan.

Chapter 41

The absence of any light coated me in deep darkness. The smell of the earth was that of damp desert sand. I did not like the idea of damp, but in the dark, I wasn't sure whether I was face down or face up. *Do not think about the grave.* I sat up so suddenly, shooting pain at the back of my head caused stars to float across my blinking eyeballs.

The hard ground beneath me trembled, little whispers of dirt shifting. I stilled, willing Mother Earth not to bury me here and now. Had the dead person who owned this grave been eaten by the ghoul? What if there were body *parts* left over?

"And this is why I tol' you I am going to stop hanging with witches," Lynx said from somewhere above me. "Can you even believe this shit?!?"

"Adriel?" White Feather sounded calmer than Lynx.

"'Trick, are you gonna die? Because if you are, what are we supposed to do with a dead vamp?" Lynx demanded.

I forced myself to my knees. Given Lynx's litany of complaints, and a lack of one about a ghoul, maybe we'd live after all.

"Is it gone?" I whispered.

White Feather's arms had hold of mine before I even knew I was being lifted. He had the advantage of finding me with his talent, while I fumbled about in the dark before remembering to scan for people by way of silver.

White Feather was obvious; my soul had known he was intact because his ring still breathed with our connection. Had I searched for gold, I might have found Lynx before finding the other packet, but my quick skim stopped short when I recognized my own magic in the silver shards that rested next to an amethyst and red garnet.

"Birthstones," I murmured. Roberto was the client who had ordered the matched packets. Since his hobbies included socializing in graveyards, maybe he wanted the packet so that he could be located easily if something went wrong. Or smarter yet, maybe he left the other half outside the graveyard so he could find his way *out*.

White Feather held me close while I shivered. "Okay?" he asked.

"Okay," I breathed against his shirt. He smelled of scorched leather. "You?"

"Good thing I knew you were planning to use fire," he said. "Although, I wasn't expecting that laser flare you threw."

"Me either."

We separated. There were bits and pieces of ghoul still burning along the ground. Two larger chunks smoldered, but the pile was eating away at itself, dissolving.

Roberto apparently carried a flashlight and decided to use it. The light wasn't as bright as the one from my ring, but I was far too tired to light the way.

On top of that, I was done linking until we high-tailed it out of this place.

Lynx beckoned us over. "'Trick is hurt."

I stumbled forward on leaden legs.

Patrick rested against a gravestone as though he might meld with it at any moment. He was quite possibly the most pathetic gargoyle I'd ever seen, although my sightings of such were very limited.

There wasn't even a glimmer of glamour about him and his skin, which had been leathery before, was stretched now as if the supple muscle underneath had disintegrated. Rather than death and decay, he was more like instant petrification. Without some kind of help, he was headed for fossil land.

"Can we assume that blood would help?" I asked.

Instead of speaking, he emitted a weak groan. It was several seconds before he managed to grate out, "Don't know. Never been here before."

Surveying the leather that was his skin, I said, "Hooking you up to an IV would be impossible. How did you find us?"

"Followed you."

"Didn't you say you were rounding up help?" My skin crawled at the thought of other vamps hanging at our back, but Patrick had been the only one who had taken a stab at the ghoul.

Patrick closed heavy eyes. "It was determined...that it was my problem to solve."

None of us said anything for thirty seconds. White Feather finally growled, "And if you failed, I guess then it would be someone else's problem?"

He had no answer.

We did the only thing we could. Lynx volunteered to escort Roberto back to the school. We called Mat, and luckily, she had returned home.

"Gordon twisted his ankle. We didn't even make it halfway up the canyon. Never found Martin. I'll meet you at the back door of the hospital. I can get the blood easier than he can."

I didn't want to know how.

We delivered Patrick to his own help ward. Near as I could tell, he wasn't bleeding. His arm was shrunken as if it had burned and failed to heal. There was a spot on his chest that had been splashed with ghoul blood and that wound did everything but continue to smoke. Something in ghoul blood was lethal to vamps. Or gargoyles. Or was that...I squeezed my head with both hands to keep my head from exploding.

Did the injuries mean that Patrick had been infected with what had been Zandy's blood?

He showed no signs of manic hunger. He barely kept his head up. Even though the ichor from the ghoul had burned through the leathery skin, the areas looked scarred and...dead.

He would not allow any of us to touch him. It was one hell of a limping crawl to the jeep.

Mat met us at the back door of the hospital with the key and four pints of blood. She held one of the bags over Patrick's lips in order for him to drink, but he barely accepted two swallows.

Whatever injuries he had sustained had not turned him rogue or feral—yet.

He shifted his feet carefully out of the car and rested on the edge for the longest time before standing. White Feather offered a hand again, but Patrick grunted him off. In slow motion, he stumbled to the open door.

How many vamps had Patrick helped? How many shifters?

And now, here he was, the caretaker with no one. Our motley crew of two witches and a warlock was hardly worth counting. Not a one of us knew how to help, and I wasn't even sure we were supposed to.

We were three steps down when White Feather stopped. "Vamp."

I swallowed hard and raised my silver crucifix, letting my remaining stock of hardware dance in front of me. I was so not in the mood. Any vamp who dared to attack us now had better be prepared to eat every silver ball I owned.

Patrick called out, "Who has welcomed you here?"

Technically it wasn't his home, but it could certainly pass as his lab. But whoever was here was already here, so what was the point in asking about being welcomed?

Vamps and their crazy rules.

The lights in the hallway slowly illuminated. A female vamp stood near the open doorway, a concrete doorway I was very tired of seeing.

"You did." She was short, slim and beautiful except for the shimmer that revealed something with impossibly long ears, leathery wings and fangs. Her human form wore business casual, khakis and a silk tee.

"Tina," Patrick acknowledged. "You shouldn't have come. It's been made perfectly clear I am persona non grata."

She hissed. I aimed. Patrick held up his hand. "Wait. If she comes to harm any of us, she is not welcome here."

"Oh, save it, Patrick," she snarled. "You've forgotten your manners. Welcome me and let me help. Perhaps you can even offer to share your dinner."

"They are friends. Not dinner." Patrick leaned heavily against the wall.

She rolled her eyes, showing all white instead of black pits. "I meant the blood the little witch carries." Tina kept her hands up and showed no teeth. Unfortunately for her, my witch sight honed in on her otherness.

Slowly, hugging the wall, Patrick eased down the steps. His clawed feet scraped the concrete, rasping in the silence. Balancing precariously, he tottered forward. One wing dragged, but he kept moving.

Tina was a full vampire with no injuries. She was no more than a blur when she flitted halfway to him.

Patrick snapped, "No!" bringing her to an instant, motionless halt. She could take Patrick out in one swipe and reach us. White Feather could keep her back long enough for me to stuff silver down her throat, but while vampires avoided silver, it wasn't all that deadly for them unless attached to a stake or used to cut their heads off. My silver crucifix was my best missile, but I only carried the one tonight. Only one of the silver balls rotating in front of us contained a lethal explosive packet. The collection might or might not be enough.

Tina smiled and raised empty hands. "Here to help."

"My friends...are leaving now. They are not the cure. Set the blood down, if you will." His politeness was for Mat. "If I cannot use it, Tina can claim it in payment for offering to help me against what was, no doubt, the wishes of every other self-vested vampire in the area."

"Every other selfish, arrogant, and stupid vampire," Tina corrected.

Mat complied, setting the bags on the steps.

I kept the beads and crucifix hovering protectively in the air and backed up, one step at a time. White Feather stayed right beside me, his wind forming a protective vortex between us and them.

From one blink to the next, the lady called Tina carried Patrick down the hall away from us. The bags remained on the steps, but she could retrieve them after we were gone.

Mat locked the door on the way out.

Chapter 42

Four days later, Lynx and I agreed on payments, and I signed the papers to sell the house to him. If it hadn't been for Patrick and the possibility that he could still enter uninvited, I'd have made Lynx rent it from me until I was sure it was the right thing to do or until I turned eighty, whichever came first. Even though I was ready to move in with White Feather, it was still difficult to sell my home.

Of course, even though Patrick had acknowledged the rescinded invitation, and he was probably trustworthy, what if he got really, really hungry? What if he went rogue from his injuries?

That was assuming he made it through his injuries at all.

Ah, well. It was time to move on. Ready or not.

After all the signing was done, I showed Lynx the hidden space in the fireplace. It was empty now, but he could store the paperwork in there.

"You really should apply for a birth certificate," I told him. "Things like buying a house would be easier."

"I don't like papers or being traceable. You don't use your real name," he pointed out.

I knew he was referring to my birth name, the witch one gifted to me by my parents. Names were powerful tools. No way did a witch flaunt her name. The wrong entities with dangerous knowledge could attempt to capture a witch's magic or her soul. "I use one of my birth names. Just not necessarily my spirit name. It's not needed for something like this."

He fiddled with the pen. "What if Bob is my real name?"

As usual with Lynx, personal questions came out of nowhere. And as usual with Lynx, I had little idea of where he was headed with his question. Names were a risky discussion to have with a witch who might know how to use your name against you. Knowing a birth name or spirit name could mean the difference between a spell—or curse—succeeding or failing. "You think Bob might be your birth name?"

"The one you witches never tell anyone. Maybe my mother gave me that name."

The kid read too many books. If I didn't know better, I'd say he read too many of *my* books, but since mine were spelled and set to me, it wasn't likely. "What makes you think you have a birth name?"

He dropped the pen as though I had slapped him. Puzzled at his shock, I said, "There's a lot of people not given the type of name you're talking about."

"You mean shit kids that are good enough to hire, but you think—" his voice shifted from a high-pitched snarl to a nasty hiss, but my hands went up, waving frantically.

"No! I mean anyone who doesn't...anyone who isn't a witch!" I sat back as far from his glare as possible. "Geez, Lynx. Not that many people know about the power of names and even for those who do, not everyone knows to guard against their use. Normals just get names. Most of the time it isn't even the right one, so it holds little or no power. Sometimes they end up with a spirit name during Baptism because it's one of the ceremonies when the magic can be imparted."

From his heavy breathing and slit-eyes, I was pretty sure this was new information to him. That, or he was too angry about my perceived insult to have heard me. "Seriously, Lynx. When have I ever had an issue with your birth? Yeah, you take some jobs you shouldn't touch, but that has nothing to do with your name, your parents or even the phase of the moon. I don't care that you're a shifter, and you could have come from Mars. Makes no difference to me at all."

He snapped his hand into a fist, withdrawing claws that he hadn't purposely revealed. "It's not the one on the birth certificate?"

"No, birth names aren't usually the one on the certificate. Quite the opposite under normal circumstances. It's way more complicated. Sure, people get," I searched for a non-witch term. "Soul names. Spirit names."

He pivoted again, a happier spark of understanding in his eyes. "Like the Indians. They get their name after they're older."

"Exactly. There was—still is sometimes—a ritual. The birth name can be the right one or it can be temporary until they earn the right name. A nasty witch might try to use a spirit name in a binding spell or to drain away power, so we protect that name. It can be used to call a person back from death or to save them from a bad spirit taking over. But that kind of name is," I floundered. "Some people are who they are right at birth. Most of us aren't that way. But my parents are both witches. They knew how to gift a name that could be used to help me. I don't use that name very often, but the longer I use my current name, the more it binds to me anyway."

"Is it the name on your certificate?"

"Adriel is on my certificate, not the gift name, the one that held the hope, the blessings and the spirit gifts they wanted to bestow on me."

He scratched the back of his ear. "So if someone like 'Trick knew my birth certificate name, it might not matter?"

I pushed my chair back from the table. "Whoa. What are you saying?" He stopped my flow of words with his cheeky cat grin.

"I thought my birth name, the one on the paper, might be important. But I don't know if I was born in a hospital and thought 'Trick could find out because he works there. But I ain't gonna hire him if he can use it against me."

"How do you even know if Patrick is still around? Have you heard?"

Lynx cocked his head as if listening, which meant he was deciding how much to tell me. "He's around. Lost an arm. I didn't know a vamp could lose an arm."

"He lost his arm?"

Lynx nodded. "Tina said he'd make it. I figured he'll be returning to his hospital shifts soon. He could check for a birth certificate."

"Lynx, arm or no, do not end up owing any vampire anything. It would not be good to have a vamp have any kind of hold on you. Although it might be worse if a witch knew. I don't think Patrick's witch knowledge is all that deep, even considering he's been around a generation or two."

"You witches hold a real grudge against vamps."

"With good reason," I defended myself.

He gave a serious nod. "Mostly they are nothing but bad news. But if he did find out for me, it wouldn't be a big deal, right? My mother wasn't a witch. She didn't give me any blessings either."

There was a long silence. I took a deep breath and plunged ahead. "Was she the cat?"

He didn't even hesitate. "Nah. Musta been someone she whored."

The simple statement made my guts clench so hard, they hurt worse than the time I tried to do sit-ups last year. Lynx, for better or worse, was my friend. "The birth certificate probably won't have anything to do with your spirit. If she wasn't a cat, she may very well have gone to a hospital. There would be a name on the certificate, but...didn't she call you something? Don't you remember what it was?" I didn't know why I was pleading with him, but I wanted a spark of hope that she wasn't all bad, that she had had some smidgeon of kindness, some motherly instincts that meant he had not been completely alone since the day he was born.

Lynx shrugged. "Do curse words count? Can those end up birth names?"

He killed my hope so easily, so calmly. I sighed. "Not really. She could have literally cursed you if she had any power, but that wouldn't necessarily be tied to any of your names. It's like a stranger on the street. Some can throw a decent curse, but most don't know enough about you to make it stick more than a second or two even if they have some latent power."

"She knew me. Enough to know what I am." He scratched his ear again.

"Why do you want to know what was on the birth certificate?"

He avoided my eyes, letting them roam. "When Tara called me," he glanced at my face, "Bob. There was this dread. Chills. I started wondering if she had guessed the name. If that was the name my mom put on the certificate."

I lent out a pent up breath, my relief palpable. "Tara is a witch. She used Bob as a curse. And a taunt because she had figured out what you are. Only Tara doesn't—didn't know how to throw a curse then. Although, with her healing ability, she has a talent for imparting magic on people that is physical." I shrugged. "Was it kind of like someone walking over your grave?"

He snorted. "How would I know? I ain't dead yet!"

I laughed. "Well, yeah. But I doubt she guessed your birth name even if your mother had the luck to have gifted you with one. And at the time, Tara's anger might have made a curse stick while she was standing there with you, but she didn't have the ability for anything much longer than that."

"What if she got lucky?"

"You aren't feeling sick or anything, are you?"

His eyes widened with excitement. "It was like that! Like I was about to barf."

"She's a healer. Her curse would be bodily like that."

"So it's not my name?"

"Not the one you're worried about." I reached out to touch his shoulder but stopped short, letting my hand hover. Lynx wasn't big on touching. Neither was I, really. "If you're worried about a spirit name, Lynx is probably the closest you have. You named yourself, and you did so with purpose and intent to fill it. You were also old enough to know your own nature, but at the same time, you kept an important part of your true nature a secret."

He tilted his head, thinking, before he finally nodded. "You witches are messed up, but you ain't dumb. Maybe I'll change my name in case Lynx is my spirit name." He smiled then, pleased with anything dealing in subterfuge. He reached up and brushed my shoulder, a whisper of a touch.

Slowly, I echoed the motion on his opposite shoulder, but I let my hand rest there.

We stayed that way long enough for me to mouth his name. I was firmly grounded, and I held it, not imparting my magic on him. If there was a spirit to his name, if there was a perfect fit, it was his to acknowledge and not my business to know.

I stood up and walked out the door, for the first time leaving the place when it wasn't mine.

I skipped down the porch and realized the railings still contained silver, as did the lock on the door. Lynx knew about it. He could remove it if he wanted. Or leave it and hide his nature from casual observers. He'd like that.

I only looked back once before hurrying to my car.

Driving home wasn't as hard as I thought it would be. I'd miss my old house, but home had not only become a new place, it had become a new person.

Wherever White Feather was, that was home, and I couldn't wait to get there.

Chapter 43

We'd never really marked Martin's grave. Mat hadn't been able to locate him the night of the ghoul because Gordon twisted his ankle, but what can you expect traipsing foolishly about a canyon on a moonless night?

A headstone wouldn't be appropriate, but Martin still deserved a gift of some sort to see him through to the other side. An earth gift was the right thing because if anyone could take it across, it would be Martin. Flowers would be a waste of time, and he couldn't drink beer, although he'd probably love to have home brew dribbled over his grave, just for old time's sake.

The collection of rock chips I selected would be something he understood. The bits were small enough that no one would notice them. Sugilite would wish him well on his spiritual journey, the turquoise would direct him in his destiny, and the quartz was for him to use as he saw fit. I was careful not to add rose quartz as that was considered a love stone.

When researching what to take, I kept running into the bloodstone again and again.

Ever since Martin's ghost had appeared, I'd felt guilty about the heliotrope. He had gifted it to Mat and she had gifted it to me, so its strength had only grown. I wasn't giving him back his heliotrope, but I'd take it along.

It was below freezing the morning we decided to visit his gravesite, so we dawdled over breakfast. Tracy was baking the last of the bricks. The outside of the house was nearly finished. He had promised to help with the drywall and the painting, but he had mentioned twice now that the road was calling.

I couldn't help but wonder if that was because the earth-baking part of the chores was done. He had an affinity to that, but much of the other stuff would be mundane tasks.

"Maybe we can find a place Tracy would be happy working for a while," I suggested while sipping my second cup of tea.

"Your dad is already asking around. He'd do well in a quarry."

"Or maybe hanging around training with Martin," I said with a sigh. "Martin never fit in with regular society either. Both of them are so talented, but I doubt either one has ever balanced a checkbook."

"Or gotten caught up in the rat race. Worried about paying bills. Owned a car."

"Martin owned a trailer and a truck. If we see him today, Mat wants me to ask about it. She'd like to inherit."

White Feather's eyebrows rose. "They were related?"

I waved my hand. "Details. We witches don't care about being an actual relative. And if Martin tells me, I get half."

"You're assuming he'll bequeath it to you. But since no one else has a claim on it—and who would want a trailer full of rocks anyway?"

I laughed. "Exactly. And we could give the truck to Tracy!"

I scooted my chair back and was on the way to rinse my mug when Tracy wandered in our new back door. He was covered in light dust and mud as usual. He never noticed the bits that fell off his boots or the larger chunk of mortar that dropped off the cuff of his jacket.

He stared down at his hand, his large digits wrapped around a chunk of earth. "Came to tell you," he said. "This petrified rock was in the oven. I didn't put it there. Black as night." He held it up for me to examine. Then he flipped it onto his open palm, letting it rest there. The bottom was flat, stable. The top was narrow and curved down into a fanned base. The very tip was pointed, like a beak.

"How do you know it's petrified rock? It looks like charcoal to me. Maybe some wood burned hot—" Oh right. I forgot who I was talking to. Tracy knew earth.

He handed it to me. "Looks like a raven. For you."

My mouth dropped open as it landed in my hand. A true fetish wasn't carved, it was found, a gift from Mother Earth. "The raven is a messenger and a sign of transformation. He represents a change of consciousness." I laughed. "It's perfect."

Tracy nodded, and for a fraction of a second, his eyes skimmed mine. "Figured maybe you needed it. I didn't think it was part of the house." Then he turned and went outside.

White Feather came over and inspected the chunk of rock. "Raven."

"It's perfect for Martin. I'll tie a little grain bundle to it."

White Feather followed me to the lab. "Corn pollen and sage? Or tobacco?"

"Hops. Barley. Wheat and rye."

"You think he needs to brew his own beer?"

"No. But it was his crutch in life, and he's transitioned now. We learn and grow by knowing our past. So it seems like the right thing for him." I tied the little bundle to the fetish using sweet grasses.

"Ah."

"It might not be exactly right," I said, frowning over it. "But that's not the point."

White Feather nodded, wisely. "Because we don't know what is on the other side anyway."

"Exactly."

It was cold but sunny and actually made for a nicer hike up Tent Rock than in the summer. The switchbacks extorted a price on White Feather's healing ribs because of the deep breathing, but that gave me an excuse to rest my legs twice.

The wind welcomed us as we came over the cusp, cool breezes against hot skin.

"I thought about making him a fetish from heliotrope, but I didn't know what to carve," I told him. "Tracy has some kind of talent to have found or made this raven."

"A turtle from heliotrope would be the right color."

"No, turtles are for a long life."

"Maybe an owl?"

"It's a little late to warn him of impending doom."

"Then a medicine bear was definitely out."

I giggled. "Probably. You know that tune that Tracy hums all the time?"

"He hums?"

"Haven't you heard him when he works?"

White Feather watched the round stones that were roving eyeballs resting on the tops of the tents. "No. But the breeze is always peaceful around him."

"Hmm. Well, I'll sing the tune anyway." I brushed out a little pocked indentation in the rock near Martin's resting place and buried the fetish. I mounded it with regular pebbles, blending it with the surrounding sand. While I worked, I hummed, keeping it low. Tracy's sound was more of a vibration, lower than a real voice. It was music, but not really a vocal chord.

I grounded and waited, but Martin didn't appear.

White Feather roamed about while I was fooling around, but there was still something missing. If White Feather hadn't heard the tune, then Tracy wasn't singing it. But if he wasn't singing it, how did I hear it?

"Maybe Mother Earth is singing to him." No, it came from Tracy. I sighed and plucked the heliotrope from my pack. There wasn't any wind left in it, but White Feather could fix that. Before I waved him over, I squeezed the heliotrope and said, "We think we closed off the holes that let the demon spit through. Not before a ghoul formed, but we either shoved it back through or killed it."

I searched the rocks around me, but none of the shadows moved or spoke.

"Mat and I are searching for your truck. We want to make use of your stones, if you don't mind. We know a guy who could use your truck, too. His name is Tracy. You'd like him. He's a bit like you."

White Feather must have sensed I was almost done because he was suddenly there, his hands on my shoulders. I held the heliotrope up to him.

"You want me to load it with helium again?"

"I guess so." His wind swirled across my hand and arm, pushing at the stone. Instead of toppling off my palm, the heliotrope absorbed it. I linked to earth automatically.

He felt my hold and fed more wind into the stone. "I wonder how much it can take?"

His voice was a silky whisper as smooth as the breeze across my hand. His eyes met mine, and he didn't bother to hide the flash of humor and challenge. He wanted to know how much I could take—how much I could control.

Which was stronger, wind or earth? We had combined them, but we hadn't explored all the boundaries.

White Feather sent a caress along my arms, all electricity.

The stone was smooth, hard and flowing with a breeze. The scent was all White Feather, a mix of forest, shaving cream, and man.

Oh yeah, he knew what he was doing. My skin tingled, and it wasn't the breeze.

How to reach it? How to *use* it?

The heliotrope had a heartbeat, much as any part of Mother Earth. Silver was an electrical current for me, a conduit straight to the heart of her, through me, through the air, through anything. The gold on my finger responded much the same way, reaching into the earth and building static that was pure energy.

The heliotrope wanted to absorb, not conduct. The flecks of red jasper seemed larger as though swelling. To use the wind, I needed it to flow.

I squeezed the stone using my left hand, the one with my wedding ring. The gold was already grounded. I knew how to push against earth. This was a case of letting the wind flow through and push against the link.

I shot up so fast, I might have catapulted myself over the side of the cliff had White Feather not caught me in a protective swirl. He spun me gently sideways, his arms spread to funnel the breeze where he wanted it.

I held the stone out and grabbed the wind into it.

His eyes widened at the audacity of stealing the wind magic.

I laughed, but without his steady support, I fell sideways, barely balancing it out with a flash of silver meeting Mother Earth in a pulse. All I really did was release the breeze and use the link to silver to slow myself down.

"This wind thing is not easy to control!"

White Feather didn't have the same problem. He pulled at the wind stored inside the stone.

"Mine," I said, curling my fingers around the stone, holding the energy back.

I wasn't stronger than him in any sense, but he let me play, his eyes laughing at me. "No, I'm pretty sure you are mine." He focused on the stone and helped his intent with a gust from behind me.

"No fair!" He could create as much of a breeze as he needed, while I was swimming against currents I could barely control.

Closer to him now, I was also close to his silver ring. There was a buffer of air between us, something that wasn't mine to manipulate, but with the heliotrope between us and silver...I pushed earth against the wind.

It lifted me another foot off the mountain, but I went nowhere. A light breeze touched my lips and danced across the back of my neck, an area that was particularly sensitive. A burst of air tilted me towards him.

"I like this. You're at my mercy," he teased.

I could tamp the stone down. Closing the conduit to earth was as natural as closing my fist and not letting the air out.

I shot sideways for no reason that I understood. "Eeep!"

White Feather laughed, the sound echoing across the tents. "You can't just draw wind, you have to direct it where you need it." Again, his caress kept me from bouncing off the nearest rock. He set me down slowly, carefully. I was back where I started. When my boots hit the earth, a chunk of rock broke free from over the spot where I had buried Martin's fetish. I picked it up, turned it over and saw a fossilized shell.

"Martin?" The pebbles I had placed were intact, but the top stone wobbled. I picked it up too. Another fossilized shell, this one tiny.

From over by the edge of the ridge White Feather shouted, "Afraid to try again?"

The sound of his voice ricocheted across the tents, but either my hearing was off or there was an extra word stuck in the backlash. "Concha."

Shell. The Spanish word for shell was Concha. "Hey! There's a road called Conchas Trail. Do you want me to look there?"

White Feather wasn't done teasing me. Or perhaps he didn't hear me talking to Martin. Perhaps I wasn't even having a conversation with Martin.

The breeze shifted again and it smelled of White Feather, sand, and magic.

My jacket and shirt suddenly danced up, one side and then the other. I nearly fell over backwards when my shirt stopped drifting and flew up across my face. "Hey!"

He moved fast. Before I could complain of the cold, his hands replaced his wind. His caress was a magic that warmed me from the inside out. He kissed me gently, teasing my lips as he had done with the breeze.

At least this was a magic where I was his equal.

Other Works

Most of my other works are mysteries. The Sedona O'Hala series (**Executive Lunch, Executive Retention, Executive Sick Days**) is a series of contemporary cozy mysteries: Sedona must solve a few crimes while fighting her way up the corporate ladder; mostly she dangles from her fingertips just trying to survive.

Catch an Honest Thief is a stand alone mystery, combining a stealthy caper in the New Mexico desert with high-tech gadgets. Alexia must try to save her career--and her life.

Dragons of Wendal, a fantasy adventure, has a touch of romance. Zoe intends to learn magic, but the mages at the university might not be willing to teach her what she needs to know.

Tracking Magic (Max Killian Investigations), **Sage**, and **Black-Tie Bingo** are all adventure-filled anthologies. You might also enjoy **Year of the Mountain Lion** and **Snitched, Snatched**, two short stories available in ebook form only.

Visit me at: www.BearMountainBooks.com.

www.ingramcontent.com/pod-product-compliance
Lightning Source LLC
Chambersburg PA
CBHW021035130626
46552CB00005B/1860